Alexandre Dumas (24 July 1802 – 5 December 1870), also known as Alexandre Dumas père (French for 'father'), was a French writer. His works have been translated into many languages, and he is one of the most widely read French authors. Many of his historical novels of high adventure were originally published as serials, including The Count of Monte Cristo, The Three Musketeers, Twenty Years After, and The Vicomte of Bragelonne: Ten Years Later. His novels have been adapted since the early twentieth century for nearly 200 films. Dumas' last novel, The Knight of Sainte-Hermine, unfinished at his death, was completed by scholar Claude Schopp and published in 2005. It was published in English in 2008 as The Last Cavalier. Prolific in several genres, Dumas began his career by writing plays, which were successfully produced from the first. He also wrote numerous magazine articles and travel books; his published works totalled 100,000 pages. In the 1840s, Dumas founded the Théâtre Historique in Paris. (Source: Wikipedia)

Literary works:
The Three Musketeers
Twenty Years After
The Vicomte of Bragelonne
Ten Years Later
Louise de la Valliere
The Man in the Iron Mask
The Count of Monte Cristo
The Women's War
The Pale Lady
The Black Tulip
Olympe de Cleves
Isaac Laquedem
Catherine Blum
Georges
Amaury

THORNE CLASSICS

TAKING THE BASTILLE
Alexandre Dumas

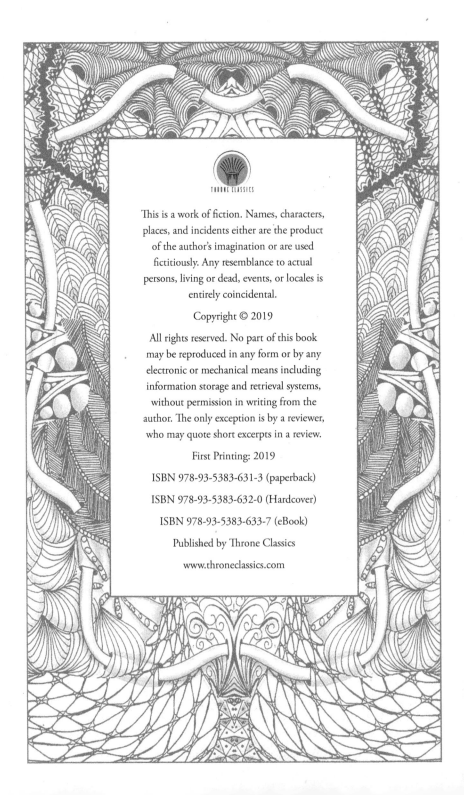

First Printing: 2019

ISBN 978-93-5383-631-3 (paperback)

ISBN 978-93-5383-632-0 (Hardcover)

ISBN 978-93-5383-633-7 (eBook)

Published by Throne Classics

www.throneclassics.com

Contents

TAKING THE BASTILLE

CHAPTER I. THE SON OF GILBERT.

It was a winter night, and the ground around Paris was covered with snow, although the flakes had ceased to fall since some hours.

Spite of the cold and the darkness, a young man, wrapped in a mantle so voluminous as to hide a babe in his arms, strode over the white fields out of the town of Villers Cotterets, in the woods, eighteen leagues from the capital, which he had reached by the stage-coach, towards a hamlet called Haramont. His assured step seemed to indicate that he had previously gone this road.

Soon above him streaked the leafless boughs upon the grey sky. The sharp air, the odor of the oaks, the icicles and beads on the tips of branches, all appealed to the poetry in the wanderer.

Through the clumps he looked for the village spire and the blue smoke of the chimneys, filtering from the cottages through the natural trellis of the limbs.

It was dawn when he crossed a brook, bordered with yellow cress and frozen vines, and at the first hovel asked for the laborer's boy to take him to Madeline Pitou's home.

Mute and attentive, not so dull as most of their kind, the children sprang up and staring at the stranger, led him by the hand to a rather large and good-looking cottage, on the bank of the rivulet running by most of the dwellings.

A plank served as a bridge.

"There," said one of the guides nodding his head towards it.

Gilbert gave them a coin, which made their eyes open still more widely, and crossed the board to the door which he pushed open, while the children, taking one another's hand, started with all their might at the handsome gentleman in a brown cloth coat, buckled shoes and large cloak, who wanted to find Madeline Pitou.

Apart from them, Gilbert, for such was the young man's name, simply so for he had no other, saw no living things: Haramont was the deserted village he was seeking.

As soon as the door was open, his sight was struck by a scene full of charm, for almost anybody, and particularly for a young philosopher like our roamer.

A robust peasant woman was suckling a baby, while another child, a sturdy boy of four or five, was saying a prayer in a loud voice.

In the chimney corner, near a window or rather a hole in the wall in which was stuck a pane of glass, another woman, going on for thirty-five or six, was spinning, with a stool under her feet, and a fat poodle on an end of this stool.

Catching sight of the visitor the dog barked in a civil and hospitable manner just to show that he had not been caught napping. The praying boy turned, cutting the devotional phrase in two, and both females uttered an exclamation between joy and surprise.

"I greet you, good mother Madeline," said Gilbert with a smile.

"The gentleman has my name," she cried out with a start.

"As you notice; but please do not interrupt me. Instead of one babe at the breast, you are to have the pair."

In the rude country-made crib he laid his burden, a little boy.

What a pretty darling!" ejaculated the spinner.

"Quite a dear, yes, Aunt Angelique," said Madeline.

"Your sister?" inquired the visitor, pointing to the spinner who was also a spinster.

"No my man's sister."

"Yes, my auntie, my aunt 'Gelique," mumbled the boy, striking into the talk without being asked.

"Be quiet, Ange," rebuked his mother: "you are interrupting the gentleman."

"My business is very plain, good woman. The child you see is son of one of my master's farmers, the farmer being ruined. My master, his godfather, wants him brought up in the country to become a good workman, hale, and with good manners. Will you undertake this rearing?"

"But, master?———"

"Born yesterday and never nursed," went on Gilbert. Besides, this is the nursling which Master Niquet, the lawyer at Villers Cotterets, spoke to you about."

Madeline instantly seized the babe and supplied it with the nourishment it craved with a generous impetuosity deeply affecting the young man.

"I have not been misled," said he: "you are a good woman. In my master's name, I confide the child to you. I see that he will fare well here, and I trust he will bring into this cabin a dream of happiness together with his own. How much does Master Niquet pay you for his children?"

"Twelve livres a-month, sir: but he is rich, and he adds a few pieces for sugar and toys."

"Mother Madeline," replied Gilbert proudly, "this child will bring you twenty livres a-month, or two hundred and forty a-year."

"Lord bless us! I thank you kindly, master," said the peasant.

"And here is the first year's money down on the nail," went on Gilbert, placing ten fine gold coins on the table, which made the two women open their eyes and little Ange Pitou stretch out his devastating hand.

"But if the little thing should not live?" queried the nurse timidly.

"It would be a great blow—such a misfortune as seldom happens," responded the gentleman; "Here is the hire settled—are you satisfied?"

"Oh, yes, sir."

"Let us now pass to the future payments."

"Then we are to keep the child?"

"Probably, and be parents to it," said Gilbert, in a stifled voice and losing color.

"Dear, dear, is he an outcast?"

Gilbert had not expected such feeling and questions: but he recovered from the emotion.

"I did not tell you the whole truth," he said; "the poor father died on the shock of hearing that his wife gave up her life in bearing him the child."

The women wrung their hands with sympathy.

"So that the child can reckon on no love from his parents," continued Gilbert, breathing painfully.

At this point in tramped Daddy Pitou with a calm and jolly manner. His was one of those round and honest characters, overflowing with health and good will, such as Greuze paints in his natural domestic pictures. A few words showed him how matters stood. Out of good nature he understood things—even those beyond his comprehension.

Gilbert made it clear that the keep-money would be paid until the boy was a man and able to live alone with his mind and arm.

"All right," said Pitou, "I rather think we shall take to the kid, though he is a tiny creature."

"Look at that," said the women together, "he thinks it a little dear just like us."

"I should like you to come over to Master Niquet's where I will leave the money required so that you may be content and the child happy."

Gilbert took leave of the women and bent over the cradle in which the new-comer had ousted the rightful heir. He wore a sombre air.

"You look little like me," he muttered, "for you have the aspect of your proud mother, the aristocratic Andrea, daughter of Baron Taverney."

The trait broke his heart: he pressed his nails into his flesh to keep down the tears flowing from his aching breast. He left a kiss timid and tremulous on the babe's fresh cheek and tottered out. He gave half a louis to little Ange, who was stumbling between his legs, and shook hands with the women who thought it an honor. So many emotions oppressed the father of eighteen years that little more would have prostrated him. Pale and nervous, his brain was spinning.

"Let us be off," he said to Pitou, waiting on the sill.

"Master!" called out Madeline from the threshold: "his name—what did you say his name is?"

"Call him Gilbert," replied the young man with manly pride.

The business at the notary's was quickly done. Money was banked for the child's keep and bringing up as became a farmhand's offspring. For fifteen years education and training was to be given him, and the balance was to be devoted to fitting him in a trade or buying a plot of land. At his eighteenth year some two thousand livres were to be paid the nurse and her husband, who would have the other sum yearly from the intermediary.

As a reward Niquet was to have the interest of the funds.

Ten years passed and the Pitou woman, who had lost her husband while Ange was hardly able to remember him, felt herself dying. Three years before she had seen Gilbert, returned a man of twenty-seven, stiff, dogmatic of speech, cold at the outset. But his mask of ice thawed when he saw his son again, hearty, smiling and strong, brought up as he had planned. He shook the good widow's hand and said:

"Rely on me if ever in need."

He took the child away, went to see the tomb of Rousseau the philosopher, musician and poet, and returned to Villers Cotterets. Seduced by the good air and the praise of the Abbe Fortier's school for youth, he left Gilbert at that institution. He had thought highly of the tutor's philosophical mien; for philosophy was a great power at this revolutionary period and had glided into the bosom of the Church. He left him his address and departed for Paris.

Ange Pitou's mother knew these particulars.

At her dying hour she remembered the pledge of Gilbert to be the friend at need. It was a bright light. No doubt Providence had brought him to Haramont to provide poor Pitou with more than he lost in losing life and family.

Not able to write, she sent for the parish priest, who wrote a letter for her, and this was given to Abbe Fortier to be sent off by the post.

It was time, for she died next day.

CHAPTER II. ANGE PITOU.

Ange was too young to feel the whole extent of his loss: but he divined that the angel of the hearth had vanished: and when the body was taken to the churchyard and interred, he sat down by the grave and replied to all pleadings for him to come away by saying that Mamma Madeline was there, that he never had left her and he would stay beside her now.

It was there that Dr. Gilbert, for Ange Pitou's future guardian was a physician, found him when he hastened to Haramont on receiving the dying mother's appeal.

Ange was very young when thus he saw the doctor for the first time. But, we know, youth can feel deep impressions, leaving everlasting memories. The previous passing of the young man of mystery through the cottage had impressed its trace. He had left welfare with the boy: every time Ange heard his mother pronounce the benefactor's name, it had been almost with worship. Finally, when he appeared, grown up, adorned with the title of Physician, joining to the past boons the future promises, Pitou had judged by his mother's gratitude that he ought himself be grateful. The poor lad, without clearly knowing what he was saying, faltered words of eternal remembrance, and profound thanks such as he had heard his mother use.

Therefore, as soon as he perceived the doctor coming among the grassy graves and broken crosses, he understood that he came at his mother's appeal and he could not say no to him as to the others. He made him no resistance except to turn his head to look backwards as Dr. Gilbert grasped his hand and led him from the cemetery.

A stylish cab was at the gates, into which the doctor made the poor boy step, and he was taken to the town tailor's, where he was fitted with clothes: they were made too large so that he would grow up to them. At the rate our hero grew this would not take long.

Thus equipped, Ange was walked in a quarter of the town called Pleux, where Pitou's pace slacked. He recalled this as being the abode of his Aunt Angelique, of whom he had preserved an appalling memory.

Indeed the old maid had no attractions for a boy who cherished true motherly affections: she was nearly sixty by this period. The minute practice of religion had brutalized her, and mistaken piety had twisted all sweet, merciful and humane feelings, so that she cultivated in their stead a natural dose of greedy intelligence, augmented daily by her association with all the prudes. She did not precisely live on public charity but besides the sale of linen thread hand-spun, and letting out chairs in the church, she received from kindly souls ensnared by her devout posturings, petty coin which she converted into silver and that into gold. Nobody suspected she accumulated them and she stuffed the gold in the cushion and frame of an old armchair in which she sat at work.

It was to this venerable relative's dwelling that Gilbert led little Pitou. We might say Big Pitou, for he was too large for his age.

Miss Rose Angelique Pitou, as they came up, was in a merry humor as she had just sent another gold piece to go and keep company with the rest of her hoard. She was going around her seat of revenue when the doctor and his ward appeared at the door, and she had to welcome the relic of her family.

The interview would have been affecting if it had not been so grotesque. The doctor, a man of keen observation, and physiognomist, read the character of the hypocritical old maid at a glance. With her long nose, thin lips and small bright eyes, she collected in one person cupidity, selfishness and hypocrisy.

As soon as the stranger stated his little text on the duty of aunts to take care of their nieces and nephews, she turned sour and replied that, whatever her love for her poor sister, and her interest in her dear little nephew, the slenderness of her means did not permit her, though she was godmother as well as aunt, to add to her expenses.

"It is this way, Master Gilbert; this would run me into six cents a day extra, for that lubberly boy would eat a pound of bread."

Ange screwed up his face, for he could tuck away a pound and a half at

16

breakfast alone.

"This is saying nothing for his washing, for he is a dirty little chap."

Considering that Ange was a regular gipsy for burrowing after moles and climbing trees, this was true enough; but it is fair to say that he tore his clothes worse than he soiled them.

"Fie!" said Doctor Gilbert; "do you who understand the Christian virtues so well, make such close calculations about a nephew and an orphan?"

"Then the keeping of his clothes in repair," went on the miser, recalling the quantity of patches she had seen sewn by her sister on the knees, and seat of Master Ange's pants.

"In short," said the doctor, "you refuse to shelter your nephew in your house—the orphan boy who will have to beg for alms at the doors of others."

Mean as she was, she felt the disgrace befalling her as if she drove her next of kin to this step.

"No, I will take charge of him," she said.

"Good," said the doctor, delighted to find a moist spot in this desert.

"I will recommend him to the Augustin Monastery and have them take him as a boy of all work."

The doctor was a philosopher, we have mentioned; which means that he was the opponent of all the churchmen. He resolved to tear this recruit from the enemy with all the warmth that the Augustines would have shown to deprive him of a disciple.

"Well," he rejoined, sticking his hand in his deepest pocket, "since you are in so hard a position, dear Miss Angelique, that you are forced to send your nephew into beggary, I will find somebody else to take him and the sum I am going to set aside for his maintenance. I am obliged to return to America. Meanwhile I must apprentice the boy to some craft, which he can choose for himself. In my absence he will grow up and then we will see what to make of him. Kiss your good aunt good-bye, and let us try our luck elsewhere," concluded the doctor.

He had barely finished before Pitou rushed into his aunt's long, bony arms to exchange the hug which he wanted to be in token of eternal separation. But the mention of a sum of money and Gilbert's movements of putting his hand in his pocket for cash, with the chink of silver, set the warmth of greed up from her old heart.

"Lord, doctor, do not you know that nobody in all the wide world can love this poor lone, lorn thing like his own dear fond auntie?"

Entwining him with her long arms, she imprinted on his cheeks a couple of kisses so sour that they made his hair stand on end and then curl with a shriveling up.

"Just what I thought; but still you are too poor to do the proper thing." ·

"Nay, good Master Gilbert," said the pious dame, "forget not that we have the Father of the fatherless above and that He has promised that a swallow shall not be sold for a penny without its being spent for the orphan's share."

"The text may be so, but it nowhere says that the orphan is to be bound out as a servant. I am afraid to do with Ange as I suggested; it would be too dear for your slight resources."

"But with the sum you spoke of, in your pocket," said the old devotee, with her eyes rivetted on the place whence the chink had sounded.

"I would give it, assuredly, but only on condition that the boy should be brought up to some livelihood."

"I promise that," cried Aunt Angelique; "I vow it, as true as the sheep are tempered for the storm-wind." And she raised her skeleton hand to heaven.

"Well," replied Gilbert, drawing out a bag rounded with coin; "I am ready to deposit the funds, but you must sign a contract at Lawyer Niquet's."

Niquet was her own business man and she raised no objections.

A bargain was made for five years: Ange Pitou was to be brought up to some trade and boarded, etc., for two hundred livres to his aunt, a-year. The doctor paid down the money.

Next day he quitted Villers, after arranging matters with a farmer on some property of his, named Billet, whose acquaintance we shall make in good time.

Miss Pitou, pouncing on the first payment in advance of the maintenance fund, buried eight bright gold pieces in her armchair bottom.

With eight livres over, she put the small change waiting to make up the amount of a gold piece to be placed, when converted, in the peculiar savings-bank.

We noticed the scant sympathy Ange felt for his aunt; he had foreseen the sorrow, disappointment and tribulations awaiting him under her roof.

In the first place, as soon as the doctor had turned his back, there was no longer a question about his learning any trade. When the good notary made a remark on this agreement, the tender aunt rejoined that her nephew was too delicate to be put out to work. The lawyer had admired his client's sensitive heart and deferred the apprenticeship question for another year. He was only twelve so that it would not waste much valuable time.

While his aunt was ruminating how to evade the contract, Ange resumed his truant life in the woods, as led at Haramont: it was the same woods and hence the same life.

As soon as he had the best spots located for bird-catching, he made some birdlime and having a four-pound loaf under his arm, he went off into the forest for the whole day.

He had foreseen a storm when he came back at nightfall, but he expected to parry it with the proceeds of his skill.

He had not presaged how the tempest would fall. In fact, Aunt Angelique had ambushed herself behind the door to deal him a cuff, as he crept in which he recognized as inflicted by her hard hand. Happily he had a hard head, too, and though the blow staggered him, he had the sense left to hold out as a peace-offering and buckler the talisman he had prepared. It was a bunch of two dozen small birds.

"What is this?" challenged his aunt, continuing to grumble for form's sake but opening her eyes more widely than her mouth.

"Birds, you see, good Aunt Angelique," replied Pitou as she grabbed the lot.

"Good to eat?" questioned the old maid who was greedy in all her senses of the word.

"Redbreasts and larks—I should bet they are good to eat—but they are better to sell. They command a good price in the market."

Where did you steal them, you little rogue?"

"Steal? they ain't stolen—I took 'em at the pool in the woods. A fellow has only to set up limed twigs anywhere round the water and the silly birds get tangled; then you run up, wring their necks, and there you have them."

"Lime? do you catch birds with lime?" queried Angelique.

"Not mortar lime, bless your innocence, but birdlime; it is made by boiling down holly sap."

"I understand, but where did you get the money to buy holly sap?"

"I should be a saphead to buy that: one makes it."

"Ah, then these birds are to be had for the picking up?"

"Yes: any day; but not everyday, for, of course, you cannot catch on Tuesday those you caught on Monday."

"Very true," returned the aunt, amazed at the brightness her nephew was for once displaying: "you are right."

This unheard of approval delighted the boy.

"But, on the days when you ought not to go to the pools, you go elsewhere. When you are not catching birds, you snare hares. You can eat

20

them, too, and sell the skins for two cents."

Angelique stared at her nephew who was coming out as a financier.

"Oh, I can do the selling!"

"Of course, just as Mother Madeline did," for Pitou had never supposed he was to enjoy the fruit of his hunting.

"When will you go snaring hares?" she asked eagerly.

"I will go snaring hares and rabbits when I have wire for snares."

"All right, make it."

"Oh, I cannot do that," Pitou said, scratching his head. "I must buy that at the store but I can weave the springes."

"What does it cost?"

"I can make a couple of dozen with four cents' worth, and it ought to catch half a dozen bunnies—and the snares are used over and over again—unless the gamekeepers seize them."

"Here are four cents," said Aunt Angelique, "go and buy wire and get the rabbits to-morrow."

Wire was cheaper in the town than at the village so that Ange got material for twenty-four snares for three cents; he brought the odd copper to his aunt who was touched by this honesty. For an instant she felt like giving him the cent but unfortunately for Ange, it had been flattened by a hammer and might be passed in the dusk for a twosous piece. She thought it wicked to squander a piece that might bring a hundred per cent, and she popped it into her pouch.

Pitou made the snares and in the morning asked mysteriously for a bag. In it she put the bread and cheese for his meals, and away he went to his hunting ground.

Meanwhile she plucked the robins intended for their dinner; she took a brace of larks to Abbe Fortier, and two brace to the Golden Ball innkeeper, who paid her three cents for them and ordered as many as she could supply at that rate.

She went home beaming: the blessing of heaven had entered the house with Ange Pitou.

"They are quite right who say a good action is never thrown away," she observed as she munched the robins, as fat as ortolans and delicate as beccaficoes.

At dark in walked Ange, with the rounded out bag on his shoulders; Aunt Angelique received him on the threshold but not with a slap.

"Here I am, with my bag," said he with the calmness of having well spent his day.

"And what have you in the bag?" cried the aunt, stretching out her hand in sharp curiosity.

"Beech-mast," replied Pitou. "It is this way. If Daddy Lajeunesse, the gamekeeper, saw me rambling without the bag he would want to know what I was lurking for and he would feel suspicion. But when he challenged me with the bag, I just answered him: 'I am gathering beechmast, father—it is not forbidden to gather mast, is it?' and not being forbidden, he could not do anything. So he said nothing except: 'You have a good aunt, Pitou; give her my compliments.'"

"So you have been collecting mast instead of catching rabbits," cried Aunt Angelique, angrily.

"No, no, I laid my snares under cover of mast-gathering: the old donkey saw me doing that and thought it right."

"But the game?" said the woman, bent on the first principle.

"The moon will be up at twelve and I will go and see how many I have snared."

"You will go into the woods at midnight?"

"Why, not? what is there to be afraid of?"

The woman was as amazed at Ange's courage as at the breadth of his speculations. But brought up in the woods, Ange was not to be scared at what terrifies the town boy.

So at midnight he set out, skirting the cemetery wall, for the innocent lad, never in his ideas offending anybody, had no more fear of the dead than of the living.

The only person he dreaded was Lajeunesse. So he made a turn round his house and stopped to imitate the barking of a dog so naturally that the gamekeeper's basset "Snorer," deceived by the provocation, replied with a full throat and came to the door to sniff the air.

Pitou ran on, chuckling, for if Snorer were home his master was surely asleep there, as the man and the dog were inseparable.

In the snares two rabbits had been strangled, Pitou stuffed them into the pockets of a coat made too long for him and now too small.

Greed kept the aunt awake, though she had lain down. She had reckoned on two brace of game.

"Only a pair," said Pitou. "It is not my fault that I have not done better but these are the cunningest rabbits for miles round."

Next day Pitou renewed his enterprises and had the luck to catch three rabbits. Two went to the tavern and one to Abbe Fortier, who recommended Aunt Angelique to the benevolent of the town.

Thus things went on for three or four months, the woman enchanted and Ange thinking life endurable. Except for his mother's loss, matters were such as at Haramont: he passed his time in rural pleasures.

But an unexpected circumstance broke the jar of illusion of the prude and stopped the nephew's trapping.

A letter from Dr. Gilbert arrived from New York. He had not forgotten his little ward on landing, but asked Master Niquet if his instructions had been followed and if young Pitou were learning the means to make his own

23

living.

It was a pinch, for there was no denying that Ange was in first-rate health. He was tall and lank but so are hickory saplings, and nobody doubts their strength and elasticity.

The aunt asked a week to put in her reply; it was miserable for both. Pitou asked no better career than he was leading, but it was quiet at the time; not only did the cold weather drive the birds away but the snow fell and as it would retain footprints, he dared not go into the woods to lay traps and snares.

During the week the old maid's claws grew; she made the stripling so wretched that he was ready to take up any trade rather than be her butt any longer.

Suddenly a sublime idea sprouted in her cruelly tormented brain, where peace reigned again.

Father Fortier had two purses for poor students attached to his school, out of the bounty of the Duke of Orleans.

Angelique resolved to beg him to enter Ange for one of them. This would cost the teacher nothing, and to say nothing of the game on which the woman had been nourishing the doctor for half a year, he owed something to the church-seat letter.

Indeed, Ange was received without fee by the schoolmaster.

The old girl was delighted for it was the school of the district where Dr. Gilbert's son was educated. He paid fifty livres and Ange got in for nothing, but nobody was to let Sebastian Gilbert or any others know that.

Whether they guessed this or not, Ange was received by his school fellows with that sweet spirit of brotherhood born among children and perpetuated among "the grown ups," in other words with hooting and teasing. But when three or four of the budding tyrants made the acquaintance of Pitou's enormous fist and were trodden under his even more enormous foot, respect began to be diffused. He would have had a life a shade less worried than when under Angelique's wing; but Father Fortier in soliciting little children to come unto him, forgot to warn them that the hands he held out were armed with the Latin Rudiments and birch rods.

Little did the aunt care whether the information was flogged or insinuated mentally into her nephew. She basked in the golden ray from dreamland that in three years Ange would pass the examination and be sent to college with the Orleans Purse.

Then would he become a priest, when he would, of course, make his aunt his housekeeper.

One day a rough awakening came to this delusion. Ange crawled into the house as if shod in lead.

"What is the matter?" cried Aunt 'Gelique, who had never seen a more piteous mien. "Are you hungry?"

"No," replied Pitou dolefully.

The hearer was uneasy, for illness is a cause of alarm to good mothers and bad godmothers, as it forces expenses.

"It is a great misfortune," Pitou blubbered: "Father Fortier sends me home from school—so no more studies, no examination, no purse, no college——"

His sobs changed into howls while the woman stared at him to try to read in his soul the reason for this expulsion.

"I suppose you have been playing truant again," she said. "I hear that you are always roaming round Farmer Billet's place to catch a sight of his daughter Catherine. Fie, fie! very pretty conduct in a future priest!"

Ange shook his head.

"You lie," shrieked the old maid, with her anger rising with the growing certainty that it was a serious scrape. "Last Sunday you were again seen rambling in Lovers-Walk with Kate Billet."

It was she who fibbed but she was one who believed the end justified the means, and a whale-truth might be caught by throwing out a tub-lie.

"Oh, no, they could not have seen me there," cried Ange; "for we were out by the Orange-gardens."

"There, you wretch, you see you were with her."

"But this is not a matter that Miss Billet is concerned in," ventured Ange, blushing like the overgrown boy of sixteen that he was.

"Yes, call her 'Miss' to pretend you have any respect for her, the flirt, the jilt, the mincing minx! I will tell her father confessor how she is carrying on."

"But I take my Bible oath that she is not a flirt."

"You defend her, when you need all the excuses you can rake up for yourself. This is going on fine. What is the world coming to, when children of sixteen are walking arm in arm under the shade trees."

"But, aunt, you are away out—Catherine will not let me 'arm' her—she keeps me off at arms-length."

"You see how you break down your own denials. You are calling her Catherine, plain, now. Oh, why not Kate, or Kitty, or some such silly nickname which you use in your iniquitous familiarity? She drives you away to have you come nearer, they all do."

"Do they? there, I never thought of that," exclaimed the swain, suddenly enlightened.

"Ah, you will have something else to think of! And she," said the old prude, "I will manage all this. I will ask Father Fortier to lock you up on bread and water for a fortnight and have her put in a nunnery if she cannot moderate her fancy for you."

She spoke so emphatically that Pitou was frightened.

"You are altogether wrong, my good aunt," pleaded he, clasping his hands: "Miss Catherine has nothing to do with my misfortune."

"Impurity is the mother of all the vices," returned Angelique sententiously.

"But Impurity has nothing to do with my being turned out of school," objected the youth: "the teacher put me out because I made too many barbarisms and solecisms which prevent me of having any chance to win that purse."

"What will become of you, then?"

"Blest if I know," wailed Pitou, who had never looked upon priesthood, with Aunt 'Gelique as housekeeper as Paradise on earth. "Let come what Providence pleases," he sighed, lamentably raising his eyes.

"Providence, do you call it? I see you have got hold of these newfangled ideas about philosophy."

"That cannot be, aunt, for I cannot go into Philosophy till I have passed Rhetoric, and I am only in the third course."

"Joke away," sneered the old maid to whom the school-jargon was Greek. "I speak of the philosophy of these philosophers, not what a pious man like the priest would allow in his holy house. You are a serpent and you have been gnawing a file of the newspapers in which these dreadful writers insult King and Queen and the Church! He is lost!"

When Aunt Angelique said her ward was lost, she meant that she was ruined. The danger was imminent. She took the sublime resolution to run to Father Fortier's for explanation and above all to try to patch up the breach.

CHAPTER III. A REVOLUTIONARY FARMER.

The departure of his aunt gave Pitou a quarter of an hour in tranquillity.

He wanted to utilize it. He gathered the crumbs of his aunt's meal to feed his lizards (he was a naturalist who was never without pets,) caught some flies for his ants and frogs, and opened the cupboard and bread-box to get a supply of food for himself. Appetite had come to him with the lonesomeness.

His preparations made for a feast, he went back to the doorway so as not to be surprised by the woman's return.

While he was watching, a pretty maid passed the end of the street, riding on the crupper of a horse laden with two panniers. One was filled with pigeons, the other with pullets. This was Catherine Billet, who smiled on Pitou, and stopped on seeing him.

According to his habit he turned red as a beet: with gaping mouth, he glared—we mean—admired Kate Billet, the last expression of feminine beauty to him. She looked up and down the street, nodded to her worshipper, and kept on in her way, Pitou trembling with delight as he nodded back.

Absorbed in his contemplation, he did not perceive his relative on the return from Fortier's. Suddenly she grabbed his hand, while turning pale with anger.

Abruptly roused from his bright dream by the electric shock always caused by Aunt Angelique's grasp, the youth wheeled and saw with horror that she was holding up his hand, which was in turn holding half a loaf with two most liberal smears of butter and another of white cheese applied to it.

The woman yelled with fury and Pitou groaned with fright. She raised her other claw-like hand and he lowered his head; she darted for the broom and the other dropped the food and took to his heels without any farewell speech.

Those two hearts knew one another and understood that they could not get on together any more.

Angelique bounced indoors and locked with a double turn of the key. The grating sound seemed a renewal of the tempest to the fugitive who put on the pace.

The result was an event the aunt was as far from expecting as the young man himself.

Running as though all the fiends from below were at his heels, Pitou was soon beyond the town bounds. On turning the burial-ground wall he bunked up against a horse.

"Good gracious," cried a sweet voice well-known to the flyer, "wherever are you racing so, Master Ange? You nearly made Younker take the bit in his teeth with the scare you gave us."

"Oh, Miss Catherine, what a misfortune is on me," replied Pitou, wide of the question.

"You alarm me," said the girl, pulling up in the mid-way; "What is wrong?"

"I cannot be a priest," returned the young fellow, as if revealing a world of iniquities.

"You won't," said the maid, roaring with laughter instead of throwing up her hands as Pitou expected. "Become a soldier, then. You must not make a fuss over such a trifle. Really, I thought your aunt had kicked the bucket."

"It is much the same thing, for she has kicked me out."

"Lor', no, for you have not the pleasure of mourning for her," observed Catherine Billet, laughing more heartily than before, which scandalized the nephew.

"You are a lucky one to be able to laugh like that, and it proves you have a merry heart, and the sorrows of others make no impression on you."

"Who tells you that I should not feel for you if you met a real grief?"

"Real? when I have not a feather to fly with!"

"All for the best," returned the peasant girl.

"But how about eating?" retorted Pitou; "a fellow must eat, and I am always sharp set."

"Don't you like to work?"

"What am I to work at?" whined he. "My aunt and Father Fortier have repeated a hundred times that I am good for nothing. Ah! if I had been bound prentice to a wheelwright or a carpenter, instead of their trying to make a priest of me. Upon my faith, Miss Catherine, a curse is on me!" said he with a wave of the hand in desperation.

"Alack!" sighed the girl who knew like everybody the orphan's melancholy tale: "there is truth in what you say, my poor Pitou. But there is one thing you might do."

"Do tell me what that is?" cried the youth, jumping towards the coming suggestion as a drowning man leaps for a twig of willow.

"You have a guardian in Dr. Gilbert, whose son is your schoolfellow."

"I should rather think he was, and by the same token I have taken many floggings for him."

"Why not apply to his father, who, certainly, will not shake you off?"

"That would be all right if I knew where to address him; but your father may know as he farms some of his land."

"I know that he sends some of the rent to America and banks the other part here at a notary's."

"America is a far cry," moaned Pitou.

"What, would you start for America?" exclaimed the maid, almost frightened at his courage.

"Me? Sakes! No, never! France is good enough for me if I could get enough to eat and drink."

"Very well," said she, falling into silence which lasted some time.

The lad was plunged into a thoughtful mood which would have much puzzled Teacher Fortier the logical man. Starting from Obscurity, the reverie brightened and then grew confused again, like lightning.

Younker had started in again for the walk home, and Pitou, with a hand on one basket, trudged on beside it. As dreamy as her neighbor, Catherine let the bridle drop with no fear about being run away with. There were no monsters on the highway and Younker bore no resemblance to the fabulous hippogriffs.

The walker stopped mechanically when the animal did, which was at the farm.

"Hello, is this you, Pitou?" challenged a strong-shouldered man, proudly stationed before a drinking pool where his horse was swilling.

"It is me, Master Billet."

"He's had another mishap," said the maid, jumping off the horse without any heed as to showing her ankles. "His aunt has sent him packing."

"What has he done to worry the old bigot this time?" queried the farmer.

"It appears that I am not good enough in Greek," said the scholar, who was lying, for it was Latin he was a bungler at.

"What do you want to be good at Greek for?" asked the broad-shouldered man.

"To explain Theocritus and read the Iliad. These are useful when you want to be a priest."

"Trash!" said Billet. "Do you need Greek and Latin? do I know my own language—can I read or write? but this does not prevent me plowing, sowing and reaping."

"But you, Master Billet, are a cultivator and not a priest: 'Agricole,' says

31

Virgil——"

"Do not you think a farmer is on a level with a larned clerk—you cussed choir-boy? Particularly when the Agricoaler has a hundred acres of tilled land in the sun and a thousand louis in the shade?"

"I have always been told that a priest leads the happiest life: though I grant," added Pitou, smiling most amiably, "I do not believe all I hear."

"You are right, my boy, by a blamed sight—you see I can make rhymes, if I like to try. It strikes me that you have the makings in you of something better than a scholard, and that it is a deused lucky thing that you try something else—mainly at the present time. As a farmer I know which way the wind blows, and it is rough for priests. So then, as you are an honest lad and larned," here Pitou bowed at being so styled for the first time—"you can get along without the black gown."

Catherine, who was setting the chickens and pigeons on the ground, was listening with interest to the dialogue.

"It looks hard to win a livelihood," said the lad.

"What do you know how to do?"

"I can make birdlime and snare game. I can mock the birds' songs, eh, Miss Kate?"

"He can whistle like a blackbird."

"But whistling is not a trade," commented Billet.

"Just what I say to myself, by Jingo!"

"Oh, you can swear—that is a manly accomplishment, any how."

"Oh, did I? I beg your pardon, farmer."

"Don't mention it," said the rustic. "I rip out myself sometimes. Thunder and blazes!" he roared to his horse, "can't you be quiet? these devilish Percherons must always be grazing and jerking. Are you lazy," he continued to the lad.

"I don't know. I have never worked at anything but learning Greek and Latin, and they do not tempt me much."

"A good job—that shows that you are not such a fool, as I took you for," said Billet.

His hearer opened his eyes immeasurably; this was the first time he had heard this order of ideas, subversive of all the theories set up for him previously.

"I mean, are you easily tired out?"

"Bless you, I can go ten leagues and never feel it."

"Good, we are getting on; we might train you a trifle lower and make some money on you as a runner."

"Train me lower," said Pitou, looking at his slender figure, bony arms and stilt-like legs; "I fancy I am thin now as it is."

"In fact, you are a treasure, my friend," replied the yeoman, bursting into laughter.

Pitou was stepping from one surprise to another; never had he been esteemed so highly.

"In short, how are you at work?"

"Don't know; for I never have worked."

The girl laughed, but her father took the matter seriously.

"These rogues of larned folk," he broke forth, shaking his fist at the town, "look at them training up the youth in the way they should not go, in laziness and idleness. What good is such a sluggard to his brothers, I want to know?"

"Not much," said Pitou; "luckily I have no brothers."

"By brothers I mean all mankind," continued the farmer; "are not all men brothers, hey?"

"The Scripture says so."

"And equals," proceeded the other.

"That is another matter," said the younger man; "if I had been the equal of Father Fortier I guess he would not have given me the whip so often; if I were the equal of my aunt, she would not have driven me from home."

"I tell you that all men are brothers and we shall soon prove this to the tyrants," said Billet. "I will take you into my house to prove it."

"You will? but, just think, I eat three pounds of bread a day, with butter and cheese to boot."

"Pooh, I see you will not be dear to feed," said the farmer, "we will keep you."

"Have you nothing else to ask father, Pitou?" inquired Catherine.

"Nothing, miss."

"What did you come along for?"

"Just to keep you company."

"Well, you are gallant, and I accept the compliment for what it is worth," said the girl, "but you came to ask news about your guardian, Pitou."

"So I did. That is funny—I forgot it."

"You want to speak about our worthy Dr. Gilbert?" said the farmer, with a tone indicating the degree of deep consideration in which he held his landlord.

"Just so," answered Pitou; "but I am not in need now; since you house me, I can tranquilly wait till he returns from America."

"You will not have to wait long, for he has returned."

"You don't say so; when?"

"I cannot exactly say: but he was at Havre a week ago; for I have a parcel in my saddlebags that comes from him and was handed me at Villers Cotterets, and here it is."

"How do you know it is from him?"

"Because there is a letter in it."

"Excuse me, daddy," interrupted Catherine, "but you boast that you cannot read."

"So I do! I want folks to say: 'There is old Farmer Billet, who owes nothing to nobody—not even the schoolmaster: for he has made himself all alone.' I did not read the letter but the rural constabulary quarter-master whom I met there."

"What does he say—that he still is content with you?"

"Judge for yourself."

Out of a leather wallet he took a letter which he held to his daughter, who read:

"My Dear Friend Billet: I arrive from America where I found a people richer, greater and happier than ours. This arises from their being free, while we are not. But we are marching towards this new era, and all must labor for the light to come. I know your principles, Friend Billet, and your influence on the farmers, your neighbors; and all the honest population of toilers and hands whom you lead, not like a king but a father.

"Teach them the principles of devotion and brotherhood I know you cherish. Philosophy is universal, all men ought to read their rights and duties by its light. I send you a little book in which these rights and duties are set forth. It is my work, though my name is not on the title-page. Propagate these principles, those of universal equality. Get them read in the winter evenings. Reading is the food of the mind as bread is that for the body.

"One of these days I shall see you, and tell you about a new kind of farming practiced in the United States. It consists, in the landlord and the tenant working on shares of the crop. It appears to me more according to the laws of primitive society and to the love of God.

"Greeting and brotherly feeling,

"HONORE GILBERT, CITIZEN OF PHILADELPHIA."

"This letter is nicely written," observed Pitou.

"I warrant it is," said Billet.

"Yes, father dear; but I doubt the quarter-master will be of your opinion. Because, this not only will get Dr. Gilbert into trouble, but you, too."

"Pooh, you are always scarey," sneered the farmer. "This does not hinder me having the book, and—we have got something for you to do, Pitou—you shall read me this in the evenings."

"But in the daytime?"

"Tend the sheep and cows. Let us have a squint at the book."

He took out one of those sewn pamphlets in a red cover, issued in great quantity in those days, with or without permission of the authorities. In the latter case the author ran great risk of being sent to prison.

"Read us the title, Pitou, till we have a peep at the book inside. The rest afterwards."

The boy read on the first page these words, which usage has made vague and meaningless lately but at that epoch they had a deep effect on all hearts:

"On the Independence of Man and the Freedom of Nations."

"What do you say to that, my lad?" cried the farmer.

"Why, it seems to me that Independence and Freedom are much of a muchness? my guardian would be whipped out of the class by Father Fortier for being guilty of a pleonasm.

"Fleanism or not, this book is the work of a real man," rejoined the other.

"Never mind, father," said Catherine, with the admirable instinct of womankind: "I beg you to hide the book. It will get you into some bad scrape. I tremble merely to look at it."

"Why should it do me any harm, when it has not brought it on the writer?"

"How do you know that, father? This letter was written a week ago, and took all that time to arrive from Havre. But I had a letter this morning from Sebastian Gilbert, at Paris, who sends his love to his foster-brother—I forgot that—and he has been three days without his father meeting him there."

"She is right," said Pitou: "this delay is alarming."

"Hold your tongue, you timid creature; and let us read the doctor's treatise?" said the farmer: "It will not only make you larned, but manly."

Pitou stuck the book under his arm with so solemn a movement that it completed the winning of his protector's heart.

"Have you had your dinner?" asked he.

"No, sir," replied the youth.

"He was eating when he was driven from home," said the girl.

"Well, you go in and ask Mother Billet for the usual rations and to-morrow we will set you regularly to work."

With an eloquent look the orphan thanked him, and, conducted by Catherine, he entered the kitchen, governed by the absolute rule of Mother Billet.

CHAPTER IV. LONG LEGS ARE GOOD FOR RUNNING, IF NOT FOR DANCING.

Mistress Billet was a fat woman who honored her husband, delighted in her daughter and fed her field hands as no other housewife did for miles around. So there was a rush to be employed at Billet's.

Pitou appreciated his luck at the full value when he saw the golden loaf placed at his elbow, the pot of cider set on his right, and the chunk of mild-cured bacon before him. Since he lost his mother, five years before, the orphan had never enjoyed such cheer, even on a feast day.

He remembered, too, that his new duties of neatherd and shepherd had been fulfilled by gods and demigods.

Besides Mrs. Billet had the management of the kine and orders were not harsh from Catherine's mouth.

"You shall stay here," said she; "I have made father understand that you are good for a heap of things; for instance, you can keep the accounts——"

"Well, I know the four rules of arithmetic," said Pitou, proudly.

"You are one ahead of me. Here you stay."

"I am glad, for I could not live afar from you. Oh, I beg pardon, but that came from my heart."

"I do not bear you ill will for that," said Catherine; "it is not your fault if you like us here."

Poor young lambs, they say so much in so few words!

So Pitou did much of Catherine's work and she had more time to make pretty caps and "titivate herself up," to use her mother's words.

"I think you prettier without a cap on," he remarked.

"You may; but your taste is not the rule. I cannot go over to the town and dance without a cap on. That is all very well for fine ladies, who have the right to go bareheaded and wear powder on the hair."

"You beat them all without powder."

"Compliments again, did you learn to make them at Fortier's."

"No, he taught nothing like that."

"Dancing?"

"Lord help us—dancing at Fortier's! he made us cut capers at the end of the birch."

"So you do not know how to dance? Still you shall come along with me on Sunday, and see Master Isidor Charny dance: he is the best dancer of all the gentlemen round here."

"Who is he?"

"Owner of Boursiennes Manor. He will dance with me next Sunday."

Pitou's heart shrank without his knowing why.

"So you make yourself lovely to dance with him?" he inquired.

"With him and all the rest. You, too, if you like to learn."

Next day he applied himself to the new accomplishment and had to acknowledge that tuition is agreeable according to the tutor. In two hours he had a very good idea of the art.

"Ah, if you had taught me Latin, I don't believe I should have made so many mistakes," he sighed.

"But then you would be a priest and be shut up in an ugly old monastery where no women are allowed."

"That's so; well, I am not sorry I am not to be a priest."

At breakfast Billet reminded his new man that the reading of the Gilbert pamphlet was to take place in the barn at ten a.m. next day. That was the hour for mass, Pitou objected.

"Just why I pitch on it, to test my lads," replied the farmer.

Billet detested religious leaders as the apostles of tyranny, and seized the opportunity of setting up one altar against another.

His wife and daughter raising some remonstrance, he said that church was good enough for womanfolks, no doubt, and they might go and sleep away their time there; but it suited men to hear stronger stuff, or else the men should not work on his land.

Billet was a despot in his house; only Catherine ever coped with him and she was hushed when he frowned.

But she thought to gain something for Pitou on the occasion. She pointed out that the doctrines might suffer by the mouthpiece; that the reader was too shabby for the phrases to make a mark. So Pitou was agreeably surprised when Sunday morning came round to see the tailor enter while he was ruminating how he could "clean up," and lay on a chair a coat and breeches of sky blue cloth and a long waistcoat of white and pink stripes. At the same time a housemaid came in to put on another chair opposite the first, a shirt and a neckcloth; if the former fitted, she was to make half-a-dozen.

It was the day for surprises: behind the two came the hatter who brought a three-cocked hat of the latest fashion so full of style and elegance that nothing better was worn in Villers Cotterets.

The only trouble was that the shoes were too small for Ange: the man had made them on the last of his son who was four years the senior of Pitou. This superiority of our friend made him proud for a space, but it was spoilt by his fear that he would have to go to the ball in his old shoes—which would mar the new suit. This uneasiness was of short duration. A pair of shoes sent for Father Billet were brought at the same time and they fitted Pitou—a fact kept hidden from Billet, who might not like his new man literally stepping into his own shoes.

When Pitou, dressed, hatted, shod and his hair dressed, looked at himself in the mirror, he did not know himself. He grinned approvingly and said, as he drew himself up to his full height:

"Fetch along your Master Charnys now!"

"My eyes," cried the farmer, admiring him as much as the women when he strutted into the main room: "you have turned out a strapper, my lad. I should like Aunt Angelique to see you thus togged out. She would want you home again."

"But, papa, she could not take him back, could she?"

"As long as he is a minor—unless she forfeited her right by driving him out."

"But the five years are over," said Pitou quickly, "for which Dr. Gilbert paid a thousand francs."

"There is a man for you!" exclaimed Billet: "just think that I am always hearing such good deeds of his. D'ye see, it is life and death for him!" and he raised his hand to heaven.

"He wanted me to learn a trade," went on the youth.

"Quite right of him. See how the best intentions are given a twist. A thousand francs are left to fit a lad for the battle of life, and they put him in a priest's school to make a psalm-singer of him. How much did your aunt give old Fortier?"

"Nothing."

"Then she pocketed Master Gilbert's money?"

"It is likely enough."

"Mark ye, Pitou, I have a bit of a hint to give you. When the old humbug of a saint cracks her whistle, look into the boxes, demijohns and old crocks, for she has been hiding her savings. But to business. Have you the Gilbert book?"

"Here, in my pocket."

"Have you thought the matter over, father?" said Catherine.

"Good actions do not want any thought," replied the farmer. "The doctor bade me have the book read and the good principles sown. The book shall be read and the principles scattered."

"But we can go to church?" ventured the maid timidly.

"Mother and you can go to the pew, yes: but we men have better to do. Come alone, Pitou, my man."

Pitou bowed to the ladies as well as the tight coat allowed and followed the farmer, proud to be called a man.

The gathering in the barn was numerous. Billet was highly esteemed by his hired men and they did not mind his roaring at them as long as he boarded and lodged them bounteously. So they had all hastened to come at his invitation.

Besides, at this period, the strange fever ran through France felt when a nation is going to go to work. New and strange words were current in mouths never pronouncing them. Freedom, Independence, emancipation, were heard not only among the lower classes but from the nobility in the first place, so that the popular voice was but their echo.

From the West came the light which illumined before it burnt. The sun rose in the Great Republic of America which was to be in its round a vast conflagration for France by the beams of which frightened nations were to see "Freedom" inscribed in letters of blood.

So political meetings were less rare than might be supposed. Apostles of an unknown deity sprang up from heaven knows where, and went from town to town, disseminating words of hope. Those at the head of the government found certain wheels clogged without understanding where the hindrance lay. Opposition was in all minds before it appeared in hands and limbs, but it was present, sensible, and the more menacing as it was intangible like a spectre and could be premised before it was grappled with.

Twenty and more farmers, field hands, and neighbors of Billet were in the barn.

When their friend walked in with Pitou, all heads were uncovered and all hats waved at arms-length. It was plain that these men were willing to die at the master's call.

The farmer explained that the book was by Dr. Gilbert which the young man was about to read out. The doctor was well-known in the district where he owned much land, while Billet was his principal tenant.

A cask was ready for the reader, who scrambled upon it, and began his task.

Common folks, I may almost say, people in general, listen with the most attention to words they do not clearly understand. The full sense of the pamphlet escaped the keenest wits here, and Billet's as well. But in the midst of the cloudy phrases shone the words Freedom, Independence and Equality like lightnings in the dark, and that was enough for the applause to break forth:

"Hurrah for Dr. Gilbert!" was shouted.

When the book was read a third through, it was resolved to have the rest in two more sessions, next time on the Sunday coming, when all hands promised to attend.

Pitou had read very well: nothing succeeds like success. He took his share in the cheers for the language, and Billet himself felt some respect arise for the dismissed pupil of Father Fortier.

One thing was lacking to Ange, that Catherine had not witnessed his oratorical triumph.

But Billet hastened to impart his pleasure to his wife and daughter. Mother Billet said nothing, being a woman of narrow mind.

"I am afraid you will get into trouble," sighed Catherine, smiling sadly.

"Pshaw, playing the bird of ill-omen again. Let me tell you that I like larks better than owls."

"Father, I had warning that you were looked upon suspiciously."

"Who said so?"

"A friend."

"Advice ought to be thanked. Tell me the friend's name?"

"He ought to be well informed, as it is Viscount Isidor Charny."

"What makes that scented dandy meddle with such matters? Does he give me advice on the way I should think? Do I suggest how he should cut his coat? It seems to me that it would be only tarring him with the same brush."

"I am not telling you this to vex you, father: but the advice is given with good intention."

"I will give him a piece, and you can transmit it with my compliments. Let him and his upper class look to themselves. The National Assembly is going to give them a shaking up; and the question will be roughly handled of the royal pets and favorites. Warning to his brother George, the Count of Charny, who is one of the gang, and on very close terms with the Austrian leech."

"Father, you have more experience than we, and you can act as you please," returned the girl.

"Indeed," said Pitou in a low voice, "why does this Charny fop shove in his oar anyhow?" for he was filled with arrogance from his success.

Catherine did not hear, or pretended not, and the subject dropped.

Pitou thought the dinner lasted a long time as he was in a hurry to go off with Catherine and show his finery at the rustic ball. Catherine looked charming. She was a pretty, black-eyed but fair girl, slender and flexible as the willows shading the farm spring. She had tricked herself out with the natural daintiness setting off all her advantages, and the little cap she had made for herself suited her wonderfully.

Almost the first of the stray gentlemen who condescended to patronize

44

the popular amusement was a young man whom Pitou guessed to be Isidor Charny.

He was a handsome young blade of twenty-three or so, graceful in every movement like those brought up in aristocratic education from the cradle. Besides, he was one of those who wear dress to the best harmony.

On seeing his hands and feet, Pitou began to be less proud over Nature's prodigality towards him in these respects. He looked down at his legs with the eye of the stag in the fable. He sighed when Catherine wished to know why he was so glum.

But honest Pitou, after being forced to own the superiority of Charny as a beauty, had to do so as a dancer.

Dancing was part of the training, then: Lauzum owed his fortune at court to his skill in a curranto in the royal quadrille. More than one other nobleman had won his way by the manner of treading a measure and arching the instep.

The viscount was a model of grace and perfection.

"Lord 'a' mercy," sighed Pitou when Catherine returned to him; "I shall never dare to dance with you after seeing Lord Charny at it."

Catherine did not answer as she was too good to tell a lie; she stared at the speaker for he was suddenly becoming a man: he could feel jealousy.

She danced three or four times yet, and after another round with Isidor Charny, she asked to be taken home; that was all she had come for, one might guess.

"What ails you?" she asked as her companion kept quiet; "why do you not speak to me?"

"Because I cannot talk like Viscount Charny," was the other's reply. "What can I say after all the fine things he spoke during the dances?"

"You are unfair, Ange; for we were talking about you. If your guardian does not turn up, we must find you a patron."

"Am I not good enough to keep the farm books?" sighed Pitou.

"On the contrary, with the education you have received you are fitted for something better."

"I do not know what I am coming to, but I do not want to owe it to Viscount Charny."

"Why refuse his protection? His brother the Count, is, they say, particularly in favor at the court, and he married a bosom friend of the Queen Marie Antoinette. Lord Isidor tells me that he will get you a place in the custom-house, if you like."

"Much obliged, but as I have already told you, I am content to stay as I am, if your father does not send me away."

"Why the devil should I," broke in a rough voice which Catherine started to recognize as her father's.

"Not a word about Lord Isidor," whispered she to Pitou.

"I—I hardly know—I kind o' feared I was not smart enough, stammered Ange.

"When you can count like one o'clock, and read to beat the schoolmaster, who still believes himself a wise clerk. No, Pitou, the good God brings people to me, and once they are under my rooftree, they stick as long as He pleases."

With this assurance Pitou returned to his new home. He had experienced a great change. He had lost trust in himself. And so he slept badly. He recalled Gilbert's book; it was principally against the privileged classes and their abuses, and the cowardice of those who submitted to them. Pitou fancied he began to understand these matters better and he made up his mind to read more of the work on the morrow.

Rising early, he went down with it into the yard where he could have the light fall on the book through an open window with the additional advantage that he might see Catherine through it. She might be expected down at any moment.

But when he glanced up from his reading at the intervention of an opaque body between him and the light, he was amazed at the disagreeable person who caused the eclipse.

This was a man of middle age, longer and thinner than Pitou, clad in a coat as patched and thread-bare as his own—for Pitou had resumed his old clothes for the working day—while thrusting his head forward on a lank neck, he read the book with as much curiosity as the other felt relish—though it was upside down to him.

Ange was greatly astonished. A kind smile adorned the stranger's mouth in which a few snags stuck up, a pair crossing another like boar's fangs.

"The American edition," said the man snuffling up his nose, "In octavo, 'On the Freedom of Man and the Independence of Nations. Boston, 1788.'"

Pitou opened his eyes in proportion to the progress of the unknown reader, so that when he had reached the end his eyes were at the utmost extent.

"Just so, sir," said Pitou.

"This is the treatise of Dr. Gilbert's?" said the man in black.

"Yes, sir," rejoined the young man politely.

He rose as he had been taught that he must not sit in a superior's presence and to simple Ange everybody was a superior. In rising something fair and rosy attracted his attention at the window: it was Catherine come down at last, who was making cautionary signs to him.

"I do not want to be inquisitive, sir, but I should like to know whose book this is?" remarked the stranger pointing at the book without touching it as it was between Pitou's hands.

Pitou was going to say it belonged to Billet, but the girl motioned that he ought to lay claim to it himself. So he majestically responded:

"This book is mine."

The man in black had seen nothing but the book and its reader and heard but these words. But he suspiciously glanced behind: swift as a bird, Catherine had vanished.

"Your book?"

"Yes; do you want to read it—'Avidus legendi libri' or 'legendie historiae?'"

"Hello! you appear much above the condition your clothes beseem," said the stranger: "'Non dives vestitu sed ingenio'—— and it follows that I take you into custody."

"Me, in custody?" gasped Pitou at the summit of stupefaction.

At the order of the man in black, two sergeants of the Paris Police seemed to rise up out of the ground.

"Let us draw up a report," said the man, while one of the constables bound Pitou's hands by a rope and took the book into his own possession, and the other secured the prisoner to a ring happening to be,by the window.

Pitou was going to bellow, but the same person who had already so influenced him seemed to hint he should submit.

He submitted with a docility enchanting the policemen, and the man in a black suit in particular. Hence, without any distrust, they walked into the farmhouse where the two policemen took seats at a table while the other—we shall know what he was after presently.

Scarcely had the trio gone in than Pitou heard the voice:

"Hold up your hands."

He raised them and his head as well, and saw Catherine's pale and frightened face: in her hand she held a knife.

Pitou rose on tiptoe and she cut the rope round his wrists.

"Take the knife," she said, "and cut yourself free from the ringbolt."

Pitou did not wait for twice telling but found himself wholly free.

"Here is a double-louis," went on the girl; "you have good legs. Make away. Go to Paris and warn the doctor."

She could not conclude for the constables appeared again as the coin fell at Pitou's feet. He picked it up quickly. Indeed the armed constables stood on the sill for an instant, astounded to see the man free whom they had left bound. But as at the dog's least stir the hare bolts, at the first move of the police, Pitou made a prodigious leap and was on the other side of the hedge.

They uttered a yell which brought out the corporal, who held a little casket under the arm. He lost no time in speech-making but darted after the escaped one. His men followed his example. But they were not able to jump the hedge and ditch, like Pitou, and were forced to go roundabout.

But when they got over, they beheld the youth five hundred paces off on the meadow, tearing away directly to the woods, a quarter of a league distant, which he would gain in a short time.

He turned at this nick, and perceiving the enemy take up the chase, though more for the name of the thing than any hope of overtaking him, he doubled his speed and soon dashed out of sight in the thicket.

He had the wind as well as the swiftness of the buck, and he ran for ten minutes as he might for an hour. But judging that he was out of danger, by his instinct, he stopped to breathe, listen and make sure that he was quite alone.

"It is incredible what a quantity of incidents have been crammed into three days," he mused.

He looked alternately at his coin and the knife.

"I must find time to change the gold and give Miss Catherine a penny for the knife, for fear it will cut our friendship. Never mind, since she bade me go to Paris, I shall go."

On making out where he was, he struck a straight line over the heath to come out on the Paris highroad.

CHAPTER V. WHY THE POLICE AGENT CAME WITH THE CONSTABLES.

About six that morning a police-agent from the capital, accompanied by two inferior policemen, had arrived at Villers Cotterets where they presented themselves to the police justice, and asked him to tell them where Farmer Billet dwelt.

Five hundred paces from the farmhouse the corporal, as the exempt's rank was in the semi-military organization of the police of the era, perceived a peasant working in the field, of whom he inquired about his master.

The man pointed to a horseman a quarter of a league off.

"He won't be back till nine," he said; "there he is inspecting the work. He comes in for breakfast, then."

"If you want to please your master, run and tell him a gentleman from town is waiting to see him."

"Do you mean Dr. Gilbert?"

"Run and tell him, all the same."

No sooner was he notified than Billet galloped home but when he entered the room where he expected to see his landlord under the canopy of the large fireplace, none were there but his wife, sitting in the middle, plucking ducks with all the care such a task demands. Catherine was up in her room, preparing finery for Sunday, from the pleasure girls feel in getting ready for fun.

"Who asked for me?" demanded Billet, stopping on the threshold and looking round.

"Me," replied a flute-like voice behind him.

"Turning, the yeoman beheld the police-agent and his two myrmidons.

"How now? what do you want?" he snarled, making three steps

backwards.

"Next to nothing, dear Master Billet," replied the unctuous speaker: "we have to make a search in your premises, that is all."

"A search, hey?" repeated Billet, glancing at his gun, on hooks over the mantelpiece. "Since we had a National Assembly," he said, "I thought citizens were no longer exposed to proceedings which smack of another age and style of things. What do you want with a peaceable and loyal man?"

Policemen are alike all the world over in their never answering questions of their victims; some bewail them while clapping on the iron cuffs, searching them or pinioning; they are the most dangerous as they appear to be the best. The fellow who descended on Farmer Billet was of the hypocritical school, those who have a tear for those they overhaul, but they never let their hands be idle to dash away the tear.

Uttering a sigh, this man waved his hand to his acolytes, who went up to Billet. He jumped back and reached out for his musket.

But his hand was turned aside from the doubly dangerous weapon to him who made use of it and her whose pair of slight hands was strong with terror and mighty with entreaty.

It was Catherine who had rushed to the spot in time to save her father from the crime of rebellion to justice.

After this first outburst, Billet made no further resistance.

The police agent ordered him to be locked up in one of the ground floor rooms which he had noticed to be barred, though Billet, who had the grating done, had forgotten the precaution. Catherine was placed in a first-floor room and Mrs. Billet was shoved into the kitchen as inoffensive. Master of the fort, the Exempt set to searching all the furniture.

"What are you doing?" roared Billet who saw through the keyhole that his house was turned out of windows.

"Looking, as you see, for something we cannot find," replied the police officer.

"But you may be robbers, burglars, scoundrels!"

"Oh, you wrong us, master," rejoined the fellow through the door; "we are honest folk like yourself—only we are in the wages of the King and we have to obey his orders."

"His Majesty's orders," repeated the farmer: "King Louis XVI. gives you orders to rummage my desk and turn my things upside down? When the famine was so dreadful last year that we thought of eating our horses; when the hail on the thirteenth of July two years back cut our wheat to chaff—his Majesty never bothered about us. What has happened at my farm at present for him to concern himself—never having seen or known me?"

"You will please excuse me," said the man, opening the door a little and warily showing a search-warrant issued by the Chief of Police but as usual commencing with "In the King's Name"—"His Majesty has heard about you, old fellow; though he may not personally know you, do not kick at the honor he does you, and try to receive properly those whom he sends in his royal name."

With a polite bow and a friendly wink, the chief policeman slammed the door, and recommenced the ferreting.

Billet held his tongue and with folded arms, trod the room: he felt he was in the men's power. The searching went on silently. These men seemed fallen from the skies. No one had seen them but the farm-hand who had pointed out the way to the farmhouse. In the yard the watch-dogs had not barked; the leader of the expedition must be a celebrated man in his line and not making his first arrest.

Billet heard his daughter wailing in the room overhead. He recalled her prophetic words, for he had no doubt that the investigation was caused by the doctor's book.

Nine o'clock struck, and Billet could count his hired men returning for their morning meal from the fields. This made him comprehend that, in case of conflict, he could have numbers of not law on his side. This made the blood boil in his veins. He had not the temper to bear inaction any longer and grasping the door he gave it such a shaking by the handle that with such another he would send the lock flying.

The police opened it at once and confronted the farmer, threatening and upright before the house turned inside out.

"But, to make it short, what are you looking for?" roared the caged lion: "Tell me, or by the Lord Harry of Navarre, I swear I'll thump it out of you."

The flocking in of the farm lads had not escaped the corporal's alert eye; he reckoned them and was convinced that, in case of a tussel, he could not crow on the battlefield.

With more honeyed politeness than before, he sneaked up to the speaker and said as he bowed to the ground:

"I am going to tell you, Master Billet, though it goes dead against the rules and regulations. We are looking for a subversive publication, and incendiary pamphlet put on the back list by the Royal Censors."

"A book in the house of a farmer who cannot read?"

"What is there amazing in that, when you are friend of the author and he sent you a copy?"

"I am not the friend of Dr. Gilbert but his humble servant," replied the other. "To be his friend would be too great an honor for a poor farmer like me."

This unreflected reply, in which Billet betrayed himself by confessing that he not only knew the author, which was natural being his landlord, but the book—assured victory to the officer of the law. This man drew himself up to his full height, with his most benignant air, and smiling as he tapped Billet on the shoulder, so that he seemed to cleave his head in twain, he said:

"You have let the cat out of the bag. You have been the first to name Gilbert, whose name we kept back out of discretion."

"That's so," muttered the farmer. "Look here, I will not merely own up but—will you stop pulling things about if I tell you where the book is?"

"Why, certainly," said the chief making a sign to his associates; "for the book is the object of the search. Only," he added with a sly grin, "don't allow you have one copy when you have a dozen."

"I swear, I have only the one."

"We are obliged to get that down to a certainty by the most minute search, Master Billet. Have five minute's farther patience. We are only poor servants of justice, under orders from those above us, and you will not oppose honorable men doing their duty—for there are such in all walks of life."

He had found the flaw in the armor: he knew how to talk Billet over.

"Go on, but be done quickly," he said, turning his back on them.

The man closed the door softly and still more quietly turned the key: which made Billet snap his fingers: sure that he could burst the door off its hinges if he had to do it.

On his part the policeman waved his fellows to the work. All three in a trice went through the papers, books and linen. Suddenly, at the bottom of an open clothespress, they perceived a small oak casket clamped with iron. The corporal pounced on it as a vulture on its prey. By the mere view, by his scent, by the place where it was stored, he had divined what he sought, for he quickly hid the box under his tattered mantle and beckoned to his bravoes that he had accomplished the errand.

At that very moment Billet had come to the end of his patience.

"I tell you that you cannot find what you are looking for unless I tell you," he called out. "There is no need to 'make hay' with my things. I am not a conspirator, confound you! Come, get this into your noddles. Answer, or, by all the blue moons, I will go to Paris and complain to the King, to the Assembly and to the people."

At this time the King was still spoken of before the people.

"Yes, dear Master Billet, we hear you, and we are ready to bow to your excellent reasons. Come, let us know where the book is, and, as we are now convinced that you have only the single copy, we will seize that and get away. There it is in a nutshell."

"Well, the book is in the hands of a lad to whom I entrusted it this morning to carry it to a friend's," said Billet.

"What is the name of this honest lad?" queried the man in black coaxingly.

"Ange Pitou; he is a poor orphan whom I housed from charity, and who does not know the nature of the book."

"I thank you, dear Master Billet," said the corporal, throwing the linen into the hole in the wall and closing the lid. "And where may this nice boy be, prithee?"

"I fancy I saw him as I came in, under the arbor by the Spanish climbing beans. Go and take the book away but do not hurt him."

"Hurt? oh, Master, you do not know us to think we would hurt a fly."

They advanced in the indicated direction, where they had the adventure with Pitou already described. Catherine had heard enough in the words about the doctor, the book, and the search-warrant, to save the innocent holder of the treasonable pamphlet.

Since the double errand of the police was fulfilled, the commander of the expedition was only too glad of the excuse to get far away. So he bounded on his men by his voice and example till they ran him into the woods. Then they came to a halt in the bushes. In the chase they were joined by two more policeman who had hidden on the farm with orders not to run up unless called.

"Faith, it is a good job the lad did not have the box instead of the book," said the organizer of the attack, "we would be obliged to take post-horses to catch up with him. Hang me if he is a man at all so much as a deer."

"But you have the prize, eh, Master Wolfstep?" said one of the subordinates.

"Certainly, comrade, for here it is," answered the police agent, to whom the nickname had been given for his sidelong "lope" or wolfish tread and its lightness.

"Then we are entitled to the promised reward, eh?"

"Ay, and here you are," said the captain of the squad, distributing gold pieces among them with no preference for those who had actively prosecuted the search and the others.

"Long live the Chief!" called out the men.

"There is no harm in your cheering the Chief," said Wolfstep: "but it is not he who cashes up this trip. It is some friend of his, lady or gentleman, who wants to keep in the background."

"I wager that he or she wants that little box bad," suggested one of the hirelings.

"Rigoulet, my friend," said the leader, "I have always certified that you are a chap full of keenness; but while we wait for the gift to win its reward, we had better be on the move. That confounded countryman does not look easily cooled down, and when he perceives the casket is missing, he may set his farm boys on our track; and they are poachers capable of keeling us over with a shot as surely as the best Swiss marksmen in his Majesty's forces."

This advice was that of the majority, for the five men kept on along the forest skirts out of sight till they reached the highroad.

This was no useless precaution for Catherine had no sooner seen the party disappear in pursuit of Pitou than, full of confidence in the last one's agility, who would lead them a pretty chase, she called on the farm-men to open the door.

They knew something unusual was going on but not exactly what.

They ran in to set her free and she liberated her father.

Billet seemed in a dream. Instead of rushing out of the room, he walked forth warily, and acted as if not liking to stay in any one place and yet hated to look on the furniture and cupboards disturbed by the posse.

"They have got the book, anyway?" he questioned.

"I believe they took that, dad, but not Pitou, who cut away? If they are sticking to him, they will all be over at Cayelles or Vauciennes by this time."

"Capital! Poor lad, he owes all this harrying to me."

"Oh, father, do not bother about him but look to ourselves. Be easy about Pitou getting out of his scrape. But what a state of disorder! look at this, mother!"

"They are low blackguards," said Mother Billet: "they have not even respected my linen press."

"What, tumbled over the linen?" said Billet, springing towards the cavity which the corporal had carefully closed but into which, opening it, he plunged both arms deeply. "It is not possible!"

"What are you looking for, father?" asked the girl as her father looked about him bewildered.

"Look, look if you can see it anywhere: the casket! that is what the villains were raking for."

"Dr. Gilbert's casket?" inquired Mrs. Billet, who commonly let others do the talking and work in critical times.

"Yes, that most precious casket," responded the farmer thrusting his hands into his mop of hair.

"You frighten me, father," said Catherine.

"Wretch that I am," cried the man, in rage, "and fool never to suspect that. I never thought about the casket. Oh, what will the doctor say? What will he think? That I am a betrayer, a coward, a worthless fellow!"

"Oh, heavens, what was in it, dad?"

"I don't know; but I answered for it to the doctor on my life and I ought to have been killed defending it."

He made so threatening a gesture against himself that the women recoiled in terror.

"My horse, bring me my horse," roared the madman. "I must let the doctor know—he must be apprised."

"I told Pitou to do that."

"Good! no, what's the use?—a man afoot. I must ride to Paris. Did you not read in his letter that he was going there? My horse!"

"And will you leave us in the midst of anguish?"

"I must, my girl, I must," he said, kissing Catherine convulsively: "the doctor said: 'If ever you lose that box, or rather if it is stolen from you, come to warn me the instant you perceive the loss, Billet, wherever I am. Let nothing stop you, not even the life of man.'"

"Lord, what can be in it?"

"I don't know a bit. But I do know that it was placed in my keeping, and that I have let it be snatched away. But here is my nag. I shall learn where the father is by his son at the college."

Kissing his wife and his daughter for the last time, the farmer bestrode his steed and set off towards the city at full gallop.

CHAPTER VI. ON THE ROAD.

Pitou was spurred by the two most powerful emotions in the world, love and fear. Panic bade him take care of himself as he would be arrested and perhaps flogged; love in Catherine's voice had said: "Be off to Paris."

These two stimulants led him to fly rather than run.

Heaven is infallible as well as mighty: how useful were the long legs of Pitou, so ungraceful at a ball, in streaking it over the country, as well as the knotty knees, although his heart, expanded by terror, beat three to a second. My Lord Charny, with his pretty feet and little knees, and symmetrically placed calves, could not have dashed along at this gait.

He had gone four leagues and a half in an hour, as much as is required of a good horse at the trot. He looked behind: nothing on the road; he looked forward; only a couple of women.

Encouraged, he threw himself on the turf by the roadside and reposed. The sweet smell of the lucerne and marjoram did not make him forget Mistress Billet's mild-cured bacon and the pound-and-a-half of bread which Catherine sliced off for him at every meal. All France lacked bread half as good as that, so dear that it originated the oft repeated saying of Duchess Polignac that "the poor hungry people ought to eat cake."

Pitou said that Catherine was the most generous creature in creation and the Billet Farm the most luxurious palace.

He turned a dying eye like the Israelites crossing the Jordan towards the east, where the Billet fleshpots smoked.

Sighing, but starting off anew, he went at a job-pace for a couple of hours which brought him towards Dammartin.

Suddenly his expert ear, reliable as a Sioux Indian's, caught the ring of a horseshoe on the road.

He had hardly concluded that the animal was coming at the gallop than he saw it appear on a hilltop four hundred paces off.

Fear which had for a space abandoned Pitou, seized him afresh, and restored him the use of those long if unshapely legs with which he had made such marvellous good time a couple of hours previously.

Without reflecting, looking behind or trying to hide his fright, Ange cleared the ditch on one side and darted through the woods to Ermenonville. He did not know the place but he spied some tall trees and reasoned that, if they were on the skirts of a forest, he was saved.

This time he had to beat a horse; Pitou's feet had become wings.

He went all the faster as on glancing over his shoulder, he saw the horseman jump the hedge and ditch from the highway.

He had no more doubts that the rider was after him so that he not only doubled his pace but he dreaded to lose anything by looking behind.

But the animal, superior to the biped in running, gained on him, and Pitou heard the rider plainly calling him by name.

Nearly overtaken, still he struggled till the cut of a whip crossed his legs, and a well-known voice thundered:

"Blame you, you idiot—have you made a vow to founder Younker?"

The horse's name put an end to the fugitive's irresolution.

"Oh, I hear Master Billet," he groaned, as he rolled over on his back, exhaustion and the lash having thrown him on the grass.

Assured of the identity he sat up, while the farmer reined in Younker, streaming with white froth.

"Oh, dear master," said Pitou, "how kind of you to ride after me. I swear to you that I should come back to the farm late. I got to the end of the double-louis Miss Catherine gave me. But since you have overtaken me, here is the gold, for it is your'n, and let us get back."

"A thousand devils," swore the yeoman, "we have a lot to do at the farm, I don't think. Where are the sleuth-hounds?"

"Sleuth hounds?" repeated Pitou, not understanding the nickname for what we call detective police officer's, though it had already entered into the language.

"Those sneaks in black," continued Billet, "if you can understand that better."

"Oh, you bet that I did not amuse myself by waiting till they came up."

"Bravo, dropped them, eh?"

"Flatter myself I did."

"Then, if certain what did you keep on running for?"

"I thought you were their captain who had taken to horse to have me."

"Come, come you are not such a dunderhead as I thought. As the road is clear, make an effort, get up behind me on the crupper and let us hurry into Dammartin. I will change horses at Neighbor Lefranc's, for Younker is done up, so we can push ahead for Paris."

"But I do not see what use I shall be there," remonstrated Pitou.

"But I think the other way. You can serve me there, for you have big fists, and I hold it for a fact that they are going to fall to hitting out at one another in the city."

Far from charmed by this prospect, the lad was wavering when Billet caught hold of him as of a sack of flour and slung him across the horse.

Regaining the road, by dint of spur, cudgel and heel, Younker was sent along at so fair a gait that they were in Dammartin in less than half an hour.

Billet rode in by a lane, not the main road, to Father Lefranc's farm, where he left his man and horse in the yard, to run direct into the kitchen where the master, going out, was buttoning up his leggings.

"Quick, quick, old mate, your best horse," he hailed him before he recovered from his astonishment.

"That's Maggie—the good beast is just harnessed. I was going out on her."

"She'll do; only I give fair warning that I shall break her down most likely."

"What for, I should like to know?"

"Because I must be in Paris this evening," said the farmer, making the masonic sign of "Pressing danger."

"Ride her to death, then," answered Lefranc; "but give me Younker."

"A bargain."

"Have a glass of wine?"

"Two. I have an honest lad with me who is tired with traveling this far. Give him some refreshment."

In ten minutes the gossips had put away a bottle and Pitou had swallowed a two-pound loaf and a hunk of bacon, nearly all fat. While he was eating, the stableman, a good sort of a soul, rubbed him down with a wisp of hay as if he were a favorite horse. Thus feasted and massaged, Pitou swallowed a glass of wine from a third bottle, emptied with so much velocity that the lad was lucky to get his share.

Billet got upon Maggie, and Pitou "forked" himself on, though stiff as a pair of compasses.

The good beast, tickled by the spur, trotted bravely under the double load towards town, without ceasing to flick off the flies with her robust tail, the strong hairs lashing the dust off Pitou's back and stinging his thin calves, from which his stockings had run down.

CHAPTER VII. THE FIRST BLOOD.

Night was thickening as the two travelers reached La Villette, a suburb of Paris. A great flame rose before them. Billet pointed out the ruddy glare.

"They are troops camping out," said Pitou; "Can't you see that, and they have lighted campfires. Here are some, so that there may naturally be more over yonder."

Indeed, on attentively looking on the right, Father Billet saw black detachments marching noiselessly in the shadow of St. Denis Plain, horse and foot. Their weapons glimmered in the pale starry light.

Accustomed to see in the dark from his night roaming in the woods, Pitou pointed out to his master cannon mired to the hubs in the swampy fields.

"Ho, ho," muttered Billet: "something new is going on here. Look at the sparks yonder. Make haste, my lad."

"Yes, it is a house a-fire. See the sparks fly," added the younger man.

Maggie stopped; the rider jumped off upon the pavement and going up to a group of soldiers in blue and yellow uniforms, bivouacking under the roadside trees, asked:

"Comrades, can you tell me what is the matter in Paris?"

The soldiers merely replied with some German oaths.

"What the deuce do they say?" queried Billet of his brother peasant.

"All I can tell is that it is not Latin," replied the youth, trembling greatly.

"I was a fool to apply to the Kaiserlicks (Kaiserlich, Imperial Austrian grenadiers)?" muttered Billet, in his curiosity still standing in the middle of the road.

"Bass on mit your vay," said an officer, stepping up; "Und bass bretty tam queeck, doo!"

"Excuse me, captain," said the farmer, "but I want to go into Paris."

"Vat next?"

"As I see you are between me and the turnpike bars, I feared I would not be let go by."

"Yah, you gan by go."

Remounting, Billet indeed got on. But it was only to run in among the Bercheny Hussars, swarming in La Villette. This time, as they were his own countrymen, he got along better.

"Please, what is the news from Paris?" he asked.

"Why, it's your crazy Parisians, who want their Necker, and fire their guns off at us, as if we had anything to do with the matter." So replied a hussar.

"What Necker? have they lost him?" questioned Billet.

"Certainly, the King has turned him out of office."

"That great man turned out?" said the farmer with the stupor of a priest who hears of a sacrilege."

"More than that, he is on the way to Brussels at present."

"Then it is a joke we shall hear some laughing over," cried Billet in a terrible voice, without thinking of the danger he ran in preaching insurrection amid twelve or fifteen thousand royalist sabres.

Remounting Maggie, he drove her with cruel digs of the heel up to the bars. As he advanced he saw the fire more plainly; a long column rose from the spot to the sky. It was the barrier that was burning. A howling and furious mob with women intermixed, yelling and capering as usual more excitedly than the men, fed the flames with pieces of the bars, the clerk's office and the custom-house officers' property.

On the road, Hungarian and German regiments looked on at the devastation, with their muskets grounded, without blinking.

Billet did not let the rampart of flame stop him: but urged Maggie through smoke and fire. She bravely burst through the incandescent barrier; but on the other side was a compact crowd stretching from the outer town to the heart of the city, some singing, some shouting:

"To arms!"

Billet looked what he was, a good farmer coming to town on his business. Perhaps he roared "Make way there!" too roughly, but Pitou tempered it with so polite a "Make way, if you please!" that one appeal corrected the other. Nobody had any interest in staying Billet in attending to his business and they let him go through.

Maggie had recovered her strength from the fire having singed her hide and all this unusual clamor worried her. Billet was obliged to hold her in now, in the fear of crushing the idlers classed before the town gate and the others who were as curiously running from the gates to the bars.

Somehow or other they pushed on, till they reached the boulevard, where they were forced to stop.

A procession was marching from the Bastile to the Royal Furniture Stores, the two stone knots binding the enclosure of Paris to its girth. This broad column followed a funeral barrow on which were placed two busts, one covered with crape, the other with flowers; the one in mourning was Necker's, the Prime Minister and eminently the Treasurer, dismissed but not disgraced; the flower-crowned bust was the Duke of Orleans', who had openly taken the Swiss financier's part.

Billet, asking, learned that this was popular homage to the banker and his defender.

The farmer was born in a country where the Orleans family had been venerated for a century and more. He belonged to the Philosophical sect and consequently regarded Necker not only as a great minister but an apostle of humanity.

There was ample to fire him. He jumped off his horse without clearly knowing what he was about and mingled with the throng, yelling:

"Long live the Duke of Orleans! Necker forever!"

Once a man mixes with a mob his individual liberty disappears. He was the more easily carried on as he was at the head of the party.

As they kept up the shouting, "Long live Necker—no more foreign troops—down with the outlandish cutthroats!" he added his lusty voice to the others.

Any superiority is always appreciated by the masses. The shrill, weak voice of the Parisian, spoilt by wine bibbing or want of proper food, was nowhere beside the countryman's fresh, full and sonorous roar, so that without too much jostling, shoving and knocking about, Billet finally reached the litter.

In another ten minutes, one of the bearers, whose enthusiasm had been too great for his strength, gave up his place to him.

Billet, you will observe, had got on.

Only the propagator of Gilbert's doctrines a day before, he was now one of the instruments in the triumph of Necker and the Duke of Orleans.

But he had hardly arrived at his post than he thought of Pitou and the borrowed horse. What had become of them?

While nearing the litter, Billet looked and, through the flare of the torches accompanying the turn-out, and by the lamps illumining all the house windows, he beheld a kind of walking platform formed of half a dozen men shouting and waving their arms. In the midst it was easy to discern Pitou and his long arms.

He did what he could to defend Maggie, but spite of all the horse was stormed and was carrying all who could clamber on her back and hang on to the harness and her tail. In the enlarging darkness she resembled an elephant loaded with hunters going for the tiger. Her vast neck had three or four fellows established on it, howling: "Three cheers for Orleans and Necker—

down with the foreigners!"

To which Pitou answered: "All right, but you will smother Maggie among ye."

The intoxication was general.

For an instant Billet thought of carrying help to his friend and horse but he reflected that he would probably lose the honor of bearing the litter forever if he gave it up; he bethought him also of the bargain made with Lefranc about swapping the horses, and anyhow, if the worst happened, he was rich enough to sacrifice the price of a horse on the altar of his country.

Meanwhile the procession made way: turning to the left it went down Montmarte Street to Victoires Place. Reaching the Palais Royale, a great throng prevented its passing on, a number of men with green leaves stuck in their hats who were halloaing:

"To arms!"

Were these friends or foes? Why green cockades, green being the color of Count Artois, the King's youngest brother?

After a brief parley all was explained.

On hearing of Necker's removal from office, a young man had rushed out of the Foy Coffeehouse, jumped on a table in the Palais Royale Gardens, and flourishing a pistol, shouted:

"To arms!"

All the loungers in the public strolling grounds took up the call.

All the foreign regiments in the French army were gathered round the capital. It looked like an Austrian invasion, as the regimental names grated on French ears. Their utterance explained the fear in the masses. The young man named them and said that the Swiss troops, camped in the Champs Elysées, with four field pieces, were going to march into the city that night, with Prince Lambesq's Dragoons to clear the way. He proposed that the town defender should wear an emblem different from theirs and, plucking a horse-chestnut leaf, stuck it in his hat. All the beholders instantly imitated him so that the three thousand persons stripped the Palais Royale trees in a twinkling.

In the morning the young man's name was unknown but it was celebrated that night; it was Camille Desmoulins.

Men recognized one another in the crowd, shook hands in token of brotherhood and all joined in with the procession.

At Richelieu Street corner Billet looked back and saw the disappearance of Maggie; the increase of curiosity during the halt was such that more had been added to the poor animal's burden and she had sunk under the surcharge.

The farmer sighed. Then collecting his powers, he called out to Pitou three times like the ancient Romans at the funeral of their king; he fancied a voice made reply out of the bowels of the earth but it was drowned in the confused uproar, ascending to heaven partly cheers and partly threatening.

Still the train proceeded. All the stores were closed; but all windows were open, and thence fell encouragement on the marchers farther to frenzy them.

At Vendome Square, an unforeseen obstacle checked the march.

Like the logs rolling in a freshet which strike up against the piles of a bridge and rebound, the leaders recoiled from a detachment of a Royal German Regiment. These were dragoons, who, seeing the mob surge into the square from St. Honore Street, relaxed the reins of their chargers, impatient at having been curbed since five o'clock, and they dashed on the people at full speed.

The bearers of the litter received the first shock, and were knocked down when it was overthrown. A Savoyard, before Billet, was the first to rise. He picked up the effigy of Prince Orleans, and fixing it on the top of his walking stick, waved it above his head, crying: "Long live the Duke of Orleans!" whom he had never seen, and "Hurrah for Necker!" whom he did not know from Adam.

Billet was going to do the same with Necker's bust, but he was forestalled. A young dandy in elegant attire had been watching it, the easier for him than

Billet as he was not burdened with the barrow poles, and he sprang for it the moment it reached the ground.

Up it went on the point of a pike, and, set close to the other, served as rallying-point for the scattered processionists.

Suddenly a flash lit up the square. At the same instant bang went the report, and the bullets whistled. Something heavy struck Billet in the forehead so that he fell, believing that he was killed. But as he did not lose his senses, and felt no hurt except pain in the head, he understood that at the worst he was merely wounded. He slapped his hand to his brow and perceived it was but a bump there, though his palm was smeared with blood.

The well-dressed stripling in front of the farmer had been shot in the breast; it was he who was slain and his blood that had splashed Billet. The shock the latter felt was from Necker's bust, falling from want of a holder, on the farmer's head.

He uttered a shout, half rage, half horror.

He sprang aloof from the youth, writhing in the death-gasp. Those around fell back in like manner, and the yell which he gave, repeated by the multitude, was prolonged in funeral echoes to the last groups in St. Honore Street.

This shout was a new proof of revolt. A second volley was heard: and deep gaps in the throng showed where the projectiles had passed.

What indignation inspired in Billet, and what he did in the gush of enthusiasm, was to pick up the blood-spattered bust, wave it over his head, and cheer with his fine manly voice in protest at the risk of being killed like the patriotic fop dead at his feet.

But instantly a large and vigorous hand came down on the farmer's shoulder and so pressed him that he had to bow to the weight. He tried to wrest himself from the grasp, but another fist, quite as strong and heavy, fell on his other shoulder. He turned, growling, to learn what kind of antagonist was this.

"Pitou?" he cried.

"I am your man—but stop a little and you will see why."

Redoubling his efforts he brought the resisting man to his knees and flat on his face. Scarcely was this done than a second volley thundered. The Savoyard bearing the Orleans bust came down in his turn, hit by a ball in the thigh.

Then they heard iron on the paving stones—the dragoons charged for the second time. One horse, furious and shaking his mane like the steed in the Apocalypse, jumped over the unhappy Savoyard, who felt the chill of a lance piercing his chest as he fell on Billet and Pitou.

The whirlwind rushed to the end of the street, where it engulfed itself in terror and death! Nothing but corpses strewed the ground. All fled by the adjacent streets. The windows banged to. A lugubrious silence succeeded the cheers and the roars of rage.

For an instant Billet waited, held by the prudent peasant; then, feeling that the danger went farther away, he rose on one knee while the other, like the hare in her form, pricked up his ear only without raising his head.

"I believe you are right, Master," said the young man; "we have arrived while the soup is hot."

"Lend me a hand."

"To help you out of this?"

"No: the young exquisite is dead, but the Savoyard is only in a swoon, I reckon. Help me get him on my back. We cannot leave so plucky a fellow here to be butchered by these cursed troopers."

Billet used language going straight to Pitou's heart; he had no answer but to obey. He took up the warm and bleeding body and loaded it like a bag of meal on to the robust farmer's back. Seeing St. Honore Street looked clear and deserted, he took that road to the Palais Royale with his man.

CHAPTER VIII. PITOU DISCOVERS HE IS BRAVE.

The street appeared void and lonesome to Billet and his friend because the cavalry in chase of the Hyers, had gone through the market and scattered after them in the side streets; but as the pair got nearer the Palais Royale, calling out in a hoarse voice by instinct "Revenge!" men began to appear in doorways, up cellars, out of alleys, from the carriage gateways, mute and frightened at the first, but, when assured that the horse-soldiers had gone on, forming the procession anew, they repeated in a low tone, but soon in a loud one: "Revenge!"

Pitou marched behind the farmer, carrying the Savoyard's cap.

Thus the mournful and ghastly cortege arrived on Palais Royale Place, where a concourse, drunk with wrath, were holding council and soliciting the French troops to help them against the foreign ones.

"What are these men in uniform?" inquired Billet, in front of a company, standing under arms, to bar the road from the Palace main doors to Chartres Street.

"The French Guards," answered several voices.

"Oh," said the countryman, going nearer and showing the body of the Savoyard which was lifeless now: "are you Frenchmen and let us be murdered by foreigners?"

The guardsmen shrank back a step involuntarily.

"Dead?" uttered several.

"Dead—murdered, along with lots more by the Royal German dragoons. Did you not hear the charging cry, the shots, the sword-slashes and the shrieks of the defenseless?"

"Yes," shouted two or three hundred voices: "the people were cut down on Vendome Square."

"And so are you the people," shouted Billet to the soldiers: "It is cowardice of you to let your brothers be hacked to pieces."

"Cowardice?" muttered some of the men in the ranks, threateningly.

"Yes, I said Cowardice, and I say it again. Look here," Billet went on, taking three steps towards the point where the protest had risen, "perhaps you will shoot me down to prove that you are not cowards?"

"That is all very good," said a soldier; "you are a honest, blunt fellow, my friend, but you are citizens and you do not understand that soldiers are bound by orders."

"Do you mean to say?" said Billet, "that if you receive orders to fire on us, unarmed men, that you, the successors of the Guards who, at Fontenoy, bade the English shoot first,—would do that?"

"I wager I would not," said the soldier.

"Nor I, nor I," echoed several of his comrades.

"Then stop the others firing on us," continued Billet: "To let the Royal Germans cut our throats is tantamount to doing it yourselves."

"The dragoons, here come the dragoons!" yelled many at the same time as the gathering began to retire over the square to get away up Richelieu Street.

At a distance but approaching, they heard the clatter of heavy cavalry.

"To arms, to arms," cried the runaways.

"Plague on you," said Billet, throwing down the dead Savoyard, "Lend us your guns if you will not use them."

"Hold on till you see whether we won't use them," said the soldier whom Billet had addressed, as he snatched back the musket which the farmer had torn from his grip. "Bite your cartridges, boys—and make the Austrians bite the dust if they interfere with these good fellows."

"Ay, they shall see," said the soldiers, carrying their hands from the

72

cartridge-boxes to their mouths.

"Thunder," muttered Billet, stamping his foot: "why did I not bring my old duck-gun along? But one of these pesky Austrians may be laid out and I can get his carbine."

"In the meantime," said a voice, "taking this gun—it is ready loaded."

A stranger slipped a handsome fowling-piece into Billet's hands.

At this very instant, the dragoons rushed into the square, upsetting everybody they ran against.

The officer commanding the French Guards came out three steps to the front.

"Halloa, you gentlemen of the heavy dragoons," he called out. "Halt, please."

Whether the cavalry did not hear him, or did not want to hear him, or, again, were carried on by the impetus of a charge too violent to check, the Germans wheeled by a half-turn to the right and trampled down an old man and a woman who disappeared under the hoofs.

"Fire," roared Billet, "why don't you fire?"

He was near the officer and the order might have been taken as coming from him. Anyway, the French Guards carried their muskets to the shoulder, and delivered a volley which stopped the dragoons short.

"Here, gentlemen of the Guards," said a German officer, coming before the squadron thrown into disorder, "do you know you are firing on us?"

"Yes, by heaven we know it, and you shall know it, too." So Billet retorted, taking aim at the speaker and dropping him with the shot.

Thereupon the reserve rank of the Guards made a discharge and the Germans, seeing that they had trained soldiery to deal with and not citizens who broke and fled at the first shot, pulled round and made off for Vendome Square in the midst of a formidable outburst of hoots and cheers of triumph so that some horses broke loose and smashed their heads against the store shutters.

"Hurrah for the French Guards!" shouted the multitude.

"Hurrah for the Guards of the Country!" said Billet.

"Thank you," said a soldier, "we are given the right name and christened with fire."

"I have been under fire, too," said Pitou, "and it is not as dreadful as I imagined it."

"Now, who owns this gun?" queried Billet, examining the rifle which was a costly one.

"My master," answered the man who had lent him it, and who wore the Orleans livery. "He thinks you use it too handsomely to have to return it."

"Where is your master?" demanded the farmer.

The servant pointed to a half-open blind behind which the prince was watching what happened.

"Is he with us, then?"

"With heart and soul for the people," replied the domestic.

"In that case, three cheers again for the Duke of Orleans!" said the farmer. "Friends the Duke of Orleans is on our side—three cheers for the duke!"

He pointed upwards and the prince showed himself for an instant while he bowed three times to the shouting; short as was the appearance it lifted enthusiasm to the utmost.

"Break open the gunsmith's," shouted a voice in the turbulence.

"Let us go to the Invalid Soldiers Hospital," added some old veterans. "General Sombreuil has twenty thousand muskets there."

"And to the City Hall!" exclaimed others: "Flesselles, Provost of the

Traders, has the keys for the town guards' armory and he must give them up."

"To the Hall!" bellowed a fraction of the assemblage.

All flowed away in one or the other of the three directions called out.

During this time the dragoons had rallied around Baron Bezenval and Prince Lambesq on Louis XV. Square.

Billet and Pitou were unaware of this as they followed none of the parties and were left pretty well alone on Palais Royale Square.

"Well, where are we off to, dear Master Billet?" inquired Ange Pitou.

"I should like to follow the crowd," replied the other: "not to the gunmakers', as I have a first-rate gun, but to the City Hall or the military Asylum. Still, as we came to town not to fight, but to learn Doctor Gilbert's address. I think we ought to go to Louis-the-Great's College, where his son is. When I shall have got through with the doctor, we can jump back into the chafing-dish."

His eyes flashed lightnings.

"This course seems logical to me," observed the young peasant.

"So take some weapon, gun or sword, from those beer drinkers lying there," said the farmer, pointing to half-a-dozen dragoons on the pave, "and let us go to the college."

"But these weapons are not mine, but the King's," objected Pitou.

"They are the people's," corrected Billet, whereupon the other who knew the speaker was incapable of wronging a man to the extent of a mustard-seed, went up to the nearest corpse with multiplied caution, and making sure he was lifeless, he took his musket, cartridge-box and sabre.

He wanted to take his hamlet but had his doubts about the defensive armor being "confisticatable" like the offensive arms; while deliberating he listened towards Vendome Square.

"It seems to me that the Royal Germans are coming back again," he said.

Indeed a troop of horse was heard coming at the walking gait.

"Quick, quick, they are returning," said Pitou.

"Billet looked around to see what means of resistance were offered, but the place was almost deserted.

"Let us be off," said he.

He went down Chartres Street, followed by Pitou who dragged the sabre after him by the scabbard-straps, not knowing how it ought to be hooked up till Billet showed him.

"You looked like a traveling-tinker," he said.

On Louis XV. Square they met the column, started off to go over the river to the Invalides but stopped short. The bridges and the Champs Elysées were blocked.

"Try the Tuileries Garden bridge," suggested Billet.

It was quite a simple proposition; the mob accepted it and followed Billet: but swords shining half way to the Gardens indicated that cavalry intercepted the march to that bridge.

"These confounded dragoons are everywhere," grumbled the farmer.

"I believe we are caught," said his friend.

"Nonsense, five or six thousand men are to be caught, and we are that strong."

The dragoons came forward, slowly, but it was an advance.

"The Royale Street is left us," said Billet; "come this way, Ange."

But a line of soldiers shut this street up.

"It looks as though you were right," said the countryman.

"Alas!" sighed Ange, who had followed him like his shadow.

All his regret at not being wrong was shown in the single word by the tone it was spoken in.

By its clamor and motion the mob showed that it was no less sensible than he about the quandary all were in.

Indeed, by a skillful manœuvre, Prince Lambesq had encircled the rioters in a bow of iron, the cord being represented by the Tuileries garden-wall, hard to climb over, and the drawbridge railing, almost impossible to force. Billet judged that the position was bad. Still, being a cool fellow, full of resources when the emergency rose, he looked round him. Seeing a pile of lumber by the riverside, he said:

"I have a notion, Pitou; come along."

Billet went up to a beam and took up one end, making a nod to his followers as much as to say, "Take your end of it."

Pitou was bent on helping his leader without questioning: he had such trust in him that he would have gone down into sheol without grumbling on the length of the road or how the heat increased as they got on. The pair returned to the waterside walk, carrying a burden which half a dozen ordinary men would have sunk under.

Strength is always an object of admiration to the crowd. Although very closely packed, way was made for the peasants. Catching an idea of the work ahead, some men walked before the joist-carriers, calling out: "Clear the way, there!"

"I say, Father Billet, are we to make a long job of this?" asked Pitou when they had gone some thirty strides.

"Up to that gateway."

"I can go it," replied the young man laconically, as he saw it was about as much farther and the crowd, having an inkling of the plan, cheered them.

Besides, some helped to carry and the beam went on much more rapidly. In five minutes they stood before the gates.

"Now, then, heave and all together," said Billet.

"I understand," said Pitou. "This is what the ancient Romans called a battering-ram."

The piece of timber set going, was banged with a terrible blow against the gate lock.

The military on guard within the gardens, ran to check this inroad. But at the third swing the gates yielded, and the multitude flowed into the dark gap.

By the movement, Prince Lambesq perceived that the netted rioters had found an outlet. Rage mastered him to see his prisoners escape. He started his horse forward to learn what was the matter, when his men, thinking he was leading a charge, followed him closely. The horses were heated with their recent work, and could not be restrained. Thirsting for retaliation for their check on Palais Royale Square, the men did not probably try hard to restrain them.

The prince, seeing that it was impossible to stop the movement, let himself be carried away, and a shriek of frightful intensity from women and children rose to heaven as a claim for its vengeance.

A dreadful scene took place in the gloom. The victims went mad with pain while they who charged were mad with fury.

A kind of defense was organized and chairs were flung at the cavalry. Struck on the head, Prince Lambesq replied with a sword cut, without thinking that he was striking the innocent for the guilty. An old man was sent to the ground. Billet saw this and he uttered a shout. At the same time he took aim with his rifle and the prince would have been killed but for his horse having reared at the very instant. It received the bullet in the neck and died instantly.

The fallen Prince was believed slain, and the dragoons rushed into the Tuileries Gardens, firing their pistols at the fugitives.

But they, having plenty of room, dodged behind the trees.

Billet tranquilly reloaded his fowling-piece.

"You are right, Pitou, we have come to town on time," he said.

"And I think I am becoming brave," remarked Pitou, standing the pistol fire of a horseman and spilling him out of the saddle with his musketoon; "it is not so hard as I thought."

"That's so," replied the other, "but useless bravery is bravado. Come along, and don't let your sword trip you up."

"Wait for me, Father Billet, for I do not know Paris like you do; and without you, I shall go astray."

"Come, come," said the farmer, leading him along the river terrace until they had distanced the troops advancing by the quays as rapidly as they could to help the Lambesq Dragoons, if needed.

At the end of the terrace, he sat on the parapet and jumped down on the embankment running along the river. Pitou did the same.

CHAPTER IX. "TO THE BASTILE!"

Once on the river edge, the two countrymen, spying arms glitter on the Tuileries Bridge, in all probability, not in friendly hands, lay down in the grass beneath the trees, and held a council.

The question was, as laid down by the elder, whether they ought to stay where they were, in comparative safety, or return into the action. He waited for Pitou's opinion.

Pitou had grown in the farmer's estimation, from the learning he had shown down in the country and the bravery he showed this evening. Pitou instinctively felt this, but he was naturally so humble that he was only the more grateful to his friend.

"Master," he said, "it is clear that you are braver and I less of a coward than was supposed by ourselves. Horace the poet, a very different character from you, flung down his weapons and took to his heels at the first conflict he was in. This proves that I am more courageous than Horace, with my musket, cartridge-box and sword to show for it. My conclusion is that the bravest man in the world may be killed by a bullet. Ergo, as your design in quitting the farm was to come to Paris on an important errand——"

"By all that is blue, the casket!"

"You have hit it; and for nothing else."

"Then, if you are killed, the business will not come off."

"Quite so. When we shall have seen the doctor, we will return to politics as a sacred duty."

"Come on then, to the college where is Sebastian Gilbert," said Billet, rising.

"Let us go," added Pitou, rising but reluctantly so soft was the grass. Besides good Pitou was sleepy.

"If anything happens me, you must know what to say to Dr. Gilbert in my stead. But be mute."

Ange was not saying anything, for he was dozing.

"If I should be mortally wounded you must go to the doctor and say— Bless me, the boy's asleep——"

Indeed, Pitou was snoring where he had sunk down again.

"After all, the college will be shut at this hour," thought Billet; "we had better take a rest."

Dawn appeared when they had slept three hours; but the day did not bring any change in the warlike aspect of Paris.

Only, there were no soldiers to be seen. The populace were everywhere. They were armed with quickly made pikes, guns of which most knew not the use, and old time weapons of which the bearers admired the ornamentation. After the military had been withdrawn they had pillaged the Royal Storage Magazines. Towards the City Hall a crowd rolled a couple of small cannon. At the Cathedral and other places the general alarm was rung on the big bells. Out from between the flagstones, so to say, oozed the lowest of the low, legions of men and women, if human they were, pale, haggard, and ill-clad, who had been yelling "Bread!" the night before, but howled for "Weapons!" now.

Nothing was more sinister than these spectres who had been stealing into the capital from all the country round during the last few months. They slipped silently through the bars and installed themselves in the town like ghouls in a cemetery.

On this day all France, represented in the capital by these starvelings, called out to the King: "Make us free!" while howling to heaven: "Feed us."

Meanwhile Billet and his pupil were proceeding to the college. On the way they saw the barricades growing up, with even children lending a hand and the richest like the poorest contributing some object that would build the wall. Among the crowds Billet recognized one or two French Guardsmen by their uniform, who were drilling squads and teaching the use of firearms, with the women and boys looking on.

The college was insurrection also. The boys had driven out the masters and were attacking the gates to get out with threats which terrified the tearful principal.

"Who of you is Sebastian Gilbert?" demanded Billet in his stentor's voice after regarding the intestine war.

"I am he," replied a boy of fifteen, of almost girlish beauty, who was helping three or four schoolfellows to bring up a ladder with which to scale the wall as they could not force the lock. "What do you want of me?"

"Are you going to take him away?" asked the head teacher, alarmed by the sight of two armed men one of whom, the speaker, was covered with blood.

The boy was also looking at them without recognizing his foster-brother who had grown out of all reason since he left him and was farther disguised by the martial harness.

"Take away Dr. Gilbert's son into that infernal rumpus?" said the yeoman: "Expose him to some ugly blow? oh, dear, no."

"You see, you mad fellow, Sebastian, that your friends do not approve of your attempt," said the principal. "For these gentlemen do appear to be your friends. Aid me, gentlemen, and ye, my children, obey me, when I command, and entreat."

"Keep my mates if you will," replied young Gilbert with a firmness marvellous at his age: "but I must go forth. I am not in the position of these; my father has been arrested and is imprisoned—he is in the tyrant's power."

"Yes, yes," shouted the boys; "Sebastian is right; they have locked up his father, and as the people are opening the prisons, they must set his father free."

"Eh? have they arrested Dr. Gilbert?" roared the farmer, shaking the gates: "Death of my life! little Catherine was right."

"Yes, they have taken away my father," continued little Gilbert, "and that is why I want to get a gun and fight till I deliver my father."

This plan was hailed by a hundred shrill voices: "Yes, give us weapons—let us fight."

At this, the mob outside the gates ran at them to give the scholars passage. The principal threw himself on his knees to supplicate both parties, crying:

"Friends, friends, spare tender youth!"

"Spare them? of course we will," said an old soldier: "they will be just the chaps to form a cadet corps with."

"But they are a sacred deposit entrusted to me by their parents," continued the head teacher; "I owe my life to them, so, in heaven's name, do not take away my lambs."

Hooting from both sides of the wall killed his doleful entreaties.

Billet stepped forward, and interposed between the soldiers and the mob and the schoolboys.

"The old gentleman is right," he said. "The youngsters are a sacred trust. Let men go and fight and get knocked over, that is their duty, but children are the seed for the future."

A disapproving murmur was heard.

"Who grumbles?" demanded the farmer; "I am sure it is not a father. Now, I am a father; I have had two men killed in my arms this last night; it is their blood on my breast—see!"

He showed the stains to the assemblage with a grand gesture electrifying all.

"Yesterday, I was fighting at the Palais Royale and in the Tuileries Garden," resumed the farmer; "and this lad fought by my side; but then he has no father or mother: and besides he is almost a man grown."

Pitou looked proud.

"I shall be fighting again to-day; but I do not want anybody to say the Parisians could not thrash the enemy until they brought the children to help them."

"The man's right," chorussed the soldiers and women. "No children in the fighting. Keep them in."

"Oh, thank you, sir," said the head master to Billet, trying to shake hands with him through the bars.

"And above all take good care of Gilbert," said the latter.

"Keep me in? I tell you they shall not," cried the boy, livid with anger as he struggled in the grasp of the school servants.

"Let me go in, and I undertake to quiet him."

The crowd divided and let the farmer and Pitou go into the schoolyard. Already three or four French Guards and a dozen other soldiers instinctively stood sentry at the gates and prevented the young insurgents from bolting out.

Billet went straight up to Sebastian and taking his fine white hands in his large, horny ones, said:

"Sebastian, do you not know Farmer Billet, who farms your father's own land?"

"Yes, sir, I know you now."

"And this lad with me?"

"It must be Ange Pitou."

Pitou threw himself on the other's neck, blubbering with joy.

"If they have taken away your father, I will bring him back. I, and the rest of us. Why not? yesterday we had a turn-up with the Austrians and we saw the flat of their backs."

"In token of which here is a cartridge-box one of them has no farther use for," added Ange.

"Will we not liberate his father?" cried Billet to the mob, who shouted an assent.

"But my father is in the Bastile," said Sebastian, shaking his head in melancholy. "None can take the Bastile." "What were you going to do then, had you got out?"

"I should have gone under the Bastile walls and when my father was out walking on the ramparts, where they tell me the prisoners come for an airing, I should have shown myself to him."

"But if the sentinels shot you when they caught you making signs to a prisoner?"

"I should have died under my father's eyes."

"Death of all the devils, you are a bad boy. To want to get killed under your father's eyes! To make him die of grief in his cell when he has nobody but you to live for, and one he loves so well. Plainly you have no good heart, Sebastian."

"A bad heart," whimpered Pitou as Billet repulsed the boy.

While the boy was musing sadly, the farmer admired the noble face, white and pearly; the fiery eye, fine and ironical mouth, eagle nose and vigorous chin, revealing nobility of race and of spirit.

"You say your father has been put in the Bastile? why?" he inquired.

"Because he is a friend of Washington and Lafayette; has fought with the sword for the Independence of America; and with the pen for France; is known in the Two Worlds as a hater of tyranny: because he has cursed this Bastile where others were suffering—and now he is there himself."

"How long since?"

"He was arrested the moment he landed at Havre; at least at Lillebonne, for he wrote me a letter from the port."

"Don't be cross, my boy: but let me have the points. I swear to deliver your father from the Bastile or leave my bones at the foot of its walls."

Sebastian saw that the former spoke from the bottom of his heart and he replied:

"He had time at Lillebonne to scribble these words in pencil in a book:

"'SEBASTIAN: I am taken to the Bastile. Patience, Hope and Labor. 7th July, 1789. P. S.—I am arrested for Liberty's cause. I have a son at Louis-the-Great College, Paris. The finder of this book is begged to bear this note on to my son Sebastian Gilbert, in the name of humanity.'"

"And the book?" inquired Billet, breathless with emotion.

"He put a gold piece in the book, tied a string round it, and threw it out of the window. The Parish Priest found it and picked out a sturdy fellow among his flock, to whom he said:

"'Leave twelve francs with your family who are without bread. With the other twelve go carry this book to Paris, to a poor boy whose father has been taken away from him because he loves the people too well.' The young man got in yesterday at noon: he handed me the book and thus I knew of the arrest."

"Good, this makes me friends with the priests again!" exclaimed Billet. "A pity they are not all built on this pattern. What about the peasant?"

"He went back last evening, hoping to carry his family the five francs he had saved on the journey."

"How handsome of him," said Billet. "Oh, the people are good for something, boy."

"Now, you know all: you promised if I told you, to restore me my father."

"I said I should or get killed. Now show me that book."

The boy drew from his pocket a copy of Rousseau's "Social Contract."

Billet kissed where the doctor's hand had traced the appeal.

"Now, be calm," he said: "I am going to fetch your father from the Bastile."

"Madman," said the principal, grasping his hands; "how will you get at a prisoner of state?"

"By taking the Bastile," replied the farmer.

Some guardsmen laughed and the merriment became general.

"Hold on," said Billet, casting his blazing glance around him. "What is this Bogey's Castle, anyhow?"

"Only stones," said a soldier.

"And iron," said another.

"And fire," concluded a third. "Mind you do not burn your fingers, my hero."

"Yes, he'll get burnt," cried the crowd.

"What," roared the peasant, "have you got no pickaxes, you Parisians, that you are afraid of stone walls? no bullets for you to shrink from steel? no powder when they fire on you? You must be cowards, then, dastards; machines fit for slavery. A thousand demons! Is there no man with a heart who will come with me and Pitou to have a go at this Bastile of the King? I am Billet, farmer in the Ile-de-France section, and I am going to knock at that door. Come on!"

Billet had risen to the summit of sublime audacity. The enflamed and quivering multitude around him shouted:

"Down with the Bastile!"

Sebastian wished to cling to Billet, but he gently put him aside.

"Your father bade you hope and have patience while you worked. Well, we are going to work, too—only the other name for our work is slaying and destroying."

The youth did not say a word, but hiding his face in his hands he went off into spasms which compelled them to take him into the sick ward.

"On, to the Bastile!" called out Billet.

"To the Bastile," echoed Pitou.

"To the Bastile," thundered three thousand persons, a cry which was to become that of the entire population of Paris.

CHAPTER X. BLOWING HOT AND COLD.

It was on the morning of the fourteenth of July that Billet opened oratorical fire against the monument which had for five centuries weighed like an incubus on the breast of France—a rock of Sisyphus. Less confident than the Titan in her power, France had never thought to throw it off.

The Bastile was the seal of feudalism on the brow of Paris.

The King was accounted too good to order people to be beheaded; but he sent people into the Bastile. Once there a man was forgotten, isolated, sequestered, buried alive, annihilated. He stayed there till the monarch remembered him, and kings have so many new matters to think of that they often forget the old ones.

There were twenty other Bastiles in France, the name being general for prison, so that, to this day, the tramp on the dusty road speaks of the "Steel," without perhaps knowing that the title of ignominy referred to the great French Statesprison.

The fortress by the St. Antoine Gate was the Bastile pre-eminently. It was alone worth all the others.

Some of the prisoners were perhaps great criminals; but others like Latude had done nothing to merit thirty years' captivity.

He had fallen in love with Lady Pompadour, the King's mistress, and wrote her a note which caused his imprisonment for a life-time.

It was not for nothing that the Bastile was hated by the people.

It was hated like a living thing—a monster like the dragoons who defy a people till a champion rises, like Billet, to show them how to attack it.

Hence one may comprehend Sebastian's hopeless grief at his father being incarcerated in the Bastile.

Hence Billet's belief that he would never be liberated but by being plucked forth.

Hence the popular transport may be felt when the shout rose of "Down with the Bastile!"

But it was, as the soldiers said, an insane project to think of capturing the King's Prison-Castle.

The Bastile had a garrison, artillery and provisions. The walls were fifteen feet thick at the top and forty at the base.

The governor was Count Launay, who had thirty thousand pounds of gunpowder in the magazine, and had promised in case of annoyance to blow up the fort and with it all that part of Paris.

Nevertheless Billet marched forward, but he did not have to do any shouting.

Liking his martial mien, the multitude felt he was one of their kind, and commenting on his words and bearing, it followed him, increasing like the flowing tide.

When Billet came out on St. Michel's quay, he had behind him more than three thousand men, armed with hatchets, cutlasses, pikes and guns.

All were shouting: "On, to the Bastile!"

Billet was making the reflections which his knowledge of the stronghold warranted, and the vapor of his enthusiasm faded gradually.

He saw clearly that the enterprise was sublime though insane.

That was easy to understand by the awed expression of those to whom he had first broached the project of taking the Bastile.

But he was only the more fortified in his resolve. But he understood that he had to answer to these mothers and fathers, girls and children, for the lives of those whom he was leading, and that he was bound to take all the precautions possible.

He commenced by collecting his followers at the City Hall.

He appointed lieutenants to control the flock—of wolves.

"Let me see," said Billet to himself; "there is more than one power in France. There are two—the head of the chief city, for one, and may be another yet."

He entered the City Hall, asking for the Chief civic magistrate. It was the Traders' Provost Flesselles.

"My lord de Flesselles," he repeated; "a noble and no friend of the people?"

"Oh, no, he is a sensible man."

Billet went up the stairs into the ante-chamber where he met an usher, who came up to him to see what he wanted.

"Speech with Lord Flesselles," replied Billet.

"Can't sir," answered the man. "He is completing the list for the militia which the City is to raise."

"Capital!" rejoined Billet; "I am also organizing a militia, and as I have three thousand men ready under arms, I am worth a Flesselles who is only going to get his together. Let me speak with him, and right off. If you like, just look out of the window at my soldiers."

One rapid glance on the waterside was enough for the servant who hastened to notify the Traders' Provost, to whom, as emphasis to his message, he pointed out the army.

This sight inspired respect in the provost for the man commanding them: he left the council and came into the ante-room. Perceiving Billet, he smiled at guessing the kind of man he must be.

"Were you wanting me?" he challenged.

"If you are Provost Flesselles," responded Billet.

"Yes; how can I serve you? please, be quick, for I am very busy."

"How many powers do you acknowledge in France, my Lord Provost?"

queried Billet.

"Hem, that is just how one looks at it," replied the politician. "If you ask Bailly the Mayor he will say 'The National Assembly.' If Lord Dreux, he would say only one—'the King.'"

"And which is yours between the two?"

"Neither one, but the nation, at present," rejoined Flesselles, playing with his ruffles.

"Ah, the nation," repeated the farmer.

"Those gentlemen waiting below there with the wood-choppers and carving-knives; the nation, all the world to me."

"You may be right and there was no mistake in their warranting you to me as a knowing man."

"Which of the three powers do you belong to?" inquired the trimmer, bowing.

"Faith, when there is a question for the Grand Spirit and the angels, I apply to the Fountain—head."

"You mean the King? What for?"

"To ask for the release of Dr. Gilbert who is in the Bastile."

"He is one of those pamhleteers I believe," said the aristocratic one saucily.

"A lover of mankind."

"That is all one. My dear M. Billet, I believe you have little chances of obtaining such a favor from the King. If he put the doctor in his Bastile, he had reasons for it."

"All right," returned Billet; "he shall offer his reasons and I will match them with mine?"

"My dear sir, the King is so busy that he will not receive you."

"Oh, if he will not let me in, I shall walk in without his leave or licence."

"But you will find Lord Dreux Breze at the door who will put you away from it. It is true he failed to do that with the National Assembly in a body; but that failure will only the more put him on his mettle and he will take his revenge out of you."

"Then I will apply to the National Assembly."

"The way to Versailles is cut off."

"I will have my three thousand men with me."

"Have a care, my dear fellow, for you will meet on the road four or five thousand Swiss soldiers and two or three thousand Austrians who will make mincemeat of your forces; in a twinkling you will be swallowed."

"What the deuse am I to do, then?"

"Do what you like: but rid me of your three thousand tatterdemalions who are cracking the flagstones with thumps of their halberds, and smoking. In the vaults are seven or eight thousand pounds of gunpowder and a spark may send us all flying to the Eternal Throne."

"In that case, turning this over in my mind," said the farmer, "I will not trouble the King or the Assembly, but call in the nation and take the Bastile myself."

"With what?"

"With the powder you have kindly told me is stored in your cellar."

"You don't tell me that?" sneered Flesselles.

"That is the very thing. The cellar keys, my lord."

"Hello, you are joking," faltered the gentleman.

"I never joke," returned Billet, grasping the provost by the collar with both hands. "Let me have the keys or I shall sling you out to my tatterdemalions who know how to pick pockets."

Flesselles turned pale as death. His lips and teeth closed so convulsively but his voice did not alter in tone from the ironical one adopted.

"To tell you the truth, sir, you do me assistance in ridding me of this combustible," he said; "So I will hand you over the keys as you desire. Only do not forget that I am your first magistrate, and that if you are so unfortunate as to handle me roughly before others as you have done, catching me privately in an unguarded time, you will be hanged within the hour by the city guards. Do you persist in removing this powder?"

"I do, and will divide it out myself right away."

"Let us have this clear, then: I have business here for an other quarter of an hour and if it makes no difference to you, I should prefer the distribution to go on during my absence. It has been foretold me that I should die of a violent death, but I own to having a deep repugnance to being blown into the air."

"You shall have the time but do me a favor in return. Come to this window, that I may make you popular."

"Much obliged: in what manner?"

"You shall see. Friends," he called out, as the two stood at the window, "you want to take the Bastile?"

"Ay, ay," replied the thousands of voices.

"But we want powder? now, here is the provost who gives us all there is in the City Hall cellars. Thank him, boys!"

"Long live the provost—Flesselles forever!" roared the mob.

"Now, my lord; there is no need for me to collar you before the crowd or when alone," said Billet: "for if you do not give the powder, the people—or the nation as you call it—will tear you to pieces."

"Here are the keys: your way of asking for anything allows no refusing."

"This encourages me," said Billet, who was meditating.

"Hang it all, have you more to ask?"

"Yes; if you know Governor Launay."

"Of the Bastile? he is a friend of mine."

"In that case, you cannot wish evil to befall him. To prevent that, ask him to give up the prison to me or at least the prisoner Gilbert."

"You cannot hope that I have any such influence?"

"That is my lookout—all I want is an introduction to him."

"My dear M. Billet, I must warn you that if you enter the Bastile, it will be alone, and it is likely that you will never come out again. Still I will give you a passport into the Bastile, on one condition, that you do not ask me another for the moon. I have no acquaintances lunatics."

"Flesselles," shrilled a harsh voice behind the speaker, "if you continue to wear two faces—one laughing with the aristocrats and the other smiling on the people, you will be signing your own passport in a day or two to the other world whence none return."

"Who speak thus?" cried the provost, turning to the ill-favored man who interrupted.

"I, Marat."

"The surgeon Marat, the philosopher," said Billet.

"Yes, the same Marat," continued Flesselles; "who as a medical man ought to attend to the insane; he will have his hands full in France at this moment."

"Provost Flesselles," replied the sombre surgeon, "this honest citizen asks a passport to Governor Launay. I would point out that you are not only keeping him waiting but three thousand other honest citizens."

"Very well; he shall have it."

Going to a table, he passed his hand over his forehead before writing with the other a few rapid lines in ink.

"Here is your introduction," he said, presenting it to the countryman.

"I do not know how to read," said Billet.

"Give it to me and I will do so," said Marat; and he saw that the pass was couched in these words:

"GOVERNOR: We, Provost of Traders of Paris, send you M. Billet to confer on the welfare of the city.

14th July, 1789.

FLESSELLES.

"All right, let me have it," said Billet.

"Oh, you think it good enough?" sneered Marat; "Wait for the provost to add a postscript, which will improve it."

He went over to the provost, who was leaning one closed hand on the table and regarding with a scornful air not only the two men who were the jaws of a vice which enclosed him, but a third, whose breeches were torn, standing before the doorway, with a musketoon in his fist.

This was Pitou who followed his friend and was ready to execute any order of his.

"I suggest the following postscript to improve the paper," said Marat.

"Speak."

Marat laid the paper again on the table and pointing with his crooked finger to the place for the addendum, he dictated:

"Citizen Billet being under flag of truce, I confide his life to your honor."

Flesselles looked at the cunning face as if he had a strongest desire to smash it with a blow than do what he was counselled.

"Do you hesitate?" demanded the surgeon.

"No, for at the most, you only ask what is fair," replied the other, writing as proposed.

"Still, gentlemen, I want you to bear in mind that I do not answer for the envoy's safety."

"But I will," said Marat, taking the paper from his hands: "for your liberty is here to answer for his—your head will guarantee his. There is your pass, my brave Billet."

Flesselles called for his coach and said loudly:

"I suppose, my friends, you are asking nothing more?"

"No," replied the two together.

"Am I to let him pass?" asked Pitou.

"My young friend," said the gentleman, "I should like to observe that you are rather too insufficiently clad to stand guard at my door. If you feel constrained to do it, at least sling your cartridge-box round and stand with your back to the wall."

"Am I to let him go?" asked Pitou again, looking at the speaker as if he did not relish the jest.

"Yes," Billet said.

"Perhaps you are wrong to let him go," said Marat as Pitou stepped aside; "he was a good hostage to hold: but in any case, be he where he may, I can lay hands on him, never fear."

"Labrie," said Flesselles to his valet, as he got into his carriage, "they are going to serve out the powder. If the City Hall goes up in an explosion I should like to be well out of the reach of splinters. Tell the coachman to whip up smartly."

The vehicle rolled under the covered way and came out on the square before some thousands of spectators. The Provost feared that his departure might be misinterpreted and taken for a flight. So he leaned out of the window and said loudly:

"Drive to the National Assembly!"

This earned him a cheer. Up on the balcony, outside, Marat and Billet heard the order.

"My head to his, that he is not going to the Assembly but to the King," commented the surgeon.

"Had he not better be stopped?" said the farmer.

"No," replied the other with a hideous grin. "Be easy: go where he may, and however quickly, we shall travel more quickly than he. Now, let us get out that powder!"

"Out with the powder," said Billet.

Flesselles was right in saying there were eight thousand pounds of gunpowder in the vaults.

Marat and Billet walked in the first with a lantern which they hung to a beam. Pitou mounted guard at the door.

The powder was in twenty-pound kegs; men were stationed in a line and the kegs were passed out, hand to hand. There was a brief confusion as it was not known what was the amount and some feared they could not get any if they did not scramble for it. But Billet had selected his lieutenants on his own model, with leg-of-mutton fists, and the distribution went on with much order.

Each man received half a pound of powder, which would fire thirty or forty shots.

But when everybody had powder it was discovered that guns were short. Only some five hundred men had them.

While the powder was being dealt out, some of the unarmed went into a council chamber where a debate was proceeding. It was about the national guards of which the usher had mentioned a word to Billet. It was settled that the force should consist of forty-eight thousand men. The army existed only on paper and yet they were wrangling about who should have the command.

In the midst of this dispute in rushed the weaponless men. The people had formed an army of their own but they wanted arms.

At this moment was heard the arrival of a carriage: it was Flesselles', for they would not let him pass though he had shown the royal order for him to go to Versailles: and he was brought back to the Hall by main force.

"Arms, arms," they yelled at him as soon as they saw him.

"No arms here, but there must be some at the Arsenal," he replied.

So five thousand men ran over to the Arsenal to find it was bare. They returned howling to the City Hall. The provost had no firearms or he would not tell of them. He packed them off to the Old Carthusian Monastery, but it was empty too. Not so much as a pocket pistol rewarded them.

Meanwhile Flesselles, learning that Marat and Billet were still busy getting out the powder, suggested sending a deputation to Governor Launay to induce him to draw in the cannon. He had made the populace howl dreadfully on the evening before by running out his guns through the embrasures. Flesselles hoped that by having them taken in, the people would be satisfied and settle down.

The deputation was starting when the arm-seekers came back enraged.

On hearing their vociferations, Billet and Marat came up out of the underground.

On a lower balcony the provost was trying to quiet the multitude. He proposed a resolution that the wards should forge fifty thousand pikes. The people were jumping at the offer.

"Truly this fellow is playing with us," said the surgeon.

He turned to his new friend, saying:

"Go and get to work at the Bastile. In an hour I shall be sending you twenty thousand muskets with a man to each butt."

At first blush Billet had felt great confidence in this leader, whose name was so popular as to have reached him down in the country. He never thought to ask him how he was going to get them. He noticed a priest in the crowd working lustily and though he had no great confidence in the cloth he liked this one to whom he confided the serving out of the amunition.

Marat jumped upon a stone horseblock. The uproar was indescribable.

"Silence," he called out; "I am Marat and I want to speak."

Like magic all was hushed and every eye was turned upon the orator.

"You want arms to take the Bastile? come with me to the Invalides where are twenty-five thousand stand of arms, and you shall have them."

"To the Invalides!" shouted the throngs.

"Now," continued Marat to Billet, "you be off to the Bastile but stay— you may want help before I come."

He wrote on a leaf of his tablets "From Marat," and tore this out to give it to Billet, who smiled to see that it also bore a masonic sign. He and Marat belonged to the Order of the Invisibles over which presided Balsamo-Cagliostro, and his work was what they were prosecuting.

"What am I to do with a paper having no name or address?" inquired the peasant.

"My friend has no address; but his name is well-known. Ask the first workingman you come across for the People's Spokesman, Gonchon."

"Gonchon—fix that on your mind, Pitou."

"Gonchon, or Gonchonius, in Latin," repeated Pitou; "I shall retain it."

"To the Invalides," yelled the voices with increasing ferocity.

"Be on your way," said Marat, "and may the spirit of Liberty march by your side!"

"Now, then, brothers, on to the Invalides," shouted Marat in his turn.

He went off with more than twenty thousand men, while the farmer took away some six hundred in his train, but they were armed. As the two leaders were departing, the provost appeared at a window, calling out:

"Friends, why do I see the green cockade in your hats, when it is the color of Artois, though it may also be that of Hope? Don't look to be sporting the colors of a prince."

"No, no," was the chorus, with Billet's loudest of the voices.

"Then, change it, and as if you must wear a color, take that good old Paris town, our mother, blue and red, my friends."

(Later, General Lafayette, making the criticism that Blue and Red were the Orleans colors also, and perhaps having the stars and stripes of the Republic he had fought for in his mind, suggested the addition of white, saying that "The Red, White and Blue, would be a flag that would go round the world.")

With approving words, everybody tore off the leaves and trampled them underfoot, while they called for ribbons. As if by enchantment all windows opened, and there was a rain of red and blue ribbons. But this was scant supply for a thousand only. Aprons, silk dresses, tapes, scarves, all sorts of tissues were torn into strips and twisted up into rosettes, streamers, favors and ties, with which decorations the improvised army of Billet went its road.

It had recruits on the line: all the side streets of the St. Antoine or working quarter sent the warmest blooded and strongest of its sons. They reached in good order Lesdigures Street, where a number of folk were staring at the Bastile towers, their red brick ruddy in the setting sunshine. Some were calm, some saucy.

In the instant the arrivals of reinforcements changed the multitude in aspect and mood: they were the drumcorps, a hundred French Guards who came down the main avenue, and Billet's rough fellows upwards of twelve thousand strong. The timid grew bold, the calm were excited, and the pert were menacing.

"Down with the cannon," howled twenty thousand throats as twice as many fists were shaken at the brazen pieces stretching their necks over the crenelations.

At that very time, as though the fortress governor obeyed the injunction, the gunners came out to the pieces and retired them until they were no longer visible from below. The throngs clapped hands, thinking they were a power because they had apparently been obeyed.

The sentries continued to pace up and down the ramparts, with alternations of the Swiss and the Veterans.

After the shout of "Down with the cannons!" that of "Draw back the Swiss!" arose, in continuation of "Down with the Germans!" of the evening before.

But the Swiss continued all the same to march up and down to meet the French Invalides.

One of the shouters was impatient, and having a gun, he fired on a sentinel: the bullet struck the grey stone wall a foot above the cornice of the tower, above the soldier's head: it left a white mark, but the man did not halt—did not do much as turn his head.

A great hubbub rose around the firer of the first shot at the Bastile: it was the signal for a mad and unheard-of attack; the tumult had more dread in it than rage; many did not understand that to fire on a royal prison was incurring the death penalty.

CHAPTER XI. THE PRISON GOVERNOR.

Billet looked at the mossgrown edifice, resembling the monsters of fable covered with scales. He counted the embrasures where the great guns might be run out again and the wall-guns which opened their ominous eye to peer through the loopholes. He shook his head, recalling Flesselles' words.

"We'll never get in," he muttered.

"Why never?" questioned a voice at his elbow.

Turning, he saw a wild-looking beggar, in rags, but with eyes glittering like stars in their hollow sockets.

"Because it is hard to take such a pile by main strength."

"Taking the Bastile is not a matter of strength," replied the mendicant, "but an act of faith: have as little faith as a grain of mustard-seed and yet you can overturn a mountain. Believe we can do it, and—Good night, Bastile!"

"Wait a bit," muttered Billet, fumbling for Marat's recommendation in his pocket.

"Wait," reiterated the vagabond, mistaking his mind: "Yes, I can understand you being willing to wait, for you are a farmer, and have always had more than enough to make you fat. But look at my mates: the deaths-heads and raw-bones surrounding us; see their veins dried up, count their bones through the holes in their tatters, and ask them if they know what waiting in patience means?" >

"This man speaks glibly, but he frightens me," remarked Pitou.

"He does not frighten me," replied Billet. Then turning to the stranger, he went on: "I say, patience, because in a quarter-hour yet we shall do."

"I can't call that much," answered the vagrant smiling, "but how much better off will we be then?"

"I shall have visited the Bastile by then," rejoined the farmer-revolutionist. "I shall know how strong the garrison is and the governor's intention—I shall in short have a glimpse of how we can get in."

"It will do, if you see how to get out."

"Well, as to that, if I do not come out, I know a man who will fetch me out."

"Who is he?"

"Gonchon, the People's Spokesman, their orator, their Mirabeau."

"You don't know him," said the man, his eyes flashing fire. "So, how do you make that out?"

"I am going to know him. I was told that the first person I addressed on Bastile Square would take me to him: you are on the spot, lead me to him."

"What do you want of him?"

"To hand him this paper from Surgeon Marat, whom I have just left at the City Hall, whence he was marching to the Invalides to get muskets for his twenty thousand men."

"In this case, hand over the paper. I am Gonchon. Friends," added the vagabond as Billet drew back a step, "here is a chap who does not know me and asks if I am really Gonchon."

The mass burst into laughter; it seemed impossible that their favorite should not be known to all.

"Long life to Gonchon!" was the shout.

"There you are," said Billet, passing the paper to him.

"Mates," said the popular leader, having read, and slapping the bearer on the shoulder, "this is a brother, whom Marat recommends. So you may rely on him. What is your name, Pal?"

"Billet."

"My name is Ax—do you see? between us I hope we shall cut something!"

The mob laughed at the ominous pun.

"Ay, somebody will get cut!" was the cry, "How are we to set about it?"

"We are going right into there," answered Gonchon, pointing to the building.

"That is the right kind of talk," said the farmer; "How many have you, Gonchon?"

"Thirty skeletons."

"Thirty thousand of yours, and twenty coming from the Soldiers' Hospital, ten thousand here; more than enough to succeed if we are to succeed."

"We shall," replied the beggar king.

"I believe you. Get your men in hand while I go in and summon the governor to surrender. If he should, so much the better as it will spare bloodshed; if not, the blood will fall on his head and it is bad luck these times. Ask those German dragoons who hewed down the inoffensive."

"How long will you be engaged with the governor?"

"As long as I can make it, so as to have the castle invested thoroughly; if possible, the moment I come out, begin the onset."

"Enough said."

"You don't distrust me?" said the countryman, holding out his hand to the city ragamuffin.

"I, distrust you?" replied the other, shaking with his emaciated hand the plump one of the farmer with a vigor he had not expected; "Wherefore? With a word or a sign, I could have you ground into dust though you were sheltered by yon towers, which to-morrow will exist not. Were you protected by those soldiers, who will be our dead-meat or we shall be theirs! Go ahead and rely on Gonchon as he does on Billet!"

Convinced, the farmer walked towards the Bastile gateway, while his new comrade proceeded towards the dwellings, under cheers for "The People's Mirabeau!"

"I never saw the other Mirabeau," thought Pitou, "but ours is not handsome."

"Towards the city, the Bastile presented two twin towers, while its two sides faced where the canal runs to-day. The entrance was defended by an outpost house, two lines of sentinels and two draw-bridges over moats.

After getting over these obstacles, one reached the Government Yard, where the governor's residence was.

Hence a corridor led to the ditches: another entrance also leading to the ditches, had a drawbridge, a guardhouse, and an iron grating as portcullis.

At the first entry they stopped Billet but he showed the Flesselles introduction and they did not turn him back. Perceiving that Pitou followed him, as he would have locked steps with him and marched up to the moon, he said:

"Stay outside: if I do not return it will be well for somebody to be around to remind the people that I went in."

"Just so; how long shall I wait?"

"An hour."

"What about the casket?" inquired the youth.

"If I do not come out, if Gonchon does not take the Bastile, or if, having taken it, I am not to be found—tell Dr. Gilbert, who may be found—that men from Paris stole the box he entrusted to me five years ago; that on arriving in town I learnt he was put in the Bastile whence I strove to rescue him but left my skin, which was entirely at his service."

"Very good, Father Billet," said the peasant; "it is rather long and I am afraid of forgetting it."

"I will repeat it."

"Better write it," said a voice hard by.

"I cannot write," rejoined Billet.

"I can, for I am clerk to the Chatelet Prison. My name is Maillard, Stanislaus Maillard."

He was a man of forty-five, tall and slim, grave, and clad in black as became such a functionary; he drew a writing-case from his pocket containing writing materials.

"He looks devilish like an undertaker," muttered Pitou.

"You say," said the clerk, imperturbably writing, "that men from Paris took from your dwelling a casket entrusted to you by Dr. Gilbert? that is an offense, to begin with."

"They belonged to the Paris Police."

"Infamous theft," said Maillard. "Here is your memorandum, young man," he added, giving the note to Ange; "if he be slain, it is to be hoped that both of us will not. I will do it if you both go down."

"Thank you," said Billet, giving his hand to the clerk who grasped it with more power than one might accredit to the meager frame.

"So I may rely on you?"

"As on Marat, and Gonchon."

"Such triplets are not born everyday," thought Pitou, who only said: "Be prudent, Father Billet!"

"Do not forget that the most prudent thing in France is courage," said the farmer with his blunt eloquence, sometimes startling in his rough body.

He passed the first line of sentinels, while Pitou backed out. At the bridge he had to parley, but it was lowered on his showing his pass, and the iron grating was raised. Behind the portcullis was the governor.

This inner yard was the prisoners' exercise ground. Eight giant towers guarded it: no window opened into it. The sun never penetrated its well-like circuit where the pavement was damp, almost muddy.

Here, a clock, the face upheld by chained captives in carving, dropped the seconds like water oozing through a ceiling on the dungeon slabs. At the bottom of this pit, the prisoner, lost in the stony gulf, would glance up at the inexorable nakedness and sue to be led back into his cell.

Governor Launay was about fifty years of age; he wore a grey linseywoolsey suit this day; it was crossed by a red sash of the Order of St. Louis, and he carried a swordcane. He was a bad man: Linguet's Memoirs had just shown him up in a sad light and he was hated almost as much as the jail. His father had been governor before him.

The officers here were on the purchase system, so that the officials tried to make all the money they could squeeze out of the prisoners and their friends. The governor, chief warder, doubled his 60,000 francs appointments by extortion.

In the way of meanness Launay out-did his foregoers: he may have had to pay more highly for the post than his father and so had to put on the screw to retrieve his outlay. He fed his household out of the prisoners' rations; he reduced the firing allowance and doubled the hire of furniture. Maybe he foresaw that he was not to enjoy the berth long.

He had the right to pass a hundred casks of wine into Paris free of duty. He sold it to a wine-shopkeeper who got in the best vintage and supplied him for the prisoners with vinegar.

The latter had one relief, one pleasure—a little garden made on a bastion where they got a whiff of sweet air and saw flowers and grass and sunshine. He let this out to a truck-gardener, robbing the prisoners for fifty livres a-year.

On the other hand he was yielding to rich captives: he let one furnish his room in his own style and have any visitors he liked.

For further particulars see "The Bastile Unveiled."

For all this Launay was brave.

He might be pale, but he was calm, although the storm had raged against him from the previous evening. He felt aware of the riot becoming a revolt for the waves broke at the foot of his castle wall.

It is true that he had four cannon and a garrison of old soldiers and Swiss—with only one unarmed man confronting him. For Billet had handed his fowling-piece to Ange on entering the stronghold.

He understood that a weapon might get him into trouble beyond the barrier.

With a glance he remarked everything; the governor's calm and menacing attitude; the Swiss ranked in the guardhouses; the Veterans on the platforms, and the silent bustle of the artillerists loading up their caissons with ammunition.

The sentinels had their muskets on their shoulders and their officers carried drawn swords.

As the commander stood still, Billet was obliged to go to him. The grating closed behind the people's parliamentarian with an ugly grinding of metal on metal which made him shudder to the marrow, brave though he was.

"What do you want again?" challenged Launay.

"Again" took up Billet. "It seems to me that this is the first time you have seen me, so that you cannot be very tired of me."

"I was told you come from the City Hall and I have just had a deputation from there to get me to promise not to open fire. I promised that much and so I had the guns drawn in."

"I was on the square as you did so, and I——"

"You thought I was giving way to the calls of the crowd?"

"It looked that way," replied the farmer.

"Did I not tell you that they would believe me just such a coward?" said

109

Launay, turning round to his officers. "Who do you come from then?" he demanded of Billet.

"I come on behalf of the people," rejoined the visitor proudly.

"That is all very well," sneered Launay, smiling; "but you must have shown some other warrant, for otherwise you would not have passed the first dead-line of sentries."

"True, I have a pass from your friend Flesselles."

"Flesselles? why do you dub him my friend?" exclaimed the prison warden, looking at the speaker to read to the bottom of his mind. "How do you conclude that he is a friend of mine?"

"I supposed as much."

"Is that all? never mind. Let us see your safe-conduct."

Billet presented the paper which Launay read more than once in order to catch a hidden meaning or concealed lines; he even held it up to the light to see if there was secret writing.

"Is that all? are you perfectly sure? nothing by word of mouth in addition?"

"Not a bit."

"Strange!" said Launay, plunging his glance by a loophole on Bastile Square. "Then tell me your want and be quick."

"The people want you to give up the Bastile."

"What do you say?" cried Launay, turning quickly as if he must be mistaken in his hearing.

"I summon you in the people's name to give up the Bastile."

"Queer animals the people," sneered Launay, snapping his fingers. "What do they want with the Bastile?"

"To demolish it."

"Why, what the mischief is the Bastile to the people? is any common man ever shut up herein? why, the people ought to bless every stone of the Bastile. Who are locked up here? philosophers, learned men, aristocrats, statesmen, princes—all the enemies of the dregs."

"This only proves that the people are not selfish and want to do good to others."

"It is plain that you are not a soldier, my friend," said the other with a kind of pity.

"It is true and come fresh from the country."

"For you do not know what the Bastile is: come with me and I will show you."

"He is going to pull the spring of some trap which will open beneath my feet," thought the adventurer, "and then good-bye, Old Billet!"

But he was intrepid and did not wince as he prepared to accede to the invitation.

"In the first place," continued Launay, "it is well to know that I have enough powder in the store to blow up the castle and lay half the suburbs in ashes."

"I knew that," was the tranquil reply.

"Do you see these cannon? They rake this gallery, which is defended by a guardhouse, and by two ditches only to be crossed by draw-bridges; lastly there is a portcullis."

"Oh, I am not saying that the Bastile will be badly defended, but that it will be well attacked."

"To proceed: here is a postern opening on the moats: observe the thickness of the walls. Forty feet here and fifteen above. You see that though the people have nails they will break against such walls."

"I am not saying that the people will demolish the Bastile to master it but that, having mastered it, they will demolish it," said the leader of the revolutionists.

"Let us go upstairs," said the governor, leading up thirty steps, where he paused to say: "This embrasure opens on the passage by which you would be bound to come. It is defended by one rampart gun, but it enjoys a fair reputation. You know the song:

"'Oh, my sweet-voiced Sackbut, I love your dear song?'"

"Certainly, I have heard it, but I do not think this a time to sing it, or anything else."

"Stay; Marshal Saxe called this gun his Sackbut, because it sang the only music he cared anything for. This is a historical fact. But let us go on."

"Oh," said Billet when upon the tower top, "you have not dismounted the cannon, but merely drawn them in. I shall have to tell the people so."

"The cannon were mounted here by the King's command and by that alone can they be dismounted."

"Governor Launay," returned Billet, feeling himself rise to the level of the emergency, "the true sovereign is yonder and I counsel you to obey it."

He pointed to the grey-looking masses, spotted with blood from the night's battling, and reflecting the dying sunlight on their weapons up to the very moats.

"Friend, a man cannot know two masters," replied theroyalist, holding his head up haughtily: "I, the Governor of the Bastile, know but one: the Sixteenth Louis, who put his sign-manual at the foot of the patent which made me the commander over men and material here."

"Are you not a French citizen?" demanded Billet warmly.

"I am a French nobleman," said the Count of Launay.

"True, you are a soldier, and speak like one."

"You are right," said the gentleman bowing. "I am a soldier and carry out my orders."

"Well, I am a citizen," went on Billet, "and as my duty as such is opposed to yours as the King's soldier, one of us must die. He who fulfills his orders or his duties."

"That is likely, sir."

"So you are determined to fire on the people?"

"Not unless I am fired at. I pledged myself to that effect to Lord Provost Flesselles' deputation. You see the guns have been retired, but at the first shot, I will roll one—say this one—forward out of the embrasure with my own hands, train it and point it, and fire with the slow-match you see there."

"If I believed that," said Billet, "before you could commit such a crime——"

"I have told you that I am a soldier and know nothing outside my orders."

"Then, look!" said Billet, drawing Launay to the gap in the battlements and pointing alternately in two different directions—the main street from the town and the street through the suburbs, "behold those who will henceforth give you orders."

Launay saw two black, dense, roaring bodies, undulating like snakes, with head and bodies in sight but the rearmost coils still waving onwards till lost in the hollows of the ground. All the bodies of these immense reptiles glittered with the scales. These were the two armies to which Billet had given the Bastile as the meeting-place, Marat's men and Gonchon's beggars. As they surged forward they brandished their weapons and yelled blood-curdling cries.

At the sight Launay lost color and said as he raised his cane:

"To your guns!" Then, threatening Billet, he added: "You scoundrel, to come here and gain time under pretence of a parley, do you know that you deserve death?"

Billet saw the attempt to draw the sword from the cane and pierce him; he seized the speaker by the collar and waistband as swift as lightning, and raising him clear off the ground, he replied:

"And you deserve to be hurled down to the bottom of the ditch to be smashed in the mud. But, never mind, thank God I can fight you in another manner."

At this instant, an immense howl, a universal one, rose in the air like a whirlwind, as Major Losme appeared on the platform.

"Oh, sir, for mercy's sake," he said to Billet: "Show yourself for the people there believe something has happened you and they call for you."

Indeed, the name of Billet, set afloat by Pitou, ascended on the clamor.

The farmer let go Launay who replaced the blade in the stick. The three men hesitated for a moment while the innumerable cries of vengeance and menace arose.

"Show yourself, sir," said Launay, "not because the noise frightens me but to prove that I have acted fairly."

The farmer thrust his head out of the porthole, waving his hand.

At this sight the populace burst with cheering: it was in a measure Revolution standing up in Billet's stead as this man of the lowest ranks trod the Bastile turret like a master.

"That is well, sir," went on Launay. "Now all is ended between us; you have no further business here. They ask for you below; go down."

Billet appreciated this moderation on the part of a man who had him in his power: he went down by the same stairs, the governor following. The major remained up there as the governor had whispered some orders to him.

It was evident that Count Launay had but one wish, that the bearer of the flag of truce should be his active enemy as soon as possible.

Without speaking a word the envoy crossed the yard, where he saw the cannoniers were at their pieces and the lintstocks were lighted and smoking. He stopped before them.

"Friends," he cried, "remember that I came to your commander to stay the shedding of blood, but that he refused me."

"In the King's name, be off from here!" said Launay, stamping his foot.

"Have a care," retorted the farmer: "I am ordered out in the King's name but I shall return in that of the People. Speak out," he added, turning to the Swiss, "who are you for?"

The foreign soldiers were silent. Launay pointed to the iron door. But Billet attempted a final effort.

"Governor, in the name of the nation, in the name of your brothers!"

"Brothers? is that what you call them who are bellowing 'Down the Bastile, and Death to the Governor?' they may be brothers of yours, but surely they are none of mine."

"In humanity's, then!"

"Humanity—which urges you to come a hundred thousand strong against one hundred hapless soldiers immured in these walls and cut their throats?"

"But by giving up the Bastile you save their lives."

"And I lose my honor."

Billet was hushed, for the soldierly argument crushed him; but again he addressed the soldiers, saying:

"Surrender, friends, while it is yet time; in another ten minutes it will be too late."

"I will have you shot unless you are out of this instantly," thundered Launay, "as true as I am a noble."

Billet stopped an instant, folded his arms in token of defiance and, crossing glances for the last time with the exasperated governor, walked forth.

CHAPTER XII. STORMING THE BASTILE.

Under the burning July sun the crowds awaited, shuddering with fever. Gonchon's men had joined in with Marat's, the suburbs hailing each other as brothers. Gonchon was at the head of his patriots but Marat had disappeared.

The scene on the open place was terrifying.

On seeing Billet the cheering was tremendous.

"He is a brave man," said Billet to Gonchon, "or rather I should say he is stubborn. He will not surrender the Bastile but will sustain the siege."

"Do you think he will hold out long?"

"To death."

"All right, he shall have that."

"But how many men will be killed by us?" said the farmer, no doubt fearing that he had not the right usurped by generals, kings and emperors, those who take out licenses to kill and maim.

"Rubbish," said Gonchon; "there are too many, since we have not enough for half the population. Is not that about the size of it, boys?" he asked of the bystanders.

"Yes, yes," was the reply in sublime abnegation.

"But the moat?" queried Billet.

"It need be filled up in only one place," responded the beggar's leader: "and I calculate that we could choke it up altogether, eh, lads?"

The friends answered unanimously in the affirmative.

"Have it so," said Billet, overpowered.

At this moment, Launay appeared on a terrace, followed by Major Losme and two or three other officers.

"Commence," shouted Gonchon.

The governor turned his back on him.

Gonchon might have put up with a threat but he would not bear contempt: he lifted his gun and fired at him. A man near him fell. Instantly a hundred, nay, a thousand gunshots sounded, as if it were awaited as a signal, and the grey towers were striped with white.

A few seconds' silence succeeded this discharge, as if the assailants were frightened at what they had done.

Then a gush of flame lost in a cloud of smoke crowned the crest of one tower. A detonation thundered. Shrieks of pain were heard in the throngs closely pressed. The first cannonshot had been fired by the royalists, the first blood shed.

The battle between people and Bastile was begun.

An instant previously menacing, the multitudes felt something like terror. By defending itself with so little of its weapons the Bastile seemed impregnable. In this period of concession the majority had no doubt supposed that they would always have their way.

That was a mistake: this cannonshot fired into them gave the measure of the Titanic work they had undertaken.

A firing of muskets, well aimed, from the platform, immediately followed.

The fresh silence was broken by renewed screams, groans and a few complaints. But nobody thought to flee, and had the thought struck any one, he must have been ashamed seeing the numbers.

Indeed all the thoroughfares were streams of human beings: the square an immense sea, with each billow a human head; the eyes flamed and the mouths hurled curses.

In a trice all the windows on the square were filled with sharpshooters who fired, though out of range. If a soldier appeared at a loophole or an embrasure, a hundred barrels were leveled at him, and the hail of bullets chipped away the edge of the stone angle shielding him.

But soon they were tired of firing at insensible stone: they wanted the flesh to aim at, and to see the blood spirt.

Everybody shouted ideas of an assault. Billet, weary of listening, caught up an ax from a carpenter's hand, and rushed forward, in the midst of a shower of missiles, striking down the men around him like a scythe lays the grain, till he reached a small guardhouse before the first drawbridge. While the grapeshot was hurling and whistling about him, he hacked at the chains till down came the bridge.

During the quarter of an hour that this insane enterprise went on, the lookers-on held their breath. At each volley they expected to see their champion laid low. Forgetting their own danger, they thought solely of that the audacious worker ran. When the drop came down, they uttered a loud whoop and dashed into the first yard.

The rush was so unexpected, rapid and impetuous that no resistance was made.

The frenziedly joyful cheers announced the first advantage to Launay. Nobody noticed that a man had been mangled under the bridge.

Then, as if at the depth of a cavern, the four guns, pointed out to Billet by the governor, were shot off with a dreadful crash and all the outer yard was swept clear. The iron hurricane cleft a long swath of blood through the mass; on the path lay ten or twelve dead and double as many wounded.

Billet had stood on the guardhouse roof to reach the chain well up; he slid down where he found Pitou, who had reached the spot he knew not how. The young man had a quick eye, a poacher's habit. He had seen the gunners step up to the touchhole with the lighted matches, and seizing his patron by the coat, he had pulled him back behind a corner of the wall which sheltered both from the cannonade.

From this period on, the war was real. The tumult was alarming; the onslaught murderous; ten thousand gunshots poured upon the fort at risk of slaying the assaulters with the garrison. To cap all, a field-piece brought up by the French Guardsmen, added its boom to the cracking of small arms.

The frightful uproar intoxicated the amateur fighters and began to daunt the besieged who felt that they could never raise a commotion equal to this deafening them. The officers saw that their soldiers were weakening: they had to snatch their muskets from them and fire themselves.

At this juncture, amid the roar of great guns and smaller ones, and the shouting, as the mob were rushing forward to carry away the injured and dead on litters, a little body of citizens appeared calm and unarmed at the yard entrance. It was a deputation of electors from the City Hall. They were sacrificing life under protection merely of the white flag before and after them to indicate they came to parley.

Wishing to stop the effusion of blood, after hearing that the attack had commenced, they forced Flesselles to renew negotiations with the governor. In the name of the city, they summoned the governor of the citadel to cease firing, and to receive in the place a hundred of the town guards to guarantee his safety, the garrison's and the inhabitants.

The deputies called this out as they marched along. Frightened by the magnitude of the task they had set themselves, the people were ready to accept the proposal, seeing, too, the dead and wounded carried by. If Launay accepted the partial defeat they would be content with a half-victory.

At sight of them, the inner-yard firing ceased; they were beckoned to approach and they scrambled over the corpses, slipped in gore and held their hands out to the maimed. Under their shelter the others grouped. The injured and lifeless were borne out, streaking the marble flags with broad purple stains.

Firing ceasing on the fort side, Billet went out to get his party to refrain. At the doors he met Gonchon, without arms, exposing his naked breast like a man inspired, calm as though invulnerable.

"What has become of the deputation?" he inquired.

"It has got in," replied Billet. "Cease firing."

"It is useless; he will not give in," said the beggar leader, with the same certainty as if he had been gifted with reading the future.

"No matter; respect the usages of war, since we have become soldiers."

"I do not mind," said Gonchon; "Elie, Hullin, go," he said to two men who seemed to rule the crowd together with him: "Do not let a shot be fired till I say so."

At the voice the two darted away, cleaving the throng, and soon the sound of the musketry dying away, stopped entirely.

During the short rest the wounded were attended to; they were upwards of forty. Two o'clock struck: they had been hammering away two hours, from noon. Billet had returned to the front where Gonchon found him. His impatience was visible as he watched the iron grating.

"What is wrong?" asked the farmer.

"All is lost if the Bastile is not taken in two hours," was the beggar's reply.

"How so?"

"Because the royal court will learn what we are at. It will send us Bezenval's Switzers and Lambesq's heavies, who will help catch us between three fires."

Billet was forced to confess the truth in the prospect. At length the deputies appeared: by their woe-begone aspect it was clear their errand had failed.

"What did I tell you?" cried the popular orator, gladly; "What was foretold by Balsamo and Cagliostro will come to pass. The accursed fortress is doomed. To arms, boys, to arms," he yelled without waiting for the deputies to relate their doings, "the commandment refuses."

In fact, scarcely had the governor read Flesselles' letter introducing the party than he brightened up in the face and exclaimed, instead of yielding to the proposition:

"You Parisian gentlemen wanted the fight and it is too late to draw back."

The citizens had protested and persisted in picturing the horrors which the defense would entail. But he would heed nothing and finishing by saying to them what he had told Billet a couple of hours anteriorly:

"Begone or I will have you shot."

The citizens were glad to get out of it.

Launay took the offensive this time. He was wild with impatience. Before the deputation crossed the threshold, the Sackbut of Marshal Saxe played its tune: three men fell—one dead and two wounded, the latter being a French guardsman and the other one of the flag-of-truce bearers. At sight of this victim, whose errand made him sacred, carried away smothered in blood, the fury of the numbers was exalted once more.

Gonchon's aid-de-camps had returned to take their places by his side; but each had run home to change his dress. Elie had been the Marquis Conflans' running-footman and his livery resembled a Hungarian officer's uniform. Elie put on the uniform he had worn when an officer of the Queen's own Regiment, and this gave more confidence to the masses with the thought that the army was on their side.

The firing recommenced more fiercely than before.

At this Major Losme approached his superior. He was a brave and honorable soldier, but he had some manhood left him and he saw with pain what had happened and foresaw with more pain what would occur.

"You know we have no food," he said.

"I know that," answered Launay.

"And we have no order to hold out."

"I ask your pardon, Military Governor of the Bastile, but I am the governor of it in all respects; my order is to shut the doors and I hold the keys."

"My lord, keys are to open locks as well as fasten them. Have a care that you do not get the garrison massacred without saving the castle. That will be two triumphs for the revolters in one day. Look at the men we kill—they spring up again from the pavement. This morning only three thousand were there: three hours ago, there were six. Now they are over sixty thousand and to-morrow they will number a hundred thousand. When our cannon are silenced, and that will be the upshot, they will be strong enough to pull down the Bastile with their bare hands."

"You do not speak like the military governor of the Bastile, Major Losme."

"I speak like a Frenchman, my lord. I say that his Majesty having given us no special order—and the Provost of the Traders having made us a very acceptable proposition, to introduce a hundred Civil Guards into the castle—you might avoid the misery I foresee by acceding to Provost Flesselles' proposition."

"In your opinion, the City of Paris is a power we ought to obey?"

"Yes, in the absence of special royal order."

"Then, read, Major Losme," said the prison chief, leading his lieutenant aside into a corner.

On the small sheet of paper which he let him read, was written:

"Hold out firmly: I will amuse the Parisians with Cockades and promises. Before day is done, Bezenval will send you reinforcements.

FLESSELLES."

"How did this advice reach you?" inquired the major.

"In the letter the deputies carried. They thought they were bearing a desire for the Bastile to be surrendered, and it was the order to defend it that they handed me."

The major bent his head.

"Go to your post and do not quit it till I command you sir," continued Launay. Losme obeying, he coldly folded up the paper, replaced it in his pocket, and went over to the cannoniers to advise them to aim true and fire low. They obeyed like the major.

But the fortalice's fate was settled. No human power could delay the accomplishment.

To every cannonshot the reply was "We mean to have the Bastile!"

While voices claimed it, arms were not idle.

Pitou's and Billet's arms and voices were among those asking most energetically and working most efficaciously.

Each worked according to his character. Courageous and confident as the bulldog, Billet had run at the enemy, heedless of shot and steel. Pitou, prudent and circumspect as the fox, endowed to the highest degree with self-preservation, utilized all his faculties to watch danger and anticipate it. His sight knew the most deadly embrasures, and distinguished the least move of the bronze tube to enter it. He could guess the exact moment when the rampart-gun was about to fire through the portcullis. His eyes having done their office, he made his limbs work for their owner.

Down went his shoulders and in went his chest, so that his frame offered no more surface than a board seen edgewise.

In these moments, of the filling-out Pitou, thin only in the legs, nothing remained but the geometrical expression of a straight line.

He chose a spot where the masonry shaped out cavities and projections so that his head was shielded by a stone, his heart by another and his knees by still another slab. Nowhere could a mortal wound be got in on him.

He fired a shot now and then, to relieve his feelings and because Billet told him to "blaze away." But he had nothing but wood and stone before him.

For his part he kept begging his friend not to expose himself to the firing. "There goes the Sackbut," or "I hear a hammer coming down."

Despite these injunctions the farmer executed prodigies of daring and energy, all in pure waste, till the idea struck him to go along the woodwork of the bridge and chop the chains of the second one, as he had done with the first.

Ange howled for him to stay and seeing that howls were useless, he followed him, from cover, saying

"Dear Master Billet, your wife will be a widow if you get killed."

The Swiss thrust their guns through the loopholes by which the Sackbut was fired to try to pick off the daring fellow who was making the chips fly off their bridge.

Billet called on his single gun to answer the Sackbut, but when the latter fired, the other artillerists retreated and the farmer was left alone to serve the cannon. This again drew Pitou out of his refuge.

"Master," he sued, "in the name of Catherine! think if you are done for, that Catherine will be an orphan."

Billet yielded to his plea, and because he had a new idea.

He ran out on the square, holloaing.

"A cart!"

"Two carts," added Pitou, "thinking you cannot have too much of a good thing."

Ten carts were immediately trundled through the multitude.

"Dry hay and straw!" shouted Billet.

"Straw and hay," repeated Pitou.

Like a flash, two hundred men brought each a truss of straw or half a bale of hay. Others brought dry fodder on litters. They were obliged to call out that they had ten times more than was wanted. In an hour they would

124

have smothered the Bastile.

Billet put himself in the rails of a bush-cart, laden with hay, and pushed it before him instead of dragging it.

Pitou did the same with another, without knowing why but thinking the farmer's example was worthy of imitation.

Elie and Hullin guessed what the farmer proposed; they supplied themselves with carts and pushed them into the prison yard.

Scarcely did they enter than small shot and canister received them but the hay and straw deadened the bullets and slugs and only a few rattled on the wheels and shafts. None of the assailants were touched.

As soon as this discharge was fired, two or three hundred musketmen dashed on behind the cart-pushers and lodged under the sloping shed of the bridge itself, under cover of the moving breastwork.

There Billet pulled out a scrap of paper, and flint and steel; he wrapped up a pinch of gunpowder in the paper, struck a light and ignited it and shoved the flaring piece into the heap of hay. Others took lighted wisps and scattered the flames. It caught the pentroof and the four blazing carts set fire to beams high up and sneaked along the bridge supports.

To put out the fire the garrison would have to come out and to show oneself was to court death.

The glad cheer, started in the yard, was caught up on the square where the smoke was seen above the towers. Something fatal to the besieged was surmised to be going on.

Indeed the redhot chains drew out and snapped from the ringbolts. The half-broken bridge fell, smoking and sending up sparks.

The firemen came up with their engines, but the governor ordered them to be fired upon though the prison might be thus burned over the garrison's heads.

The old French soldiers refused. The Swiss were willing, but as they were not artillerists they could not work the carriage-guns. These had to be abandoned.

On the other side, seeing that the cannonade ceased, the French Guards resumed their field-piece work and with the third ball sent the portcullis flying.

The governor had gone upon the tower to see if the promised succor was arriving when he suddenly found himself enwrapped in smoke. He ran downstairs and ordered the gunners to keep up the firing. The refusal of the French Veterans exasperated him.

On hearing the portcullis smashed in, he recognized that all was lost.

He was fully aware that he was hated. He guessed that there was no safety for him. During the whole of the action, he had cherished the thought of burying himself under the ruins of his castle.

As soon as he acknowledged that all resistance was useless, he snatched a lintstock from an artillerist and precipitated himself towards the powder magazine.

"The powder, the powder!" shrieked twenty terrified voices.

On seeing the governor with the burning match they divined his intention. Two soldiers crossed their bayonets before his breast at the very instant when he opened the ammunition-storeroom door.

"You may kill me," he said, "but you cannot do that so quickly that I shall not have had time to toss this brand into one of the open kegs. Then, all of us, besieged and besiegers, go up!"

The soldiers stopped with the steel at his breast, but he was still their commander and commanded, for he held the lives of all in his hands. His movement rivetted everybody to their place.

The assailants perceived that something extraordinary was going on. They peered into the yard and saw the governor threatening and being threatened.

"Hark to me," said he, "as true as I have death in my grasp for all of you, I will fire the powder if one of you dare step within this yard."

The hearers might fancy the earth quaked beneath their feet.

"What do you want?" several voices gasped with the accent of a panic.

"An honorable capitulation."

As the assailants could not fully comprehend the extent of Launay's despair and did not believe his speech, they began to enter, Billet at the head. But he suddenly turned pale and trembled, for he had thought of Dr. Gilbert. It little mattered to the farmer whether the Bastile was torn down or blown up; but at any price the arch-revolutionist must live, the pupil of Balsamo, his successor, perhaps, at the head of the Invisibles.

"Stop," shouted Billet, "for the sake of the prisoners!"

Elie and Hullin, and their men, who had not shrank from death on their own behalf, recoiled, white and trembling like he had.

"What do you want?" they demanded of the governor, renewing the question his garrison had put to him.

"Everybody must retire," replied Count Launay. "I will listen to no proposition while there is an intruder inside the Bastile walls."

"But you will take advantage of our withdrawal to repair damages," remonstrated Billet.

"If the capitulation be refused, you will find things in the same condition; you there, I at this door, on the faith of a nobleman!"

Some shook their heads.

"Is there any here who doubt a nobleman?" questioned the count.

"No, no, nobody," rejoined five hundred voices.

"Bring me pen, ink and paper," continued the governor. "That is well," he went on as his orders were executed. "Now, retire!" he said to the assaulters.

Billet, Elie and Hullin set the example, and all followed them.

Launay laid the match by his side and began to write the terms of surrender on his knee. The French Veterans and the Swiss, aware that their safety was at stake, silently looked at him in superstitious terror. When he turned, before writing the document out fair, all the yards were clear.

In a twinkling all the concourse outside had learnt what was proceeding. As Losme had said, it was the population which issued from beneath the flagstones and pavement. Not only workmen and beggars, the homeless and the imperfectly clad, but citizens of the better classes. Not only men but women and children. Each had a weapon and uttered a war-cry.

From spot to spot, amid groups, was seen a woman, disheveled, wringing her hands and waving her arms, howling curses at the giant of stone: it was a mother, a wife or a sweetheart whose dearest one had been incarcerated in its flanks.

But since a short space the giant had ceased to vomit flame and scowl in the smoke; the fire was extinct and the whole mute as a tomb. On the blackened walls the bullet grazes stood out white and were above count; everybody had wanted to leave his mark on the granite brow of his personification of tyranny.

They could hardly believe that the Bastile was about to be turned over to them; that its governor would surrender.

In the midst of this general doubt, as none ventured to congratulate another, and all waited in silence, a letter stuck on a spearpoint was seen thrust through a loophole.

Between the despatch and the besiegers was the great moat deep and wide and full of water.

Billet called for a plank, but three were too short, and the fourth, while long enough, was ill adjusted. Still he balanced himself as well as he could and unhesitatingly risked himself on the bending bridge.

All in dumbness fixed their eyes on the man who seemed suspended over the stagnant water, while Pitou, quivering, sat on the brink and hid his face.

All of a sudden, when Billet was two-thirds over, the plank shifted, and throwing up his arms he fell in the moat where he sank out of sight.

Pitou uttered a roar and dived after his master like a Newfoundland dog.

A man went right out on the plank, without hesitation, choosing the same road as Billet: it was Stanislas Maillard, the prison clerk. On reaching the point beneath which he saw two men struggling, he looked, but seeing that they could swim ashore, he continued his way.

In half a minute he was across and took the letter off the pike.

With the same tranquil nerve and steadiness of gait, he passed back over the plank.

But at the very second when all crowded round him to read the message, a hail of bullets rained down from the battlements at the same time as a tremendous report was heard.

From all breasts a cry arose, one announcing that the people meant to have revenge.

"Trust the tyrants again," said Gonchon.

Nobody cared any more about capitulations, the powder, the prisoners or himself—nothing was wanted but retaliation and the besiegers strewed into the yards not by hundreds but by thousands. The only thing preventing them entering still faster was not the muskets but the narrowness of the doorways.

On hearing the firing, the two soldiers who had not gone away from their commander, jumped at him and a third set his foot on the slow-match, and crushed it out. Launay drew the sword hidden in his cane and tried to stab with it but it was wrenched off from him and broken, while in his grip.

He was convinced that he could do no more, and he waited for his doom.

The mobs rushing in met the soldiers, holding out their hands to them—and so the Bastile was not taken under a surrender but by assault.

This came from the royal castle having ceased to enclose inert matter:

129

latterly the King had shut up human brain there and the spirit had burst the vessel.

The people entered at the breach.

As for the treacherous volley fired in the midst of silence during the suspension of hostilities, and unforeseen, impolitic and deadly aggression, it will never be known who gave the order, inspired it and accomplished it.

There are moments when the future of a nation is exactly poised in the scales of Fate. One of the plates bears up the other, even while each party thinks his side will make the other kick the beam. An invisible hand has flung into the dish a dagger or a pistol and all changes. The only cry heard is:

"Woe to the vanquished!"

CHAPTER XIII. DOWN IN THE DUNGEONS.

While the multitude poured, roaring with delight and anger at the same time, into the yards of the prison, two men were floundering in the ditch: Billet and Pitou. The latter was keeping up the other whom no bullet or blow had struck, but the fall had a trifle stunned him. Ropes were thrown to them and poles thrust down.

In five minutes they were rescued, and were hugged and carried in triumph, muddy though they were.

One gave Billet a drink of brandy, another crammed the younger peasant with bread and sausage. A third dried them off and led them into the sunshine.

Suddenly an idea or rather a memory crossed the good farmer's mind: he tore himself from the friendly arms and ran towards the fort.

"The prisoners, help the prisoners!" he shouted.

"Yes, the prisoners," repeated Pitou, darting into the tower after his leader.

Only thinking of the jailers, the mob now shuddered on remembering the captives. The cries were reiterated. A fresh flood of assailants burst any remaining barriers and seemed to enlarge the flanks of the prison to expand it with liberty.

A frightful scene was presented to Billet and his friend. The mob crowded into the court, enraged, drunken and furious. The first soldier falling under hand was torn to pieces.

Gonchon looked on quietly, no doubt thinking that popular wrath is like a great river, doing more mischief if one tries to dam it than if letting it make its course. On the contrary, Elie and Hullin leaped in between defenders and attackers; they prayed and supplicated, vociferating the holy lie that the soldiers were promised their lives.

Billet and Pitou's arrival was reinforcement to them.

Billet whom they were revenging, was alive; not even hurt; the plank had swerved underfoot and he was clear with a mud bath, that was all.

The Swiss were most detested: but they were not to be found. They had time to put on overalls and smockfrocks of dull linen, and they passed off as servants.

With sledges the invaders broke the captive images on the clock face. They raced up to the turret tops to kick the cannon which had belched death on them. They laid hands on the stones and endeavored to dislodge them.

When the first of the conquerors were seen on the battlements, all without, below, a hundred thousand or so, cast up an immense clamor.

It spread over Paris, and flew over France like a swiftwinged eagle:

"The Bastile is taken!"

At this news, hearts melted, eyes were moist with tears of gladness, and hands clasped; no longer were there opposition parties or inimical castes, for all Parisians understood that they were brothers and all men that they were free.

A million of men mutually embraced.

Billet and Pitou wanted no part in the rejoicing, they sought the liberation of the prisoners.

Traversing Government yard, they passed near a man in grey clothes, calmly leaning on a gold-headed cane: it was the governor, quietly waiting for his friends to save him or his foes to lay him low.

Billet recognized him at sight, and uttered an outcry. He walked straight up to him. Launay knew him again, also; but folded his arms and looked at Billet as much as to say:

"Is it you who will deal me the first stab?"

"If I speak to him," thought the farmer, "they will know him, and then he will be killed."

Yet how would he find Dr. Gilbert in this chaos? how wrest from the Bastile the grim secret enshrouded in its womb? Launay understood all this heroic hesitation and scruple.

"What do you want?" asked he, in an undertone.

"Nothing," rejoined Billet, pointing out that the doorways are doorless all the way to the street, "nothing; but I should like to find Dr. Gilbert."

"No. Three, Bertaudiere Tower," replied the count in a gentle voice, almost softened, but he would not flee.

At this juncture a voice behind Billet pronounced these words:

"Halloa, here is the governor!"

The voice was as emotionless as though spoken by no being of this world but every syllable was a dagger-blade cruelly dug into Launay's bosom. The voice was Gonchon's.

At the denunciation, as if from an alarm bell ringing, all the men athirst for vengeance, started and turned their flaring eyes on Launay at whom they flung themselves.

"He is lost, unless we can save him," said Billet to Elie and Hullin.

"Help us," they answered.

"I must stay here, as I have a task to do."

In a flash, Launay was taken up by numerous hands and carried out.

Elie and his comrade hurried after, calling: "Stop, he was promised his life for surrendering."

This was not true, but the sublime falsehood rushed from both of the noble hearts. In a second the governor, followed by the pair, disappeared in the corridor opening on the square, amid shouts:

"Take him to the City Hall!"

As a living prey Launay was in the eyes of most equal to the dead prey, the prison, overrun.

Strange was the sight of this sad and silent edifice, for four centuries threaded solely by the warden and his turnkeys, become the strolling ground of any tatterdemalion: the crowd roamed over the garden, up and down the stairs, buzzing like a swarm of bees, and filling the granite hive with bustle and uproar.

Billet for an instant watched Launay, carried rather than dragged, seeming to hover over the multitude. But he was gone in a space. Billet sighed and looking round him and seeing Pitou, said as he darted towards a tower:

"The Third Bertaudiere."

A trembling jailer was in the way.

"Here you are, captain," he answered: "but I have not the keys, they were taken from me."

"Brother, lend me your ax," said Billet of a neighbor.

"I give it you, for it is not wanted now we have taken the old den."

Grasping the weapon, Billet dashed into a stairway, conducted by the warder. The latter stopped before a door.

"This is No. Three, Bertaudiere Tower," said he.

"Is the prisoner here, Dr. Gilbert?"

"Don't know the names."

"Only put here a few days ago?"

"Don't know."

"Well, I shall," rejoined the farmer, attacking the door with the ax.

It was of oak, but the splinters flew freely under the chops of the vigorous yeoman. In a short time one could peep into the room. Billet looked in at the cleft. In the beam of light from a grated window in the yard a man was visible in the cell, standing a little back, holding one of his bedslates, he was in the attitude of defense, ready to knock down any one intruding.

Spite of his long beard, pale face and his hair being close cropped, Billet recognized Gilbert.

"Doctor, doctor, is it you? It is Billet who calls, your friend."

"Are you here, Billet, here?"

"Yes, yes, that's Billet, right here!" shouted the crowd; "we are here, in the Bastile, for we have taken it. You are free!"

"The Bastile is taken and I am free?" repeated the doctor.

Running both hands through the bars of the door he shook it so forcibly that the hinges and lock-bolt seemed likely to shoot out of the pockets. One of the split panels, shattered by Billet, fell clean out and was left in the prisoner's hands.

"Wait, wait," said the rescuer, seeing that such another exertion would exhaust the man's powers, too much excited; "wait."

He redoubled his blows. Through the gap the prisoner could be seen, fallen on his stool, pale as a sceptre and incapable of moving the broken beam again with which he had tried like a Samson to shake the Bastile down.

"Billet," he kept on saying.

"And me with him, doctor, poor Pitou, whom you must remember from having placed me for board and lodging at Aunt Angelique's—I came along to get you out."

"But I cannot get through that crack," objected the prisoner.

"We will widen it," cried the bystanders.

In a common effort each brought his effort to bear: while one inserted a crowbar between the wall and the door-jamb, another got a purchase on the lock with the lever, and others put their shoulders to the woodwork; the oak gave a last crack, and the stones scaled off, so that by the removed door and

135

the crumbling stone, the torrent plunged within the prison.

Gilbert was soon in the arms of his friends.

Gilbert, who was a little peasant boy on the Taverney estate, where he conceived an undying and life-long passion for his master's daughter Andrea, was now a man of thirty-five. Philip of Taverney, who tried to kill him in a cave in the Azores Islands because he had accomplished the love-design of his existence in giving Andrea the title of mother to little Sebastian Gilbert, would not recognize him he left bathed in blood. Pale without sickliness, with black hair and steady though animated eyes, one could tell that he, like his teacher Balsamo-Cagliostro, was endowed with the power of magnetism. As he could now mesmerize Andrea, he could mentally master most men.

When his gaze was idle, it did not wander in vacancy but retired into his meditations and became the gloomier and deeper.

His nose was straight, coming down from the brow in a direct line: it surmounted a disdainful lip, showing the dazzling enamel of his teeth.

Commonly he was clad with Quaker-like simplicity; but it approached elegance from its extreme primness. His stature, above the middle height, was well formed; and we have seen how strong he could be when he roused all his nervous force.

Although a week in jail, he had taken the usual care of himself. Though his beard had grown long, it was combed out and set off his clear skin, indicating by its length, not his neglect but the refusal of a razor or a shave.

After thanking Billet and Pitou, he turned to the crowd in the cell. As if he recovered all his command in a twinkling, he said:

"Then the long looked-for day has come! I thank you, all my friends, and I thank the Eternal Spirit which watches over the liberty of peoples."

He held out his hands, but they shrank from touching them, so lofty was his glance, and his voice so dignified as of a superior man.

Leaving the dungeon, he walked out before them all, leaning on the farmer and the country boy.

After Gilbert's first impulse of gratitude and friendship, a second had established the first distance between him and the subordinates.

At the door, Gilbert stopped, dazzled by the sunshine.

He stopped, folded his arms, and said as he gazed upwards:

"Hail, beautiful Liberty! I saw you spring into life in the New World, and we are old friends and battlefield comrades. Hail!"

The smile he wore showed that the cheers of a free people were not a novelty to him.

"Billet," he said, after collecting his thoughts, "Have the people overcome despotism?"

"They have."

"And you came to liberate me? how did you know of my arrest?"

"Your son told me this morning."

"Poor Emile-Sebastian! have you seen him? is he at peace in the school?"

"I left him being carried to the sick ward as he had a fit. He was wild because we would not let him have a share in the fighting to get you out."

The physician smiled, for the boy was his hope, and had borne himself as he hoped.

"I said that as you were in the Bastile we would have to take the Bastile," went on the farmer, "and now we have taken it. But that is not all: the casket is stolen which you entrusted to me."

"Stolen by whom?"

"By men wearing black, who broke into the house under guise of seizing the pamphlet which you sent me; locking me up in a room, they searched the whole house and found the casket."

"Yesterday? then there is a coincidence between my arrest and this purloining. The same person caused this arrest and abstraction. I must know whom. Where are the books of the jail?" demanded the doctor, turning round to the jailer who kept close.

"In Government yard," replied he. "Oh, master, let me go with you or say a good word to these gentlemen who will otherwise knock me about."

"Just so," replied Gilbert; "Friends, I want you not to do any harm to this poor fellow who only did his duty in opening doors and locking them; he was always gentle with the prisoners."

"Good," cried the voices all round, as they surrounded him in respect mingled with curiosity; "he need not be scared, but can come along."

"Thank you, sir," said the jailer; "but we had better make haste, for they are burning the papers."

"Then there is not an instant to be lost," cried the physician. "To the Archives."

He darted off towards the office, drawing the mob with him, at the head of which still marched Billet and Pitou.

CHAPTER XIV. THE TRIANGLE OF LIBERTY.

At the door of the Register Hall they had made a bonfire of the documents.

One of the first feelings of the masses after a victory is for destruction, unfortunately. The memorials of the prison were turned out of the large room, where the records of all the prisoners since a hundred years back were kept higgledy piggledy. The mob shut up the papers with anger, seeming to think that they gave the prisoners freedom by annulling the warrants.

Gilbert, assisted by Pitou, looked at the registers, but the present year's was missing. Though a calm and cool man, the doctor stamped his foot with impatience while he turned blanched.

At this Pitou spied a boy, such a little hero as always pops up in the reign of King Mob, who was carrying on his head the volume to throw it into the fire. With his long legs he soon overtook him. It was the register for 1789. The deal did not take long, for Ange announced himself as one who had captured the place and explained that a prisoner wanted the book. The boy gave it up with the comforting remark that there were lots more where it came from.

Pitou opened the book and on the last page he saw the entry:

"This day, ninth of July, 1789, enters Dr. Gilbert, a most dangerous writer of public matters and philosophy: keep in solitary confinement."

He carried the register to the physician. It was of course what he sought. Looking whence the order emanated, he exclaimed:

"The warrant to arrest me signed by my friend Necker? then there must be some trick played on him."

"Necker your friend?" ejaculated the crowd, for the name had great influence over them.

"Yes, my friend, and I upheld him. I am convinced that he is ignorant of my being in prison. But I will go and find him, and——"

"He is not at Versailles," said Billet, "but at Brussels; he is exiled."

"His daughter lives in the country out by St. Ouen," suggested one of the throng, whom Gilbert thanked without seeing who it was.

"Friends," he said, "in the name of history, who will find the condemnation of tyranny in these papers, cease such devastation, I entreat you. Demolish the Bastile, stone by stone, till not a trace remains, but respect documents and books, for the light of the future is in them."

The multitude had scarce heard the rebuke than its high intelligence gauged he was correct.

"The doctor is right," cried a hundred voices; "no more spoiling. Let us take these papers to the City Hall."

A fireman who had brought a small hand-engine into the fort, with half a dozen comrades, directed the horse-butt at the fire which was about to repeat a conflagration of books like that of Alexandria, and they put it out.

"At whose request were you arrested?" inquired the farmer.

"Just what I was looking for but the name is blank. I shall learn," he added after brief meditation.

Tearing out the leaf concerning himself, he folded it up and pocketed it.

"Let us be off, friends," said he, "we have no farther business here."

"It is easier to say, let us go, than manage it," remarked the countryman.

Indeed, the concourse, entering the Castle by all openings, choked up the doorways. They had liberated eight prisoners, including Gilbert. Four excited no interest; they had been locked up on a charge of forging a bank draft, without any evidence, which leads to the premise that it was a false charge; they had been in jail only two years. The next was Count Solange, a man of thirty, who was in rapture: he hugged his liberators, exalted their victory and related his captivity.

Arrested in 1782, and shut up in Vincennes Castle on a blank warrant obtained by his father, he had been transferred to the Bastile, where he remained five years without having seen a magistrate or being examined once: his father had died two years back, and nobody asked after him. Had not the Bastile been captured, he would probably have died there unasked for.

White was another wretch; he was sixty years old and jabbered incoherent words with a foreign accent. To the many questions he replied that he was ignorant how long he had been detained and for what cause. He remembered he was a kinsman of Chief of Police Sartines. A turnkey recalled having seen Lord Sartines enter White's cell and force him to sign a power of attorney. But the prisoner had utterly forgotten the incident.

Tavernier was the oldest of all. He had been ten years imprisoned in another states prison before coming to the Bastile for thirty years; he was in his ninetieth year, white in beard and hair; his eyes were so used to the gloom that he could not bear the light. When they broke open his dungeon, he did not understand what they wanted to do. When they spoke of liberty, he shook his head. When finally they said the Bastile was taken by the people, he cried:

"What will Louis XV. say?"

White was crazed, but Tavernier was an idiot.

The delight of the rest was terrible to view, so close was it to alarm; it called for vengeance.

Two or three were almost ready to expire, amid the hubbub of thousands of voices, having never heard two speaking at the same time while in the prison. They had become accustomed to the slow and odd sounds of wood cracking with dampness, or the death-watch cricket, or the spider weaving its web, or the frightened rat gnawing his Majesty's prisonwalls.

As Gilbert appeared, the resolution was unanimously adopted that the rescued ones should be carried in triumph through the town.

Gilbert wished to elude this ovation but he could not do so, as he was recognized as well as Billet and his comrade.

"To the City Hall!" shouted everybody, and Gilbert was taken up on the shoulders of twenty fellows. In vain did Gilbert resist, and Billet and Pitou shower punches and cuffs on their brothers-in-arms; joy and enthusiasm had made the people's hide tough. Fisticuffs, digs with the elbow or thrusts with musket butts, all seemed soft as strokings and only enhanced their glee.

A spear was stuck in a table and Gilbert placed on it to be carried. Thus he was above the level of the sea of heads, undulating from the Bastile to St. John's Arcade, a stormy sea which transported the delivered captives amid billows crested with bloody swords, bayonets and pikes.

At the same time another sea roiled terribly and irresistibly, a group closely serried around the prisoner Launay.

Around him the shouts were as loud and hearty as for the liberated prisoners, but they were of death not of triumph.

Gilbert, from his elevated stand, did not lose an incident of the horrible occurrence. Alone, among all his fellow captives, he enjoyed the fulness of his faculties, because five days' imprisonment was but a black speck in his career. His eye had not had time to be dimmed by the Bastile's darkness.

Usually fighting makes men hardhearted only during the action. Men coming out of the fire with their own lives intact, feel kindly towards their foes.

But in great popular uprisings, such as France had seen many from the Jacquerie or Peasants' Outbreak in 1358, those whom fear kept in the rear during the conflict, but were irritated by the turbulence, are ferocious cowards who seek after the victory to redden their hands in the blood of those they dared not face in the combat. They take their share in the reprisal.

Since he was dragged out of his castle the march of the governor was a dolorous one.

Elie, protected by his uniform and the part he had taken in the assault, marched at the head, having taken Launay's life under his special care: he was admired for the manner in which he had borne himself. On his swordpoint he carried the letter which Launay had passed out of the prison loophole to be taken by Maillard. After him came the Tax-Commissioners Guards, carrying the keys of the royal fortress; then, Maillard, bearing the Bastile flag; then, a young man who bore on a pike the Bastile's rules and regulations, an odious rescript by virtue of which many a tear had been made to flow.

Lastly came the governor, protected by Hullin and three or four others, but almost covered in with shaking fists, flourished blades and brandished pikeheads.

Beside this column, almost parallel, rolling up St. Antoine Street, leading from the main avenue to the River Seine, was to be distinguished another, no less awful and menacing, dragging Major Losme, whom we saw struggle against his superior for a space but succumb under the determination to resist to the last.

He was a kind, good and brave man who had alleviated many miseries within the jail, but the general public did not know this. On account of his showy uniform many took him to be the governor. The latter, clothed in grey, having torn off the embroidery and the St. Louis scarf, was shielded by some doubt from those who did not recognize him.

This was the spectacle which Gilbert beheld with his gloomy, profound and observant glance, amid the dangers foreseen by his powerful organization.

On leaving the Bastile, Hullin had rallied his own friends the surest and most devoted, the most valiant soldiers of the day; these four or five tried to second his generous design of shielding the governor. Impartial history had preserved the names of three: Arne, Chollat and Lepine.

These four, with Hullin and Maillard in advance, attempted to defend the life for which a hundred thousand were clamoring.

A few French Grenadiers, whose uniform had become popular within three days, clustered round them. They were venerated by the mob.

As long as his generous defenders could do it they beat off the blows aimed at Count Launay; but he could not evade the hooting, the insults and the curses.

At Jouy Street corner, all the grenadiers had been brushed aside. Not the crowd's excitement, but the calculation of murderers may have had something to do with this; Gilbert had seen them plucked away as beads are flipped off a string.

He foresaw by this that the victory would be tarnished by bloodshed; he tried to get off the table but iron hands held him to it. In his impotence he sent Billet and Pitou to the defense of the governor, and obeying his voice they made efforts to reach the threatened one. His protectors stood in strong need of reinforcement. Chollat, who had eaten nothing since the evening before, fell with exhaustion, though he tried to struggle on: had he not been assisted, he would have been trodden under foot. His falling out of line made a breach in the living wall.

A man darted in by this crevasse in the dyke and clubbing his musket, delivered a crushing blow at the governor's bared head.

Lepine saw the mace descending and had time to throw his arms around Launay and receive the blow on his own forehead. Stunned by the shock and blinded by the blood, he staggered back and when he recovered, he was twenty paces apart from the prisoner.

This was the moment when Billet fought his way up, towing Pitou after him, like a steamship-of-war bringing up a sailing man-of-war into action.

He noticed that what marked Launay out was his being without a hat: he snatched off his own and put it on the count's head.

The latter turned and recognized him.

"I thank you," he said, "but whatever you do you cannot save me."

"If I can get you inside the City Hall, I will answer for all," said Hullin.

"Yes, but can you do it?" said the victim.

"God helping us, we'll try it."

They might hope this as they reached the City Hall Square, It was packed with men with their arms bared to the pit, waving swords and spears. The rumor had run along that they were bringing the Bastile Governor and his major, and they were waiting for them like a pack of wolfhounds held back from breaking up the quarry.

As soon as they saw the party they rushed at it. Hullin saw that this was going to be the supreme peril and final struggle. If he could only get the governor up the steps and inside the building, he would save him.

"Help, Elie, and Millard, all men who hold our honor dear!" he shouted.

Elie and Maillard forged onward but the mob closed in behind them and they were isolated. The crowd saw the advantage it had won, and made a furious effort. Like a gigantic boa, it wound its coils round the knot: Billet was taken off his feet and swept away with Pitou, who stuck to him. The same whirlwind made Hullin reel on the steps where he fell. He rose but was forced down anew, and Launay fell with him this time.

He stayed down; up to the last he did not murmur or beg for mercy, but he cried in a hoarse voice:

"Do not at least keep me lingering, tigers that you are. Slay me outright."

Never had he issued an order executed more promptly than this prayer: in one instant, armed hands flourished round his stooped head. Fists and plunging blades were seen: and then a head severed from the trunk rose disgustingly on the tip of a pike; it had preserved its cold and scornful smile.

This was the first head lopped off by the Revolution.

Gilbert had foreseen the atrocity: he had tried again to dart to the rescue but a hundred hands held him down. He turned his head and sighed.

This head was lifted with its eyes glaring, up to the window where Flesselles stood, surrounded and supported by the electors—as if to bid him a last farewell. It would be hard to say which was the paler, his face or the corpses.

All at once a deafening uproar burst from where the headless body lay.

145

In searching it, in the vest pocket, was found the note addressed to him by the Provost of the Traders, the one he had shown to Losme. It will be remembered as in these terms:

"Hold out firmly; I will amuse the Parisians with cockades and promises. Before day is done, Bezenval will send you reinforcements.

FLESSELLES."

A horrible yell of blasphemy rose from the pavement to the window where the writer stood. Without divining the cause, he understood the threat and threw himself back. But he had been seen and was known to be within; the rush for him was so universal that even the bearers of Dr. Gilbert left him to join the hunters.

Gilbert sought to enter with them to protect Flesselles. He had not run up three steps before he felt himself pulled back by the coatskirts. He turned to shake off the hand but saw they were of Billet and Pitou.

From the higher standpoint he overlooked the square.

"What is going on over there?" he inquired, pointing towards a spot of commotion.

"Come, doctor, come," said the two countrymen together.

"The butchers," said the doctor.

At that instant Major Losme fell, struck down by a hatchet; in their hatred the people confounded the persecutor of the prisoners with the merciful warden.

"Let us begone," said the physician, "for I begin to be ashamed that such murderers let me out."

"Do not say that, doctor," reproved Billet, "those who stormed the Bastile are not the cutthroats yonder."

As they descended the steps which he had mounted to try to help Flesselles, the throng which had flowed through the doorway, was hurled forth. In the midst of the battling gathering one man was struggling.

146

"Take him to the Palais Royal," vociferated the thousands.

"Yes, my friends, yes, my good friends, to the Palais Royal," gasped this wretch.

But the human inundation rolled towards the river as though it intended to drown him.

"Another they mean to murder," shouted Gilbert; "let us try to save him at any rate."

But he had hardly got the words out of his mouth before a pistol-shot resounded; Flesselles disappeared in the smoke.

Gilbert covered his eyes, cursing the multitude, great but unable to remain pure, and sullying the victory by a triple murder.

When he took his hands from his eyes, he beheld three heads on pike points: Flesselles', Launay's and Losme's. One rose on the City Hall steps, another in the mouth of Tixeranderie Street and the last in Pelletier Street, so that the trio formed a triangle. He remembered the sign in the Order of the Invisibles.

"Oh, Balsamo," he muttered, "is this the emblem of Liberty?"

And sighing, he fled up Vannerie Street, dragging Billet and Pitou with him.

CHAPTER XV. THE YOUNG VISIONARY.

Meeting with a public conveyance, the doctor got into it with Billet and Pitou, and they went to Louis-the-Great College, where Sebastian was still in the sick ward.

The principal received the doctor with deep regard as he knew him to be the foremost pupil of the physicians and chemists, Cabanis and Condorcet.

He imparted his fears, as well to the doctor as to the parent of his pupil, that the boy was too much given to moody fits.

"You are right," said Gilbert, "gravity in a boy is a token of lunacy or weakness."

While Pitou was being refreshed in the principal's residence and Billet shared a bottle with the gentleman himself, the physician conferred with his son.

"I ask you about your health," said the father to the pallid, nervous youth, "and you answer that you are well. Now I ask you if your reserve towards your schoolfellows arises from pride and I hope you will answer, no."

"Be encouraged, father," said Sebastian, "It is neither pride nor ill health, but sorrow. I have a dream which frightens me and yet it is not a terror. When a little boy, I had such visions."

"Ah?"

"Two or three times I was lost in the woods, following this phantom."

Gilbert looked at the speaker in alarm.

"It was thus, father dear: I would be playing with the other children of the village when I saw nothing; but when I left them, I heard the rustle of a silk dress as if some one wearing it were going away from me; I would thrust out my hands to seize it but grasp nothing but air. But as the sound diminished, the vision appeared, more and more distinct. This cloudy vapor would gradually assume a human shape. It was a woman's, who glided rather than walked, and grew the more clear as it was buried in the woody depths.

"A strange, weird, irresistible spell drew me on in the woman's steps. I pursued her with extended arms, mute like she was. Often I tried to call her but my lips would not emit a sound; I pursued without ever overtaking, until the prodigy announcing her coming was reproduced for her departure. She became misty and faded away. Spent with weariness, I would drop on the sward, where she had disappeared. Pitou would find me there, sometimes not till the following day."

Gilbert looked at the youth with increasing disquiet. His fingers were fixed on his pulse. Sebastian seemed to understand his father's feelings.

"Do not be uneasy about it," said he; "I know that it is a phantasm."

"What did this woman look like?"

"Majestic as a queen."

"Have you seen her lately?"

"I have seen her here—that is, in the garden reserved for the teachers. I saw her glide from our grounds into that garden. And one day when Master Berardier, pleased with my composition, asked me to state a favor, I got leave to stroll in this garden. She appeared to me."

"Strange hallucination," thought Gilbert; "yet not so remarkable in the child of a mesmeric medium. Who do you think this woman is?"

"My mother."

Gilbert turned pale and clasped his hand to his heart as though to staunch a re-opening wound. "But this is all a dream and I am almost as crazed as you."

"It may be all a dream," said the youth with pensive eye, "but the reality of the dream exists. I have seen the lady alive, in a magnificent equipage drawn by four horses, in Satory Woods near Versailles, on the last holiday when we were taken out there. I nearly swooned on seeing her, I do not know

149

why. For she could not be my mother, who is dead, and she is the same as the vision."

He remarked the giddiness of his father who ran his hand over his brow, and he was frightened by his white face.

"I see I am wrong to tell you such nonsense," he said.

"Oh, no, speak all you can on the subject and we shall try to cure you," responded the doctor.

"Why? I am born to musing: it takes up half my time. I love this ghost though it avoids me and seems sometimes to repulse me. Do not expel it: I should else be all alone when you are on your travels or return to America."

"I hope we shall not part," he said to his boy whom he embraced: "for I want to take you on my journeys."

"Was my mother fair?" inquired the youth.

"Very," was answered in the doctor's stifled voice.

"And did she love you as much as I do?" continued the child.

"Sebastian, never speak her name to me!" cried the physician, kissing him a last time and bounding out of the garden.

Instead of following him, the boy dropped on a bench, disconsolate.

In the yard Gilbert found Billet and Pitou, refreshed by the feast of the principal, to whom the doctor recommended special care of his son, and the three men got into the hack again.

CHAPTER XVI. THE PHYSICIAN FOR THE STATE.

On the way back to Paris, Gilbert stopped at St. Ouen to see Necker's daughter. He had a suspicion that the financier had not gone to Brussels as everybody was led to think. Indeed, it was at Madam de Stael's country house that he was concealed, awaiting events. He made no difficulty in supplying his friend with a letter of introduction to the King.

Armed with this, the doctor, leaving Billet and Pitou in a pretty hotel of Paris where the farmer usually stayed, hurried to Versailles.

It was half past ten but Versailles could not sleep now. It was agitated about how the King would take the insult of the Bastile being captured. It was not a slap in the face like Mirabeau's refusal to obey the order of the King to vacate the Assembly-rooms, but a death-blow.

The palace and surrounding sites were packed with troops, but Gilbert managed to reach the Bulls-eye Chamber where Necker's letter passed him into the royal presence.

The doctor examined in silence the pilot given to France in stormy weather, whom he had not seen for many long years.

For the physiognomist who had studied under Lavater, the magnetiser who had read the future with Balsamo, the philosopher who had meditated with Rousseau, the traveler who had reviewed many peoples, all in this short, stout man signified degeneracy, impotence and ruin.

When Louis had read the introduction he dismissed all attendants with a wave of the hand not devoid of majesty.

"Is it true," said he, "that you are the author of the Memoirs on Administration and Politics, which much struck me? you are young for such a work?"

"I am thirty-two, but study and misfortune age a man; treat me as an old one."

"Why are you so slow to present yourself to me?"

"Because I had no need to speak to your Majesty what I could freely and easily write."

"But you ought to have been informed that I was kindly towards you," observed the monarch, suspiciously.

"Your Majesty alludes to my audacity in requesting him, in token of having read my work with gratification, to show a light in his own study window? I saw that, and was gladdened, but your Majesty offered a reward, and I want none."

"Any way you come like a true soldier when the action is on. But I am not used to meet those who do not haste when recompense is offered."

"I deserve none. Born a Frenchman, loving my land, jealous of its prosperity, confounding my individuality with that of its thirty millions of men, I work for them in toiling for myself. A selfish man deserves no recompense."

"Excuse me, you had another reason. You thought the state of events serious and held back——"

"For a more serious one? Your Majesty guesses correctly."

"I like frankness," said the King, reddening, for he was nervous. "So, you predicted ruin for the sovereign and you wanted to be out of the reach of the flying splinters."

"No, Sire, since I hasten towards the danger."

"You come fresh from Necker and you naturally speak like him. Where is he?"

"Ready at hand to obey your orders."

"All for the best, for I shall require him," returned Louis with a sigh. "In politics, nobody should sulk. A plan may be good and fail from accidents."

"Sire, your Majesty reasons admirably," said Gilbert, coming to his aid;

"but the main thing now is to see into the future clearly; as a physician, I speak bluntly at crises."

"Do you attach much importance to the riot of yesterday?"

"It is not riot, but revolution."

"And would you have me treat with rebels and murderers? Their taking the Bastile by force was an act of rebellion; their slaying of Launay, Losme and Flesselles, murder."

"They should be held apart; those who stormed the Bastile were heroes; those who murdered those gentlemen, butchers."

"You are right, sir," said the King, his lips blanching after a transient blush and perspiration appearing on his brow. "You are indeed a physician, or rather a surgeon for you cut into the tender flesh. But let us return to the subject. You are Dr. Gilbert, who wrote those articles?"

"Sire, I consider it is a great happiness that my name is retained in your memory. It must not have sounded new when spoken a week ago in your hearing. I mean that when I was arrested and put in the Bastile. I always understood that no arrest is made of any importance without the King being advised."

"You in the Bastile?" cried the astonished King.

"Here is the order to lock me up. Put in prison six days ago by the royal order, I was released by the grace of the people at three o'clock this day. Did not your Majesty hear the cannon? they broke the doors down to let me out."

"Ah, I should be glad if I might say the cannon was not fired on royalty at the same time as the Bastile." Thus the King muttered.

"Oh, Sire, do not take a prison as the emblem of the monarchy. Say on the contrary that you are glad the Bastile is taken; for, I trust, no such injustice as I was the victim of will be henceforth committed in the name of the ruler who is kept ignorant of it."

"But there must be some cause for your arrest."

"None that I am aware of, Sire; I was arrested as soon as I landed and imprisoned—that is all there is in it."

"Really, sir," said the monarch mildly, "is there not selfishness in your dilating on your troubles when I want my own dealt with?"

"I only need a word: did your Majesty have anything to do with my arrest?"

"I was unaware of your return to this kingdom."

"I am happy for this reply. I may loudly say that your Majesty is defamed when evil is attributed to you, and cite myself as example."

"You put balm on the wound, Doctor," said the other, smiling.

"Oh, Sire, I will liberally anoint it; and I will cure it, I promise. But you must strongly wish the healing done. But, before pledging yourself too deeply, I should like you to notice the note on the prison record."

The King frowned to read: "At the Queen's request."

"Have you incurred the Queen's disfavor?" he inquired.

"Sire, I am sure that her Majesty knows me less than yourself."

"But you must have committed some misdeed, for people are not put in the Bastile for nothing."

"Humph, several in this situation, have come out."

"If you run over your life——"

"I will do so, out aloud: but do not be uneasy, it will not take long. Since sixteen I have toiled without repose. The pupil of Rousseau, the companion of Joseph Balsamo, the friend of Lafayette and Washington, since I quitted France, I have not a fault to reproach myself with, not a wrongful deed. Since heaven gave me the charge of bodies, I have shed my blood for mankind and staunched its flow in others. Thousands live to bless my labors."

"In America you worked with the innovators and propagate their principles by your writings."

"Yes, Sire, I forgot this claim on the gratitude of monarchs and peoples."

This silenced the King.

"Sire, you know my life now; I have offended and injured nobody, queen or beggar; and I humbly ask your Majesty why I was imprisoned."

"I will speak to the Queen about it. Do you believe that the warrant to arrest and imprison came directly from her Majesty?"

"I do not believe this; I rather presume that her Majesty countersigned it. But when a queen approves, she commands."

"Countess of Charny," read the King on the record sheet; "is it she who wanted you imprisoned? why, what have you done to poor Charny?"

"Before this morning I never heard of any lady of that title."

"Charny," muttered the King, musing, "virtue, goodness, chastity in person!"

"You see, they have put me in prison in the name of the Christian Graces," remarked Gilbert, laughing.

"Oh, I will have this cleared up," said the King, and ringing the bell he bade the servant bring the Countess of Charny into his presence.

CHAPTER XVII. THE COUNTESS OF CHARNY.

Gilbert had retired into a window recess, while the King paced the Bulls-eye Hall, called on account of a round window in the wall, thinking now of public matters, then of his visitor's persistence though nothing but news from Paris ought to have enchained him.

Suddenly the door opened and the lady entered, dressed in the extreme of the showy and fantastic fashion of Marie Antoinette and her court.

She was lovely, this Countess Charny, with a peerless figure and her hand was aristocratic to the utmost with which she played with a small cane.

"She, Andrea Taverney!" muttered Gilbert, involuntarily shrinking behind the curtains.

"My lady, I ask your presence for a little information," began the monarch, seeing nothing of Gilbert's emotion.

"I am ready to satisfy your Majesty." The voice attracted the doctor who came a little forward.

"A week ago, or so, a blank letter under the royal seal was delivered to Minister Necker," went on the King, "for the arrest——"

Gilbert had his eye on the lady, who was pale, feverish and fretful as if bent under the weight of a secret.

"This warrant was applied for by your ladyship and countersigned by the Queen. I say this to refresh your memory. Why do you not say something, countess?"

"It is true, your Majesty," she faltered, in a feverish abstraction, "I wrote for the letter, filled up the blanks, and the Queen backed it."

"Will you please tell me what crime the person committed for whom the measure was taken?" demanded Louis.

"Sire, I may not do that, but I shall say the crime was great."

"Then you should do so to the object," continued the King; "what you refuse the King Louis XVI., you cannot Doctor Gilbert."

He stepped aside to discover the doctor, who opened the curtains and appeared as pale as the staggering lady. She tossed her head backwards as if going to swoon, and only kept her footing by aid of a table. She leaned on it in dull despair, like one whom a snake bite was filling with poison.

"My lady, let me put the question to you which the King addressed," said Gilbert.

Andrea's lips moved but no sound struggled forth.

"What did I do to you, lady, that your order threw me into a hideous dungeon?"

The voice made her leap as if it tore the very soul in her.

Suddenly lowering her cold gaze on him, she replied:

"Sir, I do not know you."

But while she was speaking the mesmerist stared at her with so much fixedness and his glance was so charged with invincible boldness that her own lost lustre under his.

"Countess, you see what this abuse of the royal signature leads to," gently reproved the monarch; "you confess you do not know this gentleman, who is a renowned physician, a learned man, whom you can blame in no way,——"

Andrea darted a withering glance at Gilbert, who bore it calmly and proudly.

"I am saying that it is wicked to visit on the innocent the faults of another. I know you have not a bad heart," he hastened to add, for he was trembling lest he offended his wife's favorite, "and that you would not pursue anybody in your hatred unless he merited it: but you will understand that such mistakes must not be made in the future. Doctor," he went on, turning to the other hearer, "these things are the fault of our period rather than of persons. We are born in corruption and we shall die in it. But we are going to try to make matters better, in which work I expect you to join us, dear doctor."

He stopped, thinking he had said enough to please both parties. If he had spoken thus at a Parliamentary session, he would have been applauded; but his audience of two personal enemies little heeded his conciliatory philosophy.

"But," recommended Gilbert, "while not knowing me, you knew another Gilbert, whose crime weighs upon his Namesake. It is not my place to question the lady; will your Majesty deign to inquire of her ladyship what this infamous man did?"

"Countess, you cannot refuse so just a request."

"The Queen must know, since she authorized the arrest," said Andrea evasively.

"But it is not enough that the Queen should be convinced," said the sovereign, "it is necessary that the King also should know. The Queen is what she is, but I am the King."

"Sire, the Gilbert for whom the warrant was intended committed a horrible crime sixteen years ago."

"Will your Majesty please inquire what age this Gilbert is to-day?"

"He may be thirty-two," replied Andrea.

"Sire, then the crime was done by a boy, not a man, and does he not deserve some indulgence who has for sixteen years deplored his boyish crime?"

"You seem to know him? has he committed no other crime than this sin of youth?" demanded the King.

"I am less indulgent to him than others, but I can say that he reproaches himself with none other."

"Only with having dipped his pen in poison and written odious libels!"

"Sire, please ask my lady if the real cause of the arrest and committal of this Gilbert was not to enable his enemies—particularly one enemy—to get possession of a certain casket containing papers possibly compromising a great lady of the court?"

Andrea shuddered from head to foot.

"Countess, what casket is this?" inquired the King, who noticed the plain pallor and agitation of the lady.

"No more shifting and subterfuges," cried Gilbert, feeling that he was master of the situation. "Enough falsehoods on both sides. I am Gilbert of the crime, the libels, the casket, and you the real great lady of the court. I take the King as the judge. Accept him and we will tell our judge, under heaven and the King will decide."

"Tell his Majesty what you please, but I shall say nothing more—for I do not know you," responded the haughty lady.

"And the casket? you do not know about that?"

"No more than of you."

But she shook with the effort to make this denial, like a statue rocking at the base.

"Beware," said the doctor, "you cannot have forgotten that I am the pupil of Balsamo-Cagliostro the Magician, who has transmitted to me the power he had over you. Once only, will you answer the question? My casket?" then, lifting his hand, full of threatening, he thundered: "Nature of steel, heart of adamant, bend, melt, shatter under the irresistible pressure of my will! You shall speak, Andrea, and none, King or any powers less than heaven's, shall subtract you from my sway. You shall unfold your mind to the august witness and he shall read what you hid in the black recesses of your soul. Sire, you shall know all through her who refuses to speak. Sleep, Andrea Taverney, Countess of Charny, sleep and speak, for I will it."

Hardly were the words uttered before the woman, stopped short in beginning a scream, held out her arms for support as if struck by blindness.

Finding none, she fell into the King's arms and he placed her in a chair.

"Ha!" exclaimed he, trembling like herself, "I have heard about hypnotism but never saw an exhibition. Is not this magnetic sleep to which you oblige her to succumb, doctor?"

"Yes, my lord. Take her hand, and ask her why she had me arrested."

Astounded by the scene, Louis receded but, interested, he did as directed. As Andrea resisted, the magnetizer touched the crown of her head with his palm, saying;

"Speak, I will it."

She sighed and her arms fell; her head sank back and she wept.

"Ugh, I hate you," she hissed.

"Hate away, but speak."

"So, countess," said the King, "you wanted to arrest and imprison the doctor?"

"Yes."

"And the casket?"

"How could I leave that in his hands?" muttered the lady, in a hollow voice.

"Tell me about that," said the King forgetting etiquette and kneeling beside the countess.

"I learnt that Gilbert, who had in sixteen years been twice back in France, purposed another voyage, to settle here. Chief of Police Crosne informed me that he had on a previous return bought an estate at Villers Cotterets: that his farmer enjoyed his trust, and I suspected that the casket with his papers was at his house."

"How could you suspect that?"

"I—I went to Mesmer's and had myself put into a trance, when, my own medium, I wrote down the revelations I wanted."

"Wonderful," exclaimed the Sovereign.

"I went to Chief Crosne and he lent me his best man, one Wolfstep, who brought me the casket."

"Where is it?" cried Gilbert. "No lying—where is my casket?"

"In my rooms at Versailles," said Andrea, trembling nervously and bursting into tears. "Wolfstep is waiting for me here by appointment since eleven."

Twelve was striking.

"Where is he?"

"Standing in the waiting room, leaning on the mantleshelf. The casket is on the table before him. Oh, haste! Count Charny, who was not to return before to-morrow, will be back to-night on account of the events. He is at Sevres now. Get Wolfstep away for fear my lord will see him."

"Your Majesty hears? This casket belongs to me. Will the King please order it to be returned to me?"

"Instantly."

Placing a screen before the countess, Louis called the officer on duty and gave him orders what to do.

This curiosity of a monarch whose throne was being undermined to a purely physical problem, would make those smile who expected him to be engrossed with politics.

But he concentrated himself on this private speculation and returned to see the mesmerizer and the medium.

In the mesmeric slumber Andrea's wondrous beauty was displayed in its entire splendor. She who had in her youth enthralled Louis XV. now enchanted his successor.

Gilbert turned his head away, sighing: he could not resist the prompting

161

to give his adored this degree of supernal beauty; and now more unhappy than Pygmalion, for he knew how insensible was the lovely statue, he was frightened by his own work.

Gilbert knew how to own his ignorance, like all superior men. He knew what he could do, but not the wherefore.

"Where did you study the art? under Mesmer?" asked the King.

"I saw the most astonishing phenomena ten years before that German came into France. My master was a more amazing man, superior to any you can name, for I have seen him execute surgical operations of incredible daring. No science was unknown to him. But I ought not to utter his name before your Majesty."

"I should like to hear it, though it was Satan's itself."

"My lord, you honor me almost with a friend's confidence in speaking thus. My master was Baron Balsamo, afterwards Count Cagliostro."

"That charlatan!" exclaimed Louis, blushing, for he could not help remembering the plot of the Diamond's Necklace, in which Cagliostro had figured as friend of Cardinal Rohan and consequently enemy of Marie Antoinette. The King believed his wife but the world thought that she had participated in the fraud on the court jewelers. We have related the story according to our lights in the volume of this series entitled "The Queen's Necklace."

"Charlatan?" repeated Gilbert warmly. "You are right. The name comes from the Italian word meaning to patter, to talk freely—and no one was more ready than Cagliostro to talk instructively where the seed would fall on fruitful ground."

"This Cagliostro whom you praise was a great enemy of kings," observed Louis.

"Rather say of queen's," retorted Gilbert.

"In the trial of Prince Rohan, his conduct was equivocal."

"Sire, then as ever he fulfilled his mission to mankind. He may have acted mistakenly then. But I studied under the physician and philosopher, not under the politician."

"Well, well," said the King, suffering under the wound to his person and his pride; "we are forgetting the countess who is in pain."

"I will awaken her presently, for here is the casket coming."

In fact the messenger was arriving with the small box which he handed to the King. He nodded his satisfaction and the officer went out.

"Sire, it is my casket: but I would remark that it contains papers damning to the countess and——"

"Carry it away unopened, sir," said the monarch coldly. "Do not awaken the lady here, I detest shrieks, groans, noise."

"She will awaken wherever you suggest her removal."

"In the Queen's apartments will be best."

"How long will it take?"

"Ten minutes."

"Awaken in fifteen minutes," ordered the mesmerizer to the lady.

Two guardsmen entered and carried out the countess, seated on the chair.

"My lady fainted here," said the King to the officer, "bear her to the Queen."

"What can I do for you, Dr. Gilbert?" he asked when they were alone.

"I wish to be honorary house physician to your Majesty. It is a position which will do nobody umbrage and is more of trust than emolument and lustre."

"Granted! Good-by, Dr. Gilbert. Remind me affectionately to Necker. Bring me supper," he added, for nothing could make the King forget a meal.

CHAPTER XVIII. THE QUEEN AT BAY.

While the King was learning to fight Revolution like a philosopher, and recreate himself with a spiritualistic seance, the Queen was rallying the combative around her in her rooms.

She sat at a table, with priests, courtiers, generals and her ladies surrounding her. At the doorways young officers, full of ardor and courage, rejoiced in the riots which gave them a chance to show their military gifts as at a tourney under view of their queens of beauty.

The Queen was no longer the sweet girl whom we saw in our work entitled "Balsamo the Magician," or the fair princess who went to Mesmer's Baths, with Princess Lamballe: but the haughty and imperious Queen who was neither Marie Antoinette, nor Queen of France, but the Austrian Eagless.

She looked up as Prince Lambesq arrived, dusty, splashed, his boots torn and his sabre bent so as not to be sheathed properly.

"Well, my lord," she said, "You come from Paris. What are the people doing?"

"Killing and burning."

"From madness or malice?"

"From ferocity."

"Nay, prince," she replied, after meditating: "the people are not ferocious. Hide nothing from me. Is it delirium or hate?"

"I believe it is hate at the point of delirium."

"Against me?"

"What does it matter?" said Dreux Breze, stepping forward. "The people may hate any one, saving your Majesty."

The Queen did not notice the flattery.

"The people," replied Lambesq, "are acting in hatred of—all above them."

"Good, that is the truth at last?" exclaimed the royal lady resolutely; "I feel that is so."

"I am speaking as a soldier," continued the cavalrist.

"Speak so. What is to be done?"

"Nothing."

"What?" cried she, emboldened by the protest from among the gold-laced coat and gold-hilted sword wearers, "nothing? do you, a Lorraine prince, tell this to the Queen of France when the people are killing and burning?"

A fresh murmur, this time approbative, hailed her speech. She turned, embraced all the gathering with flaring eyes, and tried to distinguish whose flamed the most brightly, thinking they would be the most loyal.

"Do nothing," repeated the prince, "for the Parisians will cool down if not irritated—they are warlike only when teased. Why give them the honors of a war and the risks of a battle? Keep tranquil, and in three days Paris will not talk about the matter."

"But the Bastile?"

"Shut the doors and trap all those who are inside."

Some laughs sounded among the groups.

"Take care, prince," said the lady; "now you are going to the other extreme, and too much encouraging me."

With a thoughtful mien, she went over to where her favorite, the Countess of Polignac, was in a brown study on a lounge. The news had frightened the lady; she smiled only when the Queen stood before her and that was a faint and sickly smile like a wilted lily.

"What do you say to this, countess?"

"Nothing," and she shook her head with unspeakable discouragement.

"Heaven help us, our dashing Diana is afraid," said the Queen, bending over her, "we want our intrepid Countess Charny here. It seems to me that we need her to cheer us up."

"The countess was going out when the King sent for her," explained an attendant.

Then only did Marie Antoinette perceive the isolation and stillness around her. The recent strange and unheard-of events had hit Versailles hard, making the hardest hearts tender, more by astonishment than fear. The sovereign understood that she must lift up these disheartened spirits.

"As nobody suggests any advice, I shall act on my own impulse," she said: "The people are not wicked but led astray." Everybody drew nearer. "They hate us because they do not know us; let us go up to them."

"To punish," interposed a voice, "for they know we are their masters, and to doubt us is a crime."

"Oh, baron," she said, recognizing Bezenval; "do you come to give us good advice?"

"I have given it."

"The King will punish, but as a kind father does."

"He loveth well who chasteneth soundly," replied the noble.

"Are you of this thinking, prince?" she asked of Lambesq. "The populace have committed assassinations———"

"Which they call retaliation," observed a sweet, fresh voice which made the Queen turn.

"Yes, but that is where their error lies, my dear Lamballe, so we shall be indulgent."

"But," resumed the princess with her bland voice, "before one talks of punishment one ought to be sure of winning the victory, methinks."

A general outcry rose against this piece of good sense from the noble

166

lips.

"Not vanquish—with the Swiss troops—and the Germans—and the Lifeguards?"

"Do you doubt the army and the nobility?" exclaimed a young man in Bercheny Hussian uniform, "have we deserved such a slur? Bear in mind, royal lady, that the King can put in battle array forty thousand men, throw them into Paris by the four sides and destroy the town. Forty thousand proven soldiers are worth half a million of Parisian rioters."

The young lieutenant, emboldened to be the mouthpiece of his brother officers, stopped short on seeing how far his enthusiasm had carried him. But the Queen had caught enough to feel the scope of his outburst.

"Do you know the state of affairs, sir?" she inquired.

"I was in the riots yesterday," was his confused reply.

"Then, do not fear to speak. Let us have details."

The lieutenant stepped out, though he colored up.

"My Lords of Bezenval and Lambesq know them better than I," he said.

"Continue, young sir; it pleases me to hear them from you. Under whose orders are these forty thousand men?"

"The superiors are the two gentlemen I named; under whom rule Prince Conde, Narbonne-Fritzlar and Salkenaym. The park of artillery on Montmartre could lay that district in ashes in six hours. At its signal to fire, Vincennes would answer. From four quarters as many corps of ten thousand troops could march in, and Paris would not hold out twenty-four hours."

"This is plain speaking at least, and a clear plan. What do you say to this, Prince Lambesq?"

"That the young gentleman is a perfect general!"

"At least, he is a soldier who does not despair," said the Queen, seeing the lieutenant turn pale with anger.

"Thank your Majesty," replied the latter. "I do not know what your Majesty will decide, but I beg her to count me with the other forty thousand men, including the captains, as ready to die for her."

With these words he courteously saluted the general, who had almost insulted him. This courtesy struck the Queen more than the pledge of devotedness.

"Your name, sir?" said she.

"Viscount Charny," he responded.

"Charny," repeated Marie Antoinette, blushing in spite of herself; "any relation to Count Charny?"

"I am his brother, lady," bowing more lowly than before.

"I might have known that you were one of my most faithful servitors," said she, recovering from her tremor and looking round with confidence, "by the first words you spoke. I thank you, viscount; how comes this to be the first time I have the pleasure of seeing you at court?"

"My eldest brother, head of the family, ordered me to stay with the army, and I have only been in Versailles twice during seven years on the regimental roll-call."

She let a long look dwell on his face.

"You resemble your brother," she remarked. "I shall scold him for having waited for you to present yourself at court."

Electrified by this greeting to their young spokesman, the officers exaggerated their devotion to the royal cause and from each knot burst expressions of heroism able to conquer the whole of France.

These cries flattered Marie Antoinette's secret aspirations, and she meant to profit by them. She saw herself, in perspective, the leader of an immense army, and rejoiced over the victory against the civilians who dared to rebel. Around her, ladies and gentlemen, wild with youth, love and confidence, cheered their brilliant hussars, heavy dragoons, terrible Switzers, and thunderous cannoniers, and laughed at the home-made spikes fastened on clothes-poles, without dreaming that on these coarse spears were to be carried the noblest heads of the realm.

"I am more afraid of a pike than a musket," murmured Princess Lamballe.

"Because it is uglier, my dear Therese," said the Queen. "But you need not be alarmed. Our Parisian pikemen are not worth the famous spearmen of Moat, and the good Swiss of this day carry guns much superior to the spears of their forefathers. Thank God, they can fire true with them!"

"I answer for that," said Bezenval.

Lady Polignac's disheartenment had no effect beyond saddening her royal mistress. The enthusiasm increased among the rest of the gathering, but was damped when the King, coming in abruptly, called for his supper!

The simple word chilled the assemblage. She hoped that he did it to show how cool he was; but in fact, the son of Saint Louis was hungry. That was all.

The King was served on a small table in the Queen's sitting-room. While she was trying to revive the fire, he devoured. The officers did not think this gastronomical exercise worthy of a hero, and looked on as little respectful as they dared to be. The Queen blushed, and her fretfulness was displayed in all her movements. Her fine, nervy, and aristocratic nature could not understand the rule of matter over mind. She went up to him, asking what orders he had to give.

"Oh, orders," he said, with his mouth full: "Will you not be our Egeria in the pinch?"

"My lord, Numa was a peaceful King. But at present we think a belligerent one is wanted, and if your Majesty wants to model himself on an antique pattern, be Romulus if not Tarquin."

"Are these gentlemen all bellicose, too?" he asked with a tranquillity almost beatific.

But his eyes were bloodshot with the animation of the meal and they

169

thought it was courage.

"Yes, Sire, war?" they chorussed.

"Gentlemen, you please me greatly by showing that I may rely upon you in case of need. But I have a Council and an appetite. The former advises me what to do, the other what I have done, to do."

And he chuckled while he handed the "Officer of the King's Mouth" the picked bones and chewed rejecta of his repast on the gold-fringed napkin.

A murmur of choler and stupor ran through the ranks of the nobles who were eager to shed their blood for the monarch. The Queen turned aside and stamped her foot. Prince Lambesq came up to her, saying:

"Your Majesty sees that the King thinks like me that to wait is the best course. It is prudence, and though not my strong card the best to keep in hand for the final rubber in the game we play."

"Yes, my lord, it is a highly necessary virtue," replied she, biting her lip till the blood came.

She was roused from her torpor by the sweet voice of Countess Jules Polignar who came up with her sister-in-law Diana, to propose that, as she and her party were hated by the people as the favorites of the Queen, they should be allowed to go out of the kingdom. At first the Queen would not hear of the sacrifice, but she saw that fear was at the bottom of it, and that the King's aunt Adelaide, had suggested it.

"You are right," she answered; "you run dangers from the rage of a people who are uncurbed. I cannot accept the devotion which prompts you to stay. I wish, I order you to depart."

She was choking with emotions mastering her in spite of her heroism, when the King's voice suddenly sounded in her ear. He was at the dessert.

"Madam," he said, "some one is in your rooms to see you, I am told."

"Sire," she answered, abjuring all thoughts but of royal dignity, "you have orders to give. Here are Lords Lambesq, Bezenval and the Marshal Duke

Broglie. What orders for your generals?"

"What do you think of this matter, duke?" he inquired hesitatingly of old Broglie.

"Sire, if you retire your troops, the Parisians will say they daunted them: if you let them stand they will have to defeat them."

Lambesq shook his head, but Bezenval and the Queen applauded.

"Command the forward march," went on the duke.

"Very well, since you all wish it, let it be march!" said the King.

"But at this moment a note was passed to the Queen who read:

"Do not be in a hurry! I await an audience." It was Count Charny's writing.

"Is my lord Charny waiting?" she asked of the messenger.

"Yes; dusty and, I believe, bloody with hard riding."

"Please to await me a moment," said the Queen to Broglie and the others, as she hurried into her private apartments.

CHAPTER XIX. THE QUEEN'S FAVORITE.

On entering her boudoir, the Queen beheld the writer of the missive.

Count George Oliver Charny was a tall man of thirty-five, with a strong countenance warning one of his determination. His bluish grey eyes, quick and piercing as the eagle's, his straight nose, and his marked chin, all gave his physiognomy a martial expression, enhanced by the dashing elegance with which he wore his uniform of Lieutenant in the Royal Lifeguards.

His hands were still quivering under the torn lace ruffles: his sword had been so bent as to fit the sheath badly.

He was pacing the room, a prey to a thousand disquieting thoughts.

"My Lord Charny," cried Marie Antoinette, going straight up to him. "You, here?"

Seeing that he bowed respectfully, according to the regulations, however, she dismissed her servant, who shut the door.

Hardly giving it the time to close, the lady grasped the nobleman's hand with force, and said:

"Why have you come here, count?"

"Because I believe it my duty."

"No; your duty was to flee from Versailles; to do as agreed. To obey me; to act like all my friends—who are afraid of my ill fortune. Your duty is to sacrifice nothing for me; to keep away from me."

"Who keeps away from you?"

"The wise. Whence come you?"

"From Paris, boiling with excitement, intoxicated and bathed in blood."

The Queen covered her face with her hands.

"Alas, not one, not even you, brings me good news from that quarter."

"In such a time ask but one thing of the messengers: truth."

"You have an upright soul, my friend, a brave heart. Do not tell me the truth, at present, for mercy's sake. You arrive when my heart is breaking; for the first time my friends overwhelm me with this truthfulness always used by you. It is impossible for me to trifle with it any longer: it flashes out in everything. In the red sky, the air filled with ominous sounds, the courtiers' faces, now pale and serious. No, count, for the first time in your life, do not tell me the truth."

"Your Majesty is ailing?"

"No, but come and sit beside me. George, your brow is burning."

"A volcano is raging there."

"Your hand is cold," for she was pressing it between hers.

"My heart has been touched by the chill of death," he replied.

"Poor George! I told you we had best forget. Let me no longer be the Queen, hated and threatened; but just the woman. What is the realm, the universe to me, whom one loving heart suffices?"

The count went down on one knee and kissed the hem of her dress with the reverence of the ancients for a goddess.

"Oh, count, my only friend, do you know what Countess Diana is doing?"

"Leaving the country," returned Charny.

"He guesses rightly," muttered the Queen, "how could he tell that?"

"Oh, goodness—anything can be surmised at this hour."

"But if flight is so natural, why do not you and your family take it?"

"I do not do so, in the first place, because I have pledged myself not only to your Majesty, but to myself, not to leave you during the storm. My brothers stay, as they regulate their movements by mine: and my wife remains because she loves your Majesty most sincerely, I believe."

"Yes, Andrea has a most noble heart," said the lady with visible coldness.

"That is why she will not quit Versailles," replied Charny.

"It follows that I shall always have you near me," went on the Queen, in the same glacial tone, awarded to prevent the hearer telling whether she felt disdain or jealousy.

A witness could have divined this secret, however, from their manner in this privacy.

Meeting romantically, without either knowing the other's quality, Marie Antoinette and George Charny had fallen in love with each other. The royal dame had left the passion swell to the highest point, when the King had surprised the pair in dangerous intimacy. There was only one way to save her reputation: she blurted out the first name of a lady that occurred to her, and protested that the count was at her knees sueing for this lady to be his wife, with the royal approval.

The Queen had named Andrea Taverney, her companion, and the King, his suspicions dismissed, consented that she should be withdrawn from the convent where she had taken refuge, to fulfill the pretendedly wish of Charny. Was it religion that impelled her, or love on her own side for Charny? It was love, for she eagerly accepted the proffered hand, and the wedding took place, all the more as she had had the misfortune to learn that she was used as the cover for the royal amour.

But at the churchdoor they separated and had dwelt apart ever since.

Had she been truly a wife, the experiment of Dr. Gilbert might have failed, for mesmerism succeeds best with the single.

"Your Majesty," resumed the count, "made me Lifeguards lieutenant at Versailles, and I should not have quitted my post only you ordered me to guard the Tuileries Palace, You called it a necessary exile. Your Majesty knows that the countess neither approved nor disapproved, as she was not consulted."

"True," observed the other, still cold.

"I now believe my place is here," proceeded the officer with intrepidity: "I have broken my orders and come, hoping it will not displease you. Whether Lady Charny fears the course of events and goes away or not, I remain by the Queen, unless you break my sword: then, being unable to die in your presence, I can be killed at your door or on the pavement without."

He spoke so royally and plainly these simple words straight from the heart that the sovereign fell from her high pride, behind which she had hidden a feeling more human than royal.

"Count, never utter that word, never say you will die for me, as I feel that you will do so."

"I must say so, for the time comes when those who love monarchs must die for them—I fear so."

"What gives you this fatal presentiment, my lord?"

"Alas", returned the nobleman, "at the time of the American War, I was fired like others with the fever of independence thrilling society. I also wish to take a hand in the liberation of the slaves of Great Britain, as was said in those days, and I became a Free Mason, an Invisible like the Lafayettes and Lameths, under the redoubtable Balsamo, the King-Destroyer. Do you know the aim of that secret society? the wrecking of thrones. Its motto: 'Trample down the Lilies,' expressed in Latin as 'Lilia Pedibus Destrue!' in three letters for the initiated: 'L. P. D.' I retired with honor when I learnt this, but for one who shrank, twenty took the oath. What happens to-day is merely the first act of a grand tragedy which has been rehearsed during twenty years in the darkness. I have recognized the Bounden brothers at the head of the men who govern at the City Hall, occupy the Palais Royal, and took the Bastile. Do not cheat yourself; these accomplished deeds are no accidents, but Revolution planned long beforehand."

"Do you believe this, dear friend?" sobbed Marie Antoinette.

"Do not weep, but understand," said the count.

"Understand that I, the Queen, born mistress of thousands of men, subjects created to obey, must look on at them revolting and killing my friends—No, never will I understand this."

"You must, madam: for you have become the enemy of these subjects as soon as obedience weighed upon them, and while they are lacking the strength to devour you, they are testing their teeth on your friends, whom they detest as much as you, more than you."

"Perhaps you think they are right, Master Philosopher?" sneered the Austrian.

"Alas, yes, they are right," replied the Lifeguards Lieutenant, in his bland, affectionate voice, "for when I idly rode along the street, with handsome English horses, in a gold-laced suit, and my servants wearing more gold braid than would have kept three families, your people, twenty-five thousand wretches without daily bread, asked me to my teeth what use was I, who set up as a man above his fellow-men?"

"You serve them, my lord," said the Queen, grasping the count's swordhilt, "with this blade, which your fathers used as heroes on many a celebrated battlefield. The French nobility shielded the masses in war times; they won their gold by losing their blood. Do not you ask what use you are, George, while you, a brave man, swing the sword of your fathers."

"Do not speak of the nobles' blood," returned the count, "the commoners have blood to shed also; go and see the streams of it on Bastile Square. Go and count their dead in the gutters and know that those hearts, now ceased to beat, throbbed as nobly as a knight's when your cannon thundered against them. They sang in the showers of grapeshot while handling unfamiliar weapons, and the oldest grenadiers would not make a charge with that lightness. Lady and Queen, do not look at me with that angry eye, I beseech you. What matters to the heart whether it is clad in steel or rags? The time is come to think of this: you have no longer millions of slaves, or subjects, or mere men in France—but soldiers."

176

"Who will fight against me?"

"Yes, for they fight for Liberty and you stand between them and that goddess."

A long silence succeeded the words, and the woman was first to break it.

"You have spoken the truth which I begged you to keep back," she said.

"Because it is before you, veiled, seen distorted, but there. You may sleep to forget it, but it sits on your bedside and it will be the phantom in your dreams as it is the reality of your waking moments."

"I know one sleep it will not trouble," said she, proudly.

"I do not fear that kind more than your Majesty—I may desire it as much," said the count.

"Oh, you think it our only refuge?"

"Yes: but we must not hurry towards it. We shall earn it by our exertions during the day of storm."

They were sitting beside each other, but a gulf divided them; their thoughts so diverged.

"A last word, count," said Marie Antoinette, "swear to me that you came back solely on my account? that Lady Charny did not write to you? I know that she was going out—to meet you? swear that you have not come back for her sake!"

At this was heard a slight tapping at the door.

It was the servant to announce that the King had finished supper. Charny frowned with wonder.

"Tell his Majesty," said the Queen without sitting apart from her favorite, "that I have news from the capital, and will impart to him. Continue," she added to Charny: "the King having supped must be given time to digest."

This interruption had not weakened the woman's jealousy as a loving one, or as a queen.

"Your Majesty asks if I came back on account of my wife?" he asked as soon as the door was closed. "Do you forget that I am a man of my word and the engagement I made?"

"It is the oath that goads me, for in immolating yourself to my happiness, you give grief to a fair and noble woman—a crime the more."

"You exaggerate. Be it enough that I keep my word. Call it not a crime what was born of chance and necessity. We have both deplored this union which shielded the Queen's good fame. I have been obliged to submit to it these four years."

"Yes, but do you believe that I do not see your sorrow and chagrin translated under the form of the deepest respect?" reproached the Queen.

"For mercy's sake, do me justice for what you see me do; for if I have not yet suffered and made others suffer enough, I might double the burden without rising to the level of the gratitude I owe you eternally."

His speech had irresistible power like all emanating from a sincere and impassioned heart.

"Yes, yes, I know all, and I am wrong. Forgive me. But if you worship some secret idol to whom you offer a mystic incense, if you cherish one adored woman—I dare not utter the words, they frighten me lest the syllables should scatter through the air and vibrate on my ear—oh, if one exists, keep her hidden from all; and do not forget that you have a fair and youthful wife, who should be publicly encompassed with cares and assiduity; she should lean on your arm and on your heart."

Charny frowned so that the pure lines of his visage were altered for a space.

"What are you seeking? that I should depart from the Countess of Charny? you are silent—that is your meaning. I am ready to obey you, but reflect that she is alone in the world. Andrea is an orphan, her father the baron having died last year, like a good old nobleman of the former time who did not wish to see the present. Her brother, the Knight of Redcastle, only appears once a-year at court to bow to your Majesty, kiss his sister, and go away without anybody knowing whither. Reflect, madam, that this lady of Charny, might be called unto God as a maiden, without the purest of the angels surprising in her mind any womanly memory."

"Yes, I know your Andrea is an angel on earth, and deserves to be loved. That is why I think the future will be hers when it flees from me. No, no; but I am not speaking like a queen. I forget myself, but there is a voice in my heart singing of love and happiness, while without roars war, misery and death. It is the voice of my youth which I have outlived. Forgive one, Charny, who is no longer young, and will smile, and love no more."

The unhappy woman pressed her long, thin fingers to her burning eyes and tears, regal diamonds more becoming than the finest in the Diamond Necklace, trickled between them.

"Oh, order me to quit you, but do not let me see you weep," pleaded the count, again falling on one knee.

"The dream is over," said Marie Antoinette, rising.

With a witching movement she tossed back her thick, powdered tresses, unrolling down her white and swanline neck.

"I shall afflict you no more. Let us drop such folly. Is it odd that a woman should be so weak when a queen stands in such need of comfort? Let us talk of serious matters—such as you bear from Paris."

"From Paris, madam, where I witnessed the ruin of royalty."

"This is serious with a vengeance. You call a successful revolt the ruin of royalty? Because the Bastile is taken, Lord Charny, do you say royalty is abolished? You do not reflect that the Bastile has been built but in the Fourteenth Century while royalty struck in its roots six thousand years ago all over the globe."

"I would I could deceive," said the lieutenant sadly, "and proclaim consoling news instead of saddening your Majesty. Unfortunately the instrument gives forth no other sounds than it was shaped to send."

"Stay, I will set you to a cheerier tune! though I am but a woman. You say the Parisians have revolted. In what proportion?"

"Twelve out of fifteen: the calculation is easy. The populace stand in that proportion to the classes, the other two fifteenths being the nobility and the clergy."

"But six of the rate are women, and——"

"Women and children are not the least of your foes. You are proud and courageous yourself, do not omit the women and the children. One day you may reckon them as demons."

"What do you mean, count?"

"Do you not know the part the women and children play in civil commotions? I will tell you and you will own that a woman is equal two soldiers."

"Are you mad, my lord?"

"Had you seen your sex at the taking of the Bastile," he said with a mournful smile: "hounding the men on to arm themselves, while under the fire, threatening with their naked fist your Swiss soldiers caparisoned for war, yelling maledictions over the slain in a voice which made the living bound unto death. Had you seen them boiling pitch, rolling cannon, giving the fighting men cartridges and the more timid a kiss with the cartridges! Do you know that as many women as men dashed across the Bastile draw-bridges, and that if its stones are coming down now, the picks are wielded by female hands? Oh, my lady, you must include the women, and the children who cast the bullets, sharpen the swords and hurl paving-stones from the roofs. The bullet cast by a boy will kill your best general from afar; the sword he sharpened will hamstring your finest war-horse; the blind pebble from this David's sling will put out the eye of your Dragoon Samson and your Lifeguards Goliath.

"Count the old men, too, for they who have no strength to swing the sabre, serve as buckler for the active fighters. At the taking of the Bastile old

180

men were on hand: they stood so that the younger ones could rest their guns on their shoulder so that the balls of your Switzers might be buried in the useless old body, the rampart of the able man. Include them among your foes, for they have been relating in the chimney corner for ever so many years, what affronts their mothers endured, the poverty of the estates over which the nobles hunted, the shame of their caste humbled under feudal privileges. When the sons took up the gun, they found it loaded with the curses of the aged as well as with powder and shot. In Paris now, women and children as well as the men are cheering for liberty and independence. Count them all as eight hundred thousand warriors."

"Three hundred Spartans vanquished Xerxes' army," retorted the Queen.

"Yes, but the Spartans are nearly a million and it is your army that is Xerxes."

"Oh, I would rather be hurled from the throne," she cried, as she rose with clenched fists and face flaming with shame and ire, "I would rather your Parisians hewed me to pieces, than hear from a Charny, one of my supporters, such speech as this!"

"Charny would not so address your Majesty unless every drop of blood in his veins were worthy of his sires and given to you."

"Then let us march upon Paris and let us die together!"

"Shamefully, without any battle," said the noble. "We shall not fight but disappear entirely like Philistines. March on Paris? when, as soon as we enter within her walls, all the houses will tumble down upon us, like the Red Sea waves overwhelming Pharaoh, and you will leave a cursed name, and your children will be hunted down like wolf-cubs."

"How must I fall, pray tell me, count?" demanded the sovereign haughtily; "teach me."

"As a victim," was the answer, "like a Christian queen, smiling and forgiving those who strike you. If I had five hundred thousand like myself, I might say, Let us have at them this night, and to-morrow you would sleep in the Tuileries, the throne conquered!"

"Woe is me! you despair on whom was set my final hope."

"I despair because all France thinks like Paris, and your army if victorious in the capital, will be engulfed by the other towns. Have courage enough, my lady, to sheathe the sword."

"Is this why I have gathered brave men around me? why I breathed courage into them?" wailed the Queen.

"If you are not of my opinion, madam, order, and we march at once to Paris! Speak."

So much devotion was in this offer that the hearer was appalled. She threw herself disconsolate on a sofa, where she struggled for a long time with her pride.

"Count," she said at length, "I shall remain inactive as you desire. I am not cross, though I have one thing to scold you for. I only learn by chance that you have a brother in the military service."

"Valence is in Bercheny's Hussars, yes, madam."

"Why have you never spoken of the young man? he deserves a higher grade in the regiment."

"He is young and inexperienced; he is not fit to command. If your Majesty deigned to lower your view upon me, a Charny, that is no reason for me to elevate my family at the expense of brave gentlemen worthier than brothers of mine."

"You have other brothers?"

"Isidore is another; two ready to die for your Majesty."

"Does he need nothing?"

"Nothing; we are lucky enough to place not merely life but wealth at your Majesty's feet."

As he spoke, the Queen thrilled with this delicate probity; a moan from the next room aroused them.

Rising, the Queen ran to the door, opened it and screamed loudly. She saw a woman writhing on the carpet in dreadful spasms.

"It is the countess, your wife," she faltered. "Can she have overheard us?"

"No," said he, "otherwise, she would have let us know that she could hear us."

He sprang towards Andrea and caught her up in his arms. Two paces off, the Queen stood, pale and cold, but trembling with anxiety.

CHAPTER XX. THE TRIO OF LOVE.

Without knowing who was helping her, Andrea began to recover consciousness but instinctively she knew help had come. At length, with open but ghostly eyes, she stared at Charny without yet recognizing him. She pushed him away, with a scream, then.

The Queen averted her eyes although she ought to have played the woman's part of comforter. She cast off her sister instead of supporting her.

"Pardon her, my lady," said Charny, again taking his wife in his strong arms, "but something out of the way causes this. My lady is not subject to fainting fits and this is, I believe, the first time she has had one in your presence."

"She must have felt much pain," returned the Queen, going back to her first impression that Andrea had overheard them.

"No doubt," said the count, "and you might let me have her carried to her own rooms."

The Queen rang a bell; but at the first tinkle Andrea stiffened in a culvulsion and screamed in delirium:

"Oh, our Gilbert!"

The Queen shuddered to hear the name and the astonished count placed his wife on a sofa.

The servant who ran at the call was dismissed.

Queen and nobleman looked at each other as the sufferer seemed with closed eyes to have another fit. Charny, kneeling by her, had hard work to keep her on the lounge.

"I think I know this name," said Marie Antoinette, "from its not being the first time the countess has used it."

But as though the recollection was a menace, Andrea opened her eyes and made an effort by which she stood up. Her first intelligent glance was fondly upon Charny, who was now upright. As if this involuntary manifestation of her mind was unworthy her Spartan soul, she turned her gaze only to meet the Queen's. She bowed at once.

"Good heavens, what is the matter?" inquired the count: "you alarm me, for you are usually so brave and strong—to be prey to such a swoon."

"Such dreadful things have happened at Paris where you were, that if men are trembling at them, women may be excused for fainting. I am so glad you came away from the city."

"Is it on my account that you felt so ill?" queried the noble.

"Why, certainly, count," said Marie Antoinette as the lady made no sound. "Why do you doubt it? The countess is not a Queen; she has a right to be afraid for those she loves."

"Oh, madam," rejoined Charny, perceiving jealousy in the slur, "I am sure that the countess feels more fear for her sovereign than for herself."

"Still, why do we find you in the swoon in the next room?" inquired the royal lady.

"I cannot tell, for I am ignorant, but in this life of fatigue and terror, led these three days, a woman's fainting is natural enough, meseems."

"True," said the Queen, knowing that Andrea could not be driven out of her defenses.

"For that matter, your Majesty has weeping eyes," retorted the countess, with that recovered calmness which was the more embarrassing as it was pure effort of her will and was felt to be a screen over her real feelings.

Charny thought he perceived the same ironical tone that had marked the Queen's speaking a while ago.

"It is not astonishing," reproved he, with slight sternness to which his voice was unaccustomed, "that a queen should weep who loves her people

185

and knows that their blood had flowed."

"Happily God hath spared yours," said Andrea, as coldly and impenetrably as ever.

"But her Majesty is not in question. We are talking about you. You have been frightened?"

"I, frightened?"

"You cannot deny you were in pain; has some mishap befallen you? Is there anybody you want to complain of—this Gilbert, whom you mentioned, for example?"

"Did I utter that name?" said Andrea with such a tone of dread that the count was more startled by the outcry than by the swoon. "Strange, for I did not know it, till the King mentioned it as that of a learned physician, freshly arrived from America, I believe, and who was friendly there with General Lafayette. They say he is a very honorable man," concluded Andrea with perfect simplicity.

"Then why this emotion, my dear?" said the Queen; "you spoke this Gilbert's name as though it were wrung from you by torture."

"Very likely. When I went into the royal study, I beheld a stern man clad in the grim black, who was narrating the most sombre and horrid things—with frightful realism, the murders of Flesselles and Launay. I was frightened and dropped insensible. I may have spoken in my spell and the name of Gilbert would be uttered."

"It is likely," said Charny, evidently disposed to let the discussion drop. "At least you are recovered now?"

"Completely."

"I have only one thing to entreat," said the Queen to her Lifeguardsman. "Go and tell the generals to camp where their troops are stationed and the King will issue orders to-morrow."

The count bowed but darted an affectionately anxious look on Andrea which the Queen remarked.

"Will you not return to the King with me?" inquired she of the countess.

"Oh, no," replied the latter eagerly; "I beg leave to retire."

"Oh, the King has been pleasant but you would rather not see him again? I understand. You may go, and let the count carry out his instructions."

She glanced at the lord as much as to say: "Return soon!"

And his look replied: "As soon as possible."

Andrea, with a heaving and oppressed bosom, watched her husband's movements, but as soon as he had disappeared, her forces failed her and the Queen had to run to her with the smelling salts as she sank on a stool, apologizing for the breach of etiquette in sitting in the royal presence.

The feeling between the pair was strange. The Queen seemed to have affection for her attendant and the latter respect for her mistress, but they were like enemies at times.

"You know, dear countess, that etiquette is not made for you. But you have nothing to say to me about this Dr. Gilbert, whose sight made so profound an impression on you?"

The woman had reflected in an instant. Whatever the relation between the Queen, who was suspected of having paramours, and the King, perhaps not so gullible as he looked, Marie Antoinette might draw from her royal consort the particulars of the mesmeric trance in which Gilbert had thrown the Lady of Charny. Better her relation than the King's.

With the energy of lunacy, she ran from one door to another, fastened them all, and when assured that nobody could hear or see, she flung herself on her knees before her mistress.

"Save me, in heaven's name, save me!" she wailed: "and I will tell you everything!"

CHAPTER XXI. THE QUEEN AND HER MASTER.

Andrea's confession was a long one for it was not until eleven at night that the royal boudoir door opened, and on the sill was seen the Countess of Charny, kissing her mistress's hand.

She went away with weeping eyes but the Queen's were scorching, as she paced her room.

She gave order that she was to be disturbed on no account unless for news from Paris.

At the supposition that Charny had at last perceived that his wife was still young and fair, the Queen found that misfortune is nothing to a heart-chagrin.

But in the midst of her feverish torment came the cruel consolation. According to Andrea's confession she had been wronged in a mesmeric trance and Gilbert had humbled her pride forever. Somewhere was the visible token of her defeat—like a trophy of his shameful triumph, the young man had borne away in the wintry night the offspring of the occult love of the gardener's boy for his suzerain's daughter!

She could not but be wonderstricken at the magical combination of wayward fortune, by which a peasant lad had been made to love the fine lady who was to be the favorite of the Queen of France.

"So the grain of dust has been lifted up to glitter like the diamond in the lustre of the skies," she mused.

Was not this lowborn lover the living symbol of what was happening at the time, a man of the people swaying the politics of a great empire, one who personified, by privilege of the evil spirit who soared over France, the insult to its nobility and the attack on royalty by the plebeians?

While shuddering, she wanted to look upon this monster who by a crime had infused his base blood into the aristocratic blue: who had caused a Revolution that he should be delivered from the castle; it was his principles which had armed Billet, Gonchon, Marat, and the others.

He was a venomous creature and terrible; for he had ruined Andrea as her lover and wrecked the Bastile as the hater of kings.

She ought to know him to avoid him or the better to fight him. Better still to make use of him. At any price she must see him and judge him.

Two thirds of the night were passed in reverie before she sank into troubled slumber.

But even here the Revolution was her nightmare. She had a dream that she was walking in one of her German forests when a gnome seized her from behind a tree and she knew that it was Gilbert.

She shrieked and, waking, found Lady Tourzel, an attendant, by her pillow.

"The Queen is sick," she called out. "Fetch the doctor."

"What doctor is in waiting?" asked the Queen.

"Dr. Gilbert, the new honorary physician whom the King has appointed."

"You speak as if you knew him, and yet he has only been a week in this country from America, and only a day out of the Bastile?"

"Your Majesty, I read his writings, and I was so curious to see the author," said the lady, "that I had him pointed out to me as he was in his rooms."

"Ah! well, let him begin his duties. Tell him I am ailing and request his presence."

Surprised and profoundly affected, though he seemed but a little uneasy, Gilbert appeared before the Queen. With her aristocratic intelligence she read that he felt timid respect for the woman, tranquil audacity for the patient and no emotion whatever for the sovereign. She was vexed, too, that he could look so well in the black suit worn by the third class of society and one the Revolutionists chose.

The less provoking he was in bearing, the more her anger grew. She had fancied the man an odious character, one of the heroes of impudence whom she had often seen around her. She had represented as a Mirabeau, the man she hated next to Cardinal Rohan and General Lafayette, this author of Andrea's woes. He was guilty in her eyes for looking the gentleman. The proud Austrian conceived a wild hatred against one whom she thought had stolen the semblance of the rank he had no business to aspire to.

As he had not ceased to look at her while she was dismissing all her ladies, his persistency exasperated her like importunity.

"Well, sir," she snapped at him like a pistol-shot, "what are you doing in staring at me instead of telling what ails me?"

This furious apostrophe, accompanied with visual lightning, would have blasted any courtier into dropping at her feet and sueing for mercy though he was a hero, a marshal, or a demigod.

But Gilbert made answer quietly:

"The physician judges by the eyes in the first place, my lady. As your Majesty summoned me, I come not from idle curiosity but to obey your orders and fulfill my duty. As far as in my power lays, I study your Majesty."

"Am I sick?"

"Not in the usual meaning of the word, but your Majesty is superexcited."

"Why not say I am out of temper?" she queried with irony.

"Allow me to use the medical term, since I am a medical man called in."

"Be it so. Whence this superexcitement?"

"Your Majesty is too intelligent not to know that a man of medicine only judges the material state: he is not a wizard to sound at the first glance the mind of man."

"Do you mean to imply that at the second, or third time, you could not merely tell me my bodily ail but a mental one?"

"Possibly," returned Gilbert coldly.

She darted at him a withering look while he was simply staring at her with desperate fixedness. Vanquished, she tried to wrench herself away from what was alarming while fascinating, and she upset a stand so that a chocolate cup was smashed on the floor. He saw it fall and the cup shiver, but did not budge. The color flew to her brow, to which she carried her chilly hand; but she dared not direct her eyes again on the magnetizer.

"Under what master did you study?" she inquired, using a scornful tone more painful than insolence.

"I cannot answer without wounding your Majesty."

The Queen felt that he gave her an advantage and she leaped in at the opening like a lioness on a prey.

"Wound me?" she almost screamed. "I vow that you mistake. Dr. Gilbert, you have not studied the French language in as good sources as medicine, I fear. Members of my class are not wounded by inferiors, only tired."

"Excuse me, madam," he returned, "I forgot I was called in to a patient. You are about to stifle with excitement and I shall call your women to put you to bed."

She walked up and down the room, infuriated at being treated like a great child, and, turning, said:

"You are Dr. Gilbert? Strange—I have a girlish memory of one of your name. A boy who looked unkempt, tattered and torn like a little Jean Jacques Rousseau when a vagabond, who was delving the ground with the spade held in his dirty, crooked hands."

"It was I," replied the other calmly. "It was in 1772, that the little gardener's boy to whom you kindly allude, was earning his bread by working in the royal gardens of Trianon. That is seventeen years ago, and much has happened in that time. It needed no longer to make the wild boy a learned man: revolutionary eras are the forcing-beds of mind. Clear as your glance is, your Majesty does not see that the youth is a man of thirty; it is wrong to be astonished that little Gilbert, simple and uncouth, should have become a learned philosopher in the breath of two revolutions."

"Simple? perhaps we will recur to that on another occasion," said the Queen vindictively: "but let us have to do with the learned philosopher, the improved and perfect man whom I have under my eyes."

Gilbert did not notice the sneer though he knew it was a fresh insult.

"You are appointed medical attendant to the King," she continued: "it is clear that I have the welfare of my husband too near my heart to entrust his health to a stranger."

"I offered myself, madam," responded Gilbert, "and his Majesty accepted me without any doubts on my capacity and zeal. I am mainly a political physician, vouched for by Minister Necker. But if the King has need of my knowledge of the scalpel and drugs, I can be as good a healer as human science allows one of our race to be. But the King most wants, besides the good adviser and physician, a good friend."

"You, a friend of the King?" exclaimed the lady, with a new outbreak of scorn. "By virtue of your quackery and charms? have we gone back to the Dark Ages and are you going to rule France with elixirs and jugglery like a Faust?"

"I have no pretentions that way."

"Oh, why have you given that branch? you might, in the same way as you sent Andrea to sleep, put the monsters under a spell who howl and spit fire on our threshold."

This time Gilbert could not help blushing at the allusion to mesmerizing Andrea, which was of inexpressible delight to her who baited him as she believed she had left a wound.

"For you can send people to sleep," she pursued: "you no doubt have studied magnetism with those villains who make slumber a treacherous weapon and read our secrets in our sleep."

"Indeed, madam, I have studied magnetism under the wise Cagliostro."

"That teacher of moral theft, who taught his disciples how to rifle bodies and souls by his infamous practice!"

Gilbert understood all by this, and she shuddered with joy to the core at seeing him lose color.

"Wretch," she rejoiced, "I have stung him to the quick and the blood flows."

But the deepest emotions did not long hold the mesmerizer in their spell. Approaching the Queen who was rash enough to look up in her triumph and let her eyes be caught, he said:

"You are wrong to judge fellow-creatures so harshly. You denounce Cagliostro as a quack when you had a proof of his real science; when you were the Archduchess of Austria and first came to France. When I saw you at Taverney, did not that wonder-worker whom you decry show to your Majesty in a clear cup of water such a picture of your fate that you swooned away?"

Gilbert had not seen the forecast, but he knew from his master, no doubt, what Marie Antoinette had been shown. He struck so hard that she turned dreadfully pale.

"Yes," she said in a hoarse voice, "he showed me a hideous machine of bloodshed. But I do not yet know that such a thing exists."

"I know not that, but he cannot be denied the rank of sage who held such might over his fellow-beings."

"His fellows?" sneered the Queen.

"Nay, his power was so great that crowned heads sank beneath his level," went on Gilbert.

"Shame! I tell you that Cagliostro was a cowardly charlatan, and his mesmeric sleep a crime. In one case it resulted in a deed for which human justice, represented by me, shall seize the author and punish him."

"Madam, be indulgent for those who have sinned."

"Ho, ho! you confess then?"

She thought by the gentleness of his tone that he was imploring her mercy. Some forgot herself and looked at him to scorch him with her indignation.

But her glance crossed his only to melt like a steel blade on which the electric fluid falls and she felt her hatred change to fright, while she recoiled a step to elude coming wrath.

"Ah, madam, do you understand what the power is I had from the master whom you defamed? believe that if I were not the most respectful of your subjects, I could convince you by a terrible experiment. I might constrain you to write down with your own hands lines that would convince you when you read them at your release from the charm. But mark how solid is the patience and the generosity of the man whom you have been insulting, and whom you placed in the Bastile. You regret it was broken open because he was released by the people. And you will hate me, and continue to doubt when I relax the bond with which I hold you."

Ceasing to govern her with glances and magnetic passes, he allowed her to regain some self-control, like the bird in the vacuum, to whom a little air is restored.

"Send me to sleep—force me to speak or write while sleep-bound," cried the Queen, white with terror. "Have you dared? Do you know that your threat is high-treason? a crime punishable with death!"

"Do not cry out too soon. If I thus charmed you and forced you to betray your inmost secrets it would be with a witness by. He would repeat your revelations so as to leave you no doubt."

"A witness? but, think, sir, that a witness to such a deed would be an accomplice."

"A husband is not the accomplice to an experiment he favors on his wife."

"The King?" screamed Marie Antoinette with dread, revealing rather the wife than the medium reluctant to make a scene for the spiritualist: "fie, Dr.

Gilbert!"

"The King, your natural defender, your sustainer," replied Gilbert quietly. "He would relate, when you were awakened, how respectful I was, while proud in proving my science on the most venerated of sovereigns."

He left her to meditate on the depth of his words.

"I see," she said at length, "you must be a mortal enemy——"

"Or a proven friend——"

"Impossible; friendship cannot dwell beside fear or distrust."

"Between subject and monarch, friendship cannot live but on the confidence the subject inspires. I have made the vow not to use my weapons but to repulse the wrongs done me. All for defense, nothing for offence!"

"Alas," moaned the Queen: "I see that you set a trap. After frightening the woman, you seek to rule the Queen."

"No, lady, I am not a paltry speculator. You are the first woman in whom I have found all feminine passions with all the dominant faculties of man. You can be a woman and a friend. I admire you and would serve you. I will do it without receiving aught from you—merely to study you. I will do more to show you how I serve you: if I am in the way send me forth."

"Send you hence," said she with gladness.

"But no doubt you will reflect that my power can be exercised from afar. It is true: but do not fear—I shall not employ it."

The Queen was musing, unable to reply to this strange man when steps were heard in the corridor.

"The King," she exclaimed.

"Then point out the door by which I may depart without being seen by him."

"Stay," she said.

He bowed, and remained impassible while she sought to read on his brow to what point triumph rose in him more plain than anger or disquiet.

"At least he might have shown his delight," she thought.

CHAPTER XXII. THE PRIVATE COUNCIL.

Louis entered briskly but heavily as was his wont. His manner was busy and curious, strongly contrasting with the Queen's cold rigidity.

His high color had not left him. An early riser and proud of the heartiness he had imbibed with the morning breeze, he breathed noisily and set his foot vigorously on the floor.

"The doctor—what has become of the doctor?" he inquired.

"Good morning, Sire! how do you feel this morning? are you tired?"

"I have slept six hours, my allowance. I feel very well, and my head is clear. But you are a little pale. I heard you had sent for the new doctor."

"Here is Dr. Gilbert," said the Queen, standing aside from a window recess where the doctor had been screened by the curtains.

"But were you unwell that you sent for him?" continued the monarch: "You blush—you must have some secret, since you consult him instead of the regular doctors of the household. But have a care! Dr. Gilbert is one of my confidential friends, and if you tell him anything he will repeat it to me."

The Queen had become purple from being merely red.

"Nay, Sire," said Gilbert, smiling.

"What, has the Queen corrupted my friends?"

Marie Antoinette laughed one of those dry, half-suppressed laughs signifying that the conversation has gone far enough or it fatigues: Gilbert understood but the King did not.

"Come, doctor, since this amuses the Queen, let me hear the joke."

"I was asking the doctor why you called him so early. I own that his presence at Versailles much puzzles me," said the Queen.

"I was wanting the doctor to talk politics with him," said Louis, his brow darkening.

"Oh, very well," said she, taking a seat as if to listen.

"But we are not going to talk pleasant stuff; so we must go away to spare you an additional pang."

"Do you call business matters pangs?" majestically said the Queen. "I would like you to stay. Dr. Gilbert, surely you will not disobey me."

"But I want the doctor's opinion and he cannot give it according to his conscience if you are by us."

"What risk does he run of displeasing me by speaking according to his conscience?" she demanded.

"That is easy to understand, madam; you have your own line of policy, which is not always ours; so——"

"You would clearly imply that the Gilbert policy runs counter to mine?"

"It should be so, from the ideas your Majesty knows me to entertain," said Gilbert. "But your Majesty should know that I will speak the truth before you as plainly as to his Majesty."

"That is a gain," said Marie Antoinette.

"Truth is not always good to speak," observed the monarch.

"When useful?" suggested Gilbert.

"And the intention good," added the Queen.

"We do not doubt that," said King Louis. "But if you are wise, madam, you will leave the doctor free use of his language, which I stand in need of."

"Sire, since the Queen provokes the truth, and I know her mind is too noble and powerful to dread it, I prefer to speak before both my sovereigns."

"I ask it."

"I have faith in your Majesty's wisdom," said Gilbert, bowing to the lady. "The question turns on the King's glory and happiness."

"Then you were right to have faith in me. Commence, sir."

"Well, I advise the King to go to Paris."

A spark dropping into the eight thousand pounds of gunpowder in the City Hall cellars would not have caused the explosion of this sentence in the Queen's bosom.

"There," said the King who had been startled by her cry, "I told you so, doctor."

"The King," proceeded the indignant woman, "in a city revolted; among scythes and pitchforks, borne by the villains who massacred the Swiss, and murdered Count Launay and Provost Flesselles; the King crossing the City Hall Square and slipping in the blood of his defenders: you are insane to speak thus, sir!"

Gilbert lowered his eyes as in respect but said not a word. The King writhed in his chair as though on a red hot grid.

"Madam," said the doctor at last, "I have seen Paris, and you have not even been out of the palace to see Versailles, Do you know what Paris is about?"

"Storming some other Bastile," jeered the Queen.

"Assuredly not; but Paris knows there is another fortress between it and the King. The city is collecting the deputies of its forty-eight wards and sending them here."

"Let them come," said the Queen, with fierce joy. "They will be hotly received."

"Take care, madam, for they come not alone but escorted by twenty thousand National Guards."

"What is that?"

"Do not speak lightly of an institution which will be a power one day.

It will bind and unbind."

"My lord," you have ten thousand men who are equal to these twenty thousand," said the Queen: "call them up to give these blackguards their chastisement, and the example which all this revolutionary spawn has need of. I would sweep them all away in a week, if I were listened to."

"How deceived you are—by others," said Gilbert, shaking his head, sadly. "Alas! think of civil war excited by a queen. Only one did so, and she went down to the grave with the epithet of the Foreigner."

"Excited by me? what do you mean? did I fire on the Bastile without provocation?"

"Pray, instead of urging violence, hearken to reason," interposed the King. "Continue," he said to Gilbert.

"Spare the King a battle with doubtful issue; these hates which grow hotter at a distance, these boastings which become courage on occasion. You may by gentleness soften the contact of this army with the palace. Let the King meet them. These twenty thousand are coming perhaps to conquer the King: let him conquer them, and turn them into his own body-guard; for they are the people."

The King nodded approval.

"But do you not know what will be said?" she cried, "that the King applauds what was done, the slaying of his faithful Switzers, the massacre of his officers, the putting his handsome city to fire and blood. You will make him dethrone himself and thank these gentlemen!"

A disdainful smile passed over her lips.

"No, madam, there is your mistake. This conduct would mean, there was some justice in the people's grievances. 'I come to pardon where they overstepped the dealing of wild justice. I am the King and the chief; the head of the French Revolution as Henry Fourth was head of the League and the nation. Your generals are my officers, your National Guards my soldiers; your magistrates my own. Instead of urging me on, follow me if you can. The length of my stride will prove that I lead in the footsteps of Charlemagne.'"

"He is right," the King said ruefully.

"Oh, Sire, for mercy's sake, do not listen to this man, your enemy."

"Her Majesty tells you what she thinks of my suggestion," said Gilbert.

"I think, sir, that you are the only person who has ever ventured to tell me the truth," commented Louis XVI.

"The truth? is that what you have told?" exclaimed the Queen. "Heaven have mercy!"

"Yes, madam," said Gilbert, "and believe me that it is the lamp by which the throne and royalty will be prevented rolling into the abyss."

He bowed very humbly as he spoke, to the Queen, who appeared profoundly touched this time—by his humility or the reasoning?

The King rose with a decisive air as though determined on realization. But from his habit of doing nothing without consulting with his consort, he asked:

"Do you approve?"

"It must be," was her rejoinder.

"I am not asking for your abnegation but support to my belief."

"In that case I am convinced that the realm will become the meanest and most deplorable of all in Christendom."

"You exaggerate. Deplorable, I grant, but mean?"

"Your ancestors left you a dreary inheritance," said Marie Antoinette sorrowfully.

"Which I grieve you should share," added Louis.

"Allow me to say, Sire, that the future may not be so lamentable," interposed Gilbert, who pitied the dethroned rulers; "a despotic monarchy has ceased, but a constitutional one commences."

"Am I the man to found that in France?" asked the King.

"Why not?" exclaimed the Queen, catching some hope from Gilbert's suggestion.

"Madam, I see clearly. From the day when I walk among men like themselves, I lose all the factitious strength necessary to govern France as the Louis before me did. The French want a master and one who will wield the sword. I feel no power to strike."

"Not to strike those who would rob your children of their estate," cried the Queen, "and who wish to break the lilies on your crown?"

"What am I to answer? if I answer No, I raise in you one of those storms which embitter my life. You know how to hate—so much the better for you. You can be unjust; I do not reproach you, for it is an excellent trait in the lordly. Madam, we must resign ourselves: it takes strength to push ahead this car with scythe-bladed wheels, and we lack strength."

"That is bad, for it will run over our children," sighed Marie Antoinette.

"I know it, but we shall not be pushing it."

"We can draw it back, Sire."

"Oh, beware," said Gilbert, deeply, "it will crush you then."

"Let him speak what the newspapers have been saying for a week past. At any rate he wraps up the bitterness of his free speech," said the King. "In short, I shall go to Paris."

"Who knows but you will find it the gulf I fear?" said the Queen in a hollow, irritated voice. "The assassin may be there with his bullet, who will know among a thousand threatening fists, which holds the dagger?"

"Fear nothing of that sort, they love me," said Louis.

"You make me pity you for saying that. They love you who slay and mangle and cut the throats of your representatives? The Governor of the

Bastile was your image. They killed that brave and faithful servitor, as they would kill you in his stead. The more easy as they know you and that you would turn the other cheek to the smiter. If you are killed, what about my children?" concluded the Queen.

"Madam," struck in Gilbert, deeming it time he intervened, "the King is so respected that I fear that his entry will be like that of Juggernaut, under whose wheels the fanatics will throw themselves to be crushed. This march into Paris will be a triumphal progress."

"I am rather of the doctor's opinion," said the monarch.

"Say you are eager to enjoy this triumph," said the Queen.

"The King is right, and his eagerness proves the accuracy of his judgment on men and events. The sooner his Majesty is, the greater will be his triumph: by delay the gain may be lost. This promptness will change the King's position and make the act in some way his order. Lose time, Sire, and their demand will be an order."

"Not to-day, Master Gilbert," said the Queen, "to-morrow. Grant me till then, and I swear not to oppose the movement."

"But who knows what will happen meanwhile?" expostulated the King in despair. "Marie, you seem doomed to ruin me. The Assembly will send me some addresses which will rob me of all the merit in taking the first step."

Gilbert nodded.

"Better so," said the Queen with sullen fury, "refuse and preserve your regal dignity: go not to Paris but wage war from here; and if we must die here, let us fall like rulers, like masters, like Christians, who cling to their God as to their crown."

The King saw from her excitement that he must give way.

"But what do you expect between whiles?" he inquired: "A reinforcement from Germany? or news from town?"

It was a coat of mail which the King refused to wear, but her misapprehension of the monarch who knew he was not of the times when kings wore armor, cost a precious time.

Without other safeguard than Gilbert's breast, as the latter rode in the coach beside the monarch, the visit to Paris was made.

In the Queen's drive, in the Champs Elysées, Mayor Bailly offered him the city keys, saying:

"Sire, I bring your Majesty the keys of the good city. They are the same offered to Henry Fourth. He won his people, but the people have now won their King."

On the return, all having passed smoothly, crossing Louis XV. Place, a shot was fired from across the river and Gilbert felt a stroke. The bullet had hit one of his steel vest buttons and glanced off into the crowd and killed an unfortunate woman.

The King heard her scream and heard the shot.

"Burning powder in my honor?" he said.

"Yes, Sire," was Gilbert's easy reply.

It was never known what hand fired this regicidal shot which justified the Queen's fear that her husband would be assassinated.

While all was festivity at Paris, gloom settled down on Versailles at eventide. With darkness came its retinue of fears and sinister visions, when suddenly uproar was heard at the end of the town.

The Queen shuddered and ran to a window which she opened with her own hand.

A hussar came up to the palace; it was a lieutenant sent by Charny who had gone on towards Paris to get the news. He reported that the King was safe and sound, and that he would arrive shortly.

Taking her two children by the hand, Marie Antoinette went down and out upon the grand staircase, where were grouped the servants and the courtiers.

Her piercing eye perceived a woman in white leaning on the stone balustrade and eagerly looking into the shadows: it was Countess Andrea, enrapt in expectation of her husband so that she did not see her royal mistress, or disdained to notice her.

Whether she bore the Queen rancor or merely yearned to see her husband, it was a double stab for the beloved of Charny.

But she had determined on the righteous course: she trod her jealousy underfoot; she immolated her secret joys and wrath to the sanctity of the conjugal oath. No doubt from heaven was sent this salutary love to raise her husband and children above all else. Her pride, too, lifted her above earthly desires and she could be selfish without deserving blame.

As the coach came up, she descended the steps, and when its door was opened, and Louis stepped out, she did not notice how the grooms and footmen hastened to tear off the rosettes and streamers of the new popular colors with which Billet and Pitou and others of the throng had decorated the vehicle and horses.

With an outcry of love and delight the Queen embraced the King. She sobbed as though she had fully expected never again to see him.

In her impulse of an overburdened heart, she did not remark the hand-grasp the Charnys exchanged in the darkness.

As the royal children kissed their father, the elder boy spied the cockade reddened by the torchlight on his father's hat and exclaimed with his childish astonishment:

"Oh, papa, what is on your white cockade—blood?"

It was the national Red.

Spying it herself, the Queen plucked it off with profound disgust as the King stooped as if to kiss his daughter but really to hide his shame. The mad woman did not think that she was insulting the nation, which would repay her at an early day.

"Throw the thing away," she cried, casting it down the steps so that all the escort tramped over it.

This strange transition extinguished her phase of marital love. She looked round for Charny without appearing to do so; he had fallen back into the ranks like a soldier.

"I thank you, my lord," she said to him, at last: "you have kept your promise to restore the King to me unhurt."

"Who is that?" inquired the sovereign: "Oh, Charny? But where is Gilbert, whom I do not see?"

"Come to supper," said the Queen to change the subject; "Go to the countess, my Lord Charny, and bring her. We shall have a family supper party, to-night."

She was the Queen again; but still she was vexed that the count, who had been sad, should cheer up at the prospect of his wife being in the company.

CHAPTER XXIII. WHY THE QUEEN WAITED.

A little calm succeeded at Versailles the political and mental tempests which we have chronicled.

The King breathed again: and consoled himself with his regaled popularity for what his Bourbon pride had suffered in truckling to the Paris mob. The Nobility prepared to flee or to resist. The people watched and waited.

Assured that she was the butt of all the slings and arrows of hatred, the Queen made herself as inconspicuous as possible: she knew that for her party she was the centre of all hopes.

Since the King went to Paris she had not seen Dr. Gilbert, but the chance was offered her when they met in the vestibule of the royal apartments.

"Going to the King?" she challenged as he bowed deeply. "As physician or counsellor?" she continued with a smile betraying some irony.

"As doctor; it is my day on duty," he replied.

She beckoned him to follow her into a little sideroom.

"You see, sir," she began, "that you were wrong the other day when you assured me that the King ran no risk of murder. A woman was killed by a shot aimed at him and striking you, without injury. Who told me so? gentlemen of the escort who saw your button fly."

"I do not believe it was a crime, or, if so, one to be imputed to the people," returned Gilbert, hesitatingly.

"Who are we to attribute it to, then?" she demanded, fixing her eyes upon him.

"I have been studying the masses some time," he responded: "when in fury the mobs tear and slay like a tiger; but in cold blood, they seek no go-betweens. They want to make the blood fly with their own claws and fangs."

"As witness, Foulon and his son-in-law Berthier Savigny, accused of complicity in the Great Grain Fraud, and ripped to pieces by the crowd? and Flesselles, slain by a pistol! But the accounts of their atrocious executions may be untrue, we crowned heads are so engirt by flatterers."

"Madam, you do not believe any more than I, that Flesselles was killed by the mob. Others of higher degree were more interested in his death. As for the King, those who love their country believe he is useful to it, and these stand between him and the assassin eagerly."

"Alas," said she, "there was a time when a good Frenchman would have expressed his sentiments in better terms than those. It was not possible then to love his country without loving his rulers."

Gilbert blushed and bowed, feeling the thrill at his heart which the Queen could impart in her periods of winning intimacy.

"Madam, I beg to boast that I love the monarchy better than many."

"Are we not at an era when it is not enough to say so, but actions should speak?"

"Madam, I was your enemy yesterday, when you had me imprisoned, and now I am your servant."

"But whence the change? it is not in your nature, doctor, to change your feelings, opinion and belief so readily. You are a man with a deep-rooted memory; you know how to lengthen out your vengeance. Tell me the aim of your change?"

"Madam, you reproach me with loving my country too dearly."

"You love it so as to stoop to serve me, the foreigner? no I am a Frenchwoman—I love my country. You smile—but it is my country. I have adopted it. German by birth, I am French through the heart; but I love France through the King and the respect due the God which consecrated me to it. But I understand you; it is not the same thing. You love France purely and simply for France's sake."

"Madam, I cannot be outspoken without disrespect," replied the doctor.

"Oh," she said, "dreadful is this epoch when men pretending to be honorable isolate two principles that should never be parted, and have always marched forward together: France and her King. Is there not a tragedy in which a queen, abandoned by all, is asked: What remains? and she answers 'I!' Well, like Medea, I am here—and we shall see the outcome."

She passed out, in vexation, leaving Gilbert in stupor. By her fiery breath she had blown aside a corner of the veil beyond which simmered the hell-broth of the Anti-Revolution.

"Let us look to ourselves," thought Gilbert, "the Queen is nursing a scheme."

"Plainly nothing can be done with this man," muttered the sovereign, regaining her rooms. "He is a strong one, but he lacks devotion."

Poor princess, to whom servility is thought to be devotion!

Marie Antoinette felt the weight upon her most when alone.

As woman and queen, she had nothing to lean upon or help her support the crushing burden.

Doubt or wavering was on either hand. Uneasy about their fortune, the sycophants fled. Her relatives and friends brooded on exile. The proudest of all, Andrea, gradually drew aside from her, body and soul.

The noblest and dearest man of all, Charny, was wounded by her fickleness and was a prey to doubt.

She who was instinct and sagacity themselves, was fretted by the crisis.

"This pure, unalloyed heart has not changed, but it is changing," she reasoned.

A dreadful conviction for the woman who loved with passion, and insupportable for one who loved with pride, as the Queen did Charny.

Being a man, all that George understood was that the Queen was unfairly jealous of his wife. Nothing pains a heart incapable of false play so much as to be suspected of it. Nothing so points attention on the person unjustly accused of inspiring an attachment than jealousy. The suspected one reflects. It looks from the jealous heart to the one believed to be its rival.

Indeed, how suppose that a noble and elevated creature should be vexed over a trifle? What has a lovely woman to be worried about? what, the powerful lady?

Charny knew that Andrea had been the bosom friend of the Queen, and wondered why their love had cooled and the confidante stood away. He had to look to her and the idol lost so much of the eye-adulation as Andrea gained. By her unfairness and anger Marie Antoinette told Charny that he must feel less a lover for her. He sought for the cause, and naturally whither the Queen was frowning.

He pitied Andrea, who had married him by royal command, and was but nominally his wife.

Marie Antoinette's burst of affection in receiving her husband on his return from Paris had opened the eyes of the count.

He began to steel himself against her, and she, while ill-treating him, resumed showering favor on Andrea.

The latter submitted, without astonishment but also with no gratitude. Long since, she reckoned herself as belonging to her royal mistress and she let the Queen do what she liked.

The result was a curious situation, such as women act and comprehend best.

Andrea felt all her husband underwent, and she pitied him and showed her pity, from her love being of the angelic kind which is not fed on hope.

This compassion led to a gentle approach. She tried to comfort George without letting him see that she needed the same consolation. This was done with that delicacy called womanly because the softer sex best practice it.

Marie Antoinette, trying to reign by dividing, saw she was on the wrong road, and was forcing together the souls which she wanted to keep aloof.

Hence, in the silence of night and the lonesomeness, she felt such wrestlings with Giant Despair as must give the spirit a high idea of its power since it can struggle with so vast a might.

She would have succumbed had it not been for the diversion of politics.

In her pride she ascribed her decay to the depreciation she had let herself as a woman suffer lately. In her active mind, to think was to act.

She set to work without losing a moment, but unfortunately the work was for her perdition.

Seeing that the Parisians had turned into soldiers and appeared to intend war, she resolved to show them what war really is.

For two months the King had been striving to retain some shred of royalty: with the peerage and Mirabeau, he had tried to neutralize the democratic spirit effacing it in France. In this strife the monarch had lost all his power and part of his popularity; the Queen had gained the nickname of "Lady Veto." She had been known as The Austrian, then as Lady Deficit, on account of the hole in the Treasury attributed to her generosity to her favorites; now, Lady Veto; she was to bear lastly the title of The Widow Capet.

After the conflict in which the Queen had endeavored to engage her friends by showing them that they were endangered with her, she remarked that only sixty thousand passports had been applied for by the higher classes, fleeing to foreign parts. This had struck the Queen.

She purposed her own escape, so as to leave the true royalists in France to wage a civil war. Her plan was not bad, and it must have succeeded had it not been for the evil genius who was plotting behind the Queen. Strange destiny! this woman who inspired great devotion, nowhere could attach discretion.

It was known all over town that she intended to take to wing before she had settled herself: and from that time it was impracticable.

Meanwhile, the Flanders Regiment, famous for its royalist fervor, arrived at Versailles, asked for by the town council, as the guarding of the palace exceeded their powers at command.

It made a solemn entrance into the court-town, and received an ovation from the courtiers, other soldiers, and a band of young nobles who had set up a company of their own with a special uniform, to which were joined the Knights of St. Louis, officers on the retired list and adventurers.

Only one black spot marred the sky: Liege had revolted against the Austrian Emperor and this made it difficult for him to succor the daughter whom he had wedded to his brother on the French throne.

After the Flanders Regiment had been welcomed, the Lifeguards officers voted to give them a dinner: it was fixed for the First of October. As the King had no politics to trouble him, since the new government took all business on themselves, he passed the days in hunting. The Queen was applied to for the dinner to take place in the palace. She let the guards officers have the theatre, which was boarded over to make more room, and a hall adjoining.

She shut herself up alone, save for her children and Andrea, sad and thoughtful, where the toasts and the clink of glasses should not disturb her.

At the palace gates a crowd peeped in and sniffed the air, puffing the fumes of roasts and wines, from the large dinner table. It was imprudent to let the hungry inhale the vapor of good cheer and the morose hear songs and cheers of hope and joy.

The feast went on without any interruption, however. At the second course the Colonel of the Flanders Regiment proposed the regular toasts of the Royal Family, which were hailed so loudly that the Queen may have heard the echoes in her refuge.

An officer stood up. He was a man of wit and courage who foresaw the issue of this banquet and was sincerely attached to the Royal Family; or else he was a plotter who tried to challenge the anti-popular opinion. He proposed the Health of the Nation.

It was hooted down, and the feast took its plain meaning—the torrent resumed its down-hill rush.

To forget the country might pass: but to insult it was too much; it would take revenge.

From that moment discipline was at an end: the privates hobnobbed with their superiors, and it was really a brotherly meeting.

What a pity that the unfortunate King and sorrowful Queen could not witness such a gathering!

Officious servants ran with exaggerated accounts of the festivities to Marie Antoinette and urged that she should go with the young heir to the throne by her side, in the monarch's absence.

"Madam, I entreat you to keep away," pleaded Count Charny. "I have come away from the scene; they are too excited to make it seemly for your Majesty."

She was in one of her sulky, whimsical moods and it suited her to tease Charny by going counter to his advice. She looked at him with disdain and was going to answer him tartly when he respectfully said:

"At least, see what the King says about it."

The King had just returned from hunting.

Marie Antoinette ran to meet him and dragging him with her, in his riding boots and dusty as he was, she led him away, without a glance at Charny, and crying:

"Come, my lord, to see a sight worthy of a King of France's regard!"

With her left hand, she led her son. The courtiers flowed before and after the trio: she reached the theatre doors just as the glasses were being emptied for the twentieth time to shouts of:

"God save the King! Long live the Queen!"

The applause burst like a mine exploding when the King and Queen and Prince Royal were seen on the floor. The drunken soldiers and heated officers waved their hats on their swords and shouted. The band began to play from the Opera of Richard Coeur-de-lion, Blondel's song of "Oh, Richard, oh, my King!" which so transparently alluded to the King in a kind of bondage that all voices took up the song.

The enthusiastic Queen did not see that the soldiers were intoxicated: the surprised King had too much good sense not to see more clearly, but he was weak and flattered by this reception, so that he let the general frenzy overcome him.

Charny, who had drunk nothing but water during the part of the banquet which he attended, stood pale at this participation of the Royal Family in what would now be a historical event by their presence.

But his apprehension was still greater when he saw his brother Valence, the hussar lieutenant, approach the Queen and speak to her when encouraged by a smile. It was consent, for she unpinned from her cap the cockade she was wearing and presented it to her imprudent Knight. It was not even a royal rosette, but that of Austria: the black insignia of the foreign foe! This was not rashness but treason to the country. So mad was the concourse that they to whom Valence Charny presented the black cockade, tore off their white ones and they who were wearing the tricolors trampled them under foot.

The exultation became so high that the august guests had pains to return to their rooms without trampling on those who prostrated themselves in their passageway.

All this might have been overlooked as the freak of an orgie, but after the Royal Family departed, the guests turned the banquet hall into a town taken by assault. The soldiers whooped and as the bugles blew the charge—against what enemy? the absent nation! they climbed the balconies where the ladies held over helping hands.

The first soldier to reach the boxes was a grenadier whom a nobleman decorated with the ribbon he was wearing in his buttonhole: the Order of Limburg, that is, of no value. But all the sham battle was fought under the Austrian colors while the national one was shouted down. Only a few dull protests were heard, drowned under the trumpet blasts, the hurrahs, and the music of the band. The tumult came menacingly to the crowd at the doors. Astonished at first, they were soon indignant as it was known that the tricolor had been spurned and the black streamer flaunted in its stead.

An officer of the National Guard had been badly beaten in the scuffle to uphold the honor of the latter, but it was not known that Charny, the Queen's favorite, had taken all the blame of the outrages on himself.

The Queen had returned to her rooms, dazed by the scene. A swarm of flatterers and adulators assailed her.

"See the true spirit of your troops," they said. "When the fury of the mob is bragged of, think how it would melt away in the blast of this wild ardor of the military for monarchical ideas."

She was still under the illusion that this fire would spread over the kingdom from the palace, at her will, when, next day, receiving the National Guard to whom she had promised to distribute their new flags, she made this address:

"I am happy to make this presentation. The Nation and the army ought to love the King, as we love them both. I was delighted with the rejoicing yesterday!"

At these words, emphasized by her glittering glance and sweetest voice, the crowd grumbled while the soldiers applauded noisily.

"She upheld us," said one party while the other muttered: "We are betrayed!"

"Am I not brave?" she asked of Charny who looked on with sorrow and listened with terror.

"To the point of folly," he replied with a deeply clouded face.

CHAPTER XXIV. THE ARMY OF WOMEN.

The Queen was reposing after the day of felicitation. She had her janissaries around her, her cohort of young bravoes, and having reckoned up her foes, she was wishful for the onslaught.

Had she not the defeat of the Fourteenth of July, the Loss of the Bastile, to avenge?

She treated Andrea with the former friendship for a time deadened in her bosom. But Charny? she only looked where he was when she was forced to give him an order. But this was no spite against the family, for it was noticed that she paid special attention to young Valence Charny, the hussar who had been given her Austrian rosette at the officers' dinner.

Indeed, as he was crossing the gallery to announce to the Master of the Buckhound's that the King would go hunting that day, Marie Antoinette who came out of the chapel, perceived him and greeted him.

"The King goes hunting?" she repeated; "what a mistake when the weather is threatening—is it not, Andrea?"

"Yes," answered the lady of honor absently.

"Where will the chase be?"

"In Meudon Wood, my lady."

"Well, accompany him and watch over him."

At this moment the head of the Charnys appeared. He smiled to Andrea and remarked:

"That is advice which my brother will bear in mind during the dangers to the King as well as during his pleasures."

At the sound of the voice, for she had not seen him coming, Marie Antoinette started and rejoined with studied rudeness:

"I should have been astonished if that speech had come from any but your lordship, for it contains a foreboding."

Andrea saw her husband blanch, but he bowed without retort. He noticed her surprise that he bore it so patiently, for he quickly said:

"I am most unhappy that I can no longer speak to the Queen without offense."

"The 'No longer' was spoken with a fine actor's due stress on the important words in a line.

"Speech is only bad when the intention is so," snapped the Queen, through her teeth, locked with anger.

"The ear hears hostilely when the mind is hostile," was the repartie of Charny, more aptly than politely.

"I shall wait to reply till the Count of Charny is happier in his attacks," went on the Queen.

"And I shall wait to attack till the Queen's Most Excellent Majesty is more happy in servitors than lately."

Andrea grasped her husband's hand hastily and prepared to go out of the gallery with him, when a glance from her mistress retained her.

"In short, what does your husband have to say to me?" she inquired.

"Sent to Paris yesterday by the King, I found it in great turmoil."

"Yes, the Parisians are going to pull down the Bastile! The Dutch have taken Holland! Anything fresher, my lord?"

"It is true that they are pulling down the prison, but that affords them nothing but stones and they want for bread."

"Let them be hungry," said the Queen. "What are we to do in the matter since others rule the roost?"

"There was a day when the Queen was the first to be compassionate in times of general distress," said the count; "when she went up into the garrets and the prayers of those she helped rose from the garrets unto God."

"Yes, and I have been nicely repaid for this pity for others," returned the lady bitterly. "One of my worst miseries came from my going into a garret."

She alluded, of course, to the incident of the "Queen's Necklace," already described in this series.

"Because your Majesty was once deceived, is all humanity to be measured by that bushel? Oh, how our gracious lady was loved at that period!"

She darted a flaming look at him.

"To be brief," she said, "what is happening in the capital? Only tell me what you have actually seen, for I want to depend on the accuracy of your words."

"I saw people packed on the waterside waiting for the flour boats; others crowding the bakers' doors, waiting for bread. A famishing people—husbands watching their wives sadly, mothers mourning over their babes. Their fists were clenched and shaken in the direction of Versailles. Alas, I fear that the dangers which my brothers and I are ready to brave, and under which we may die, will not long be forthcoming——"

The Queen had leaned on a window sill and with a view of expressing unconcern, she looked out instead of towards the count. They saw her start, and she exclaimed:

"Andrea, who is this rider?—he seems by his speed to bear news in hot haste."

Andrea went up, but almost instantly retreated, turning pale, and gasped in reproach:

"To call me to see him?"

Charny had looked also, and he said:

"It is Dr. Gilbert."

"So it is," said Marie Antoinette in such a tone that it was not possible to tell whether she had or had not visited on Andrea her personal spite.

Gilbert arrived with the sequel to the ominous scenes which Charny described. The famished women had started for Versailles; they were escorted by ragamuffins willing to be shielded by their petticoats and ripe for any deeds.

"Seven or eight thousand women," repeated the Queen when Gilbert had delivered his message of coming woe. She spoke with scorn.

"But they have been reinforced to double that number on the way. They are hungry and come to ask bread of the King."

"Just what I feared," said Charny.

"What is to be done?"

"Prepare the King to receive them," suggested Gilbert.

"Why expose him?" she expostulated, with that bravery and personal consciousness of her traits and of her husband's weakness which ought not to be exhibited before strangers.

But were Charny and Gilbert strangers—one destined to guard the King, the other the Queen?

The count replied for both, having resumed all his command, for he had sacrificed his pride.

"Madam, Dr. Gilbert is right; the King is still loved, he will make a speech and disarm these furies."

"But who will apprise the King? he is in Meudon Woods and the ways may be blocked."

"Will your Majesty see in me not the courtier but the man of war?" returned the Count, simply. "A soldier is made to be slain."

He did not wait for an answer or to hear the sigh, but rapidly went out and, mounting a guardman's horse, sped away for Meudon.

The sky was menacing and rain began to dot the dust, but Versailles was filling with people who had heard a noise like approaching thunder.

The soldiers took up their muskets slowly and the horseguards got into the saddle with the hesitation of the soldier when his adversaries are beneath his notice.

What could be done against women who had thrown down their weapons on the road and had scarce the power to drag themselves into the town? Half way they had divided eight loaves found at Sevres—thirty-two pounds of bread among seven thousand!

Maillard had accompanied them and induced the last who were armed to lay aside their weapons at the first houses of the place. He suggested that they should sing "Long live Henry Fourth!" to show that they had no ill feelings against royalty. They sang in a feeble whine.

Great was the amazement at the palace, where the harpies and Furies were expected, to see the tottering singers, hunger giving the giddiness of intoxication, pressing their haggard, thinned, livid, blotched and dusty faces against the gilded bars of the gates, and hanging on by their bony hands. From the weird groups came wails and howls while the dull eyes emitted sparks.

Now and again the hands let go the bars to be brandished in threat or held out imploringly.

It was a gloomy sight.

"What do you want?" challenged St. Priest, Minister of Paris.

"Bread," was the cry.

"When you had but one master you were never hungry," he replied testily; "you see how you stand since you have twelve hundred."

He came away, yelled at while he ordered the gates to be kept closed. But they had soon to be opened to a deputation from Parliament which Maillard had obtained. Unfortunately, Valence Charny with the guards had ridden against the mob. Two women of the twelve with the deputation were wounded, to whom Charny who had returned to announce the arrival of the King, and Gilbert rushed to assist.

"Open the doors," called out the King. "A palace is a sanctuary—it must receive all callers."

"An asylum for all but the kings and queens," muttered Marie Antoinette.

Deputy Mounier spoke for the deputation while a flowergirl who had started this woman's war by beating the "fall in" on a drum, undertook to address the King. Unfortunately she was so weak that she fainted after gasping:

"Bread, my lord!"

"Help," cried the King.

Andrea ran up with her smelling bottle and Charny gave the Queen a reproachful glance for not having thought of this act.

Turning pale, she retired to her own rooms.

"Get the coaches ready," she said: "the King and I are going to Rambouillet."

Meanwhile the flowergirl, finding herself in the King's arms on coming to her senses, screamed with bashfulness and tried to kiss his hand.

"I will give you a kiss, my pretty one," he said; "you are well worth it."

"Oh, how good you are! so you will give the order that the grain shall come into Paris to stop the famine?"

"I will sign the order, my child," the King said, "though I am afraid it will do no good."

Sitting at a table he was about to write when a discharge of fire arms followed a solitary shot.

A second charge of cavalry had been made on the women and a man of their supporters had fired a gun to break the arm of Lieutenant Savonnieres of the Guards. He was going to strike a young soldier who was defending with naked hands a woman who had dropped behind him for protection. The bullets from the Lifeguards' carbines had killed one woman; the mob replied and two soldiers were knocked off their horses.

At the same time shouts of "Make room for the Guns!" were heard as the Men of St. Antoine's Ward dragged up three field-pieces which they levelled at the palace gates. Luckily the rain had damped the priming powder and the match.

Suddenly a whisper came to Gilbert without his knowing who spoke.

"General Lafayette is half an hour's march away and coming."

It was a valuable hint.

Gilbert ran and caught one of the horses of the dismounted guards, and as he dashed off the other followed his stable-companion. Hearing the hoofs, Gilbert thought he was pursued and looked back over his shoulder. He saw the animal caught by the reins and his throat cut; then the people fell on the carcase with knives and cut it up.

While Gilbert was racing to meet Lafayette, who arrived with the National Guards, the King was signing the acceptation of "the Resolution of the Rights of Man," for Mounier, and the older to let grain pass into Paris for Louison Champry the flowergirl.

As the first drum beats were heard of the National Guards entering Versailles, the King felt his arm respectfully touched: it was by Andrea.

"Sire, the Queen supplicates your Majesty not to wait for the Parisians, but take the head of your Lifeguards and the Flanders Regiment which will cut their way through."

"Is this your advice, Count Charny?"

"Yes, Sire, if without stopping, you cross the frontier; otherwise, you should stay."

The King shook his head; he stayed, not from having courage but because he had not strength to go.

"A runaway King," he muttered. "Tell the Queen to depart alone," he said to Andrea who went on her errand.

Five minutes afterwards the Queen came and stood by her husband's side.

"I have come to die with you," she said unaffectedly.

"How handsome she is now," muttered Charny, but she heard him for she started.

"I believe, in all truth, that it is better to die than live!"

"Sire," said Dr. Gilbert, running in, "fear nothing now—General Lafayette is here."

The King did not like Lafayette, but there his feelings stopped, while the Queen hated him and let her hate be seen. She took three steps back, but the King stayed her with an imperative gesture.

The courtiers formed two groups; Charny and Gilbert stood next the King. Steps were heard up to the door of many persons, but all alone General Lafayette entered. As he did so, some voice exclaimed:

"Here comes Cromwell."

"No, sir," said the marquis smiling, "Cromwell would not have walked unguarded into the presence of Charles First!"

Louis XVI. turned to those imprudent friends who had made an enemy of the man hurrying to his relief.

"Count," he said to Charny, "I remain. Now that General Lafayette is here, there is nothing to fear. Retire the troops on Rambouillet. The National Guards will take the outposts and the Lifeguards the palace. Come, general, he said to Lafayette, "I have to confer with you. Come with us, Doctor." he added to Gilbert.

"We must get away to-day," thought the Queen, "to-morrow it will be too late."

As she was going to her own rooms, she was lighted by a red glare outside the palace; the mob had made a barbecue of the soldiers horses.

CHAPTER XXV. THE NIGHT OF HORRORS.

The night went by quietly. At midnight the Queen had tried to go out to the Trianon Palace but the National Guards had refused to let her pass. When she spoke of feeling fear, they answered that she was safer here than any other place.

She felt encouraged indeed on her return home by having her most faithful guards around her. At the door was Valence Charny, leaning on the carbine used by the Lifeguards as well as the dragoons in those days. It was not the habit of the indoor guards to carry swords on duty. "Oh, it is you, Viscount, always faithful?" she said.

"Am I not at my post, where my brother set me, while he is by the King. He is the head of our family, and his place is to die before the head of the kingdom."

"Yes," said the royal lady with marked bitterness, "you only have the right to die for the Queen."

"It will be a great honor for me if God permits me to accomplish that duty," said the young man bowing.

"What has become of the countess?" she asked, returning after making a step to go, for a suspicion had stung her in the heart.

"She came past, ten minutes ago, and is having her bed made in your Majesty's ante-chamber."

The Queen bit her lip: it was impossible to surprise the Charnys in default in matters of duty: "Thank you, sir," she said with a winning nod and wave of the hand, "for so well guarding the Queen. Thank your brother from me for so well guarding the King."

In the ante-room Andrea was respectfully awaiting her.

"I thank you as I have thanked the viscount, and your husband through him."

Andrea made a courtesy and moved aside for her to go by. The Queen did not ask her to follow, for this cold devotion which lasted unto death put her ill at ease.

Gilbert had gone away with General Lafayette who had been twelve hours on horseback and was ready to drop. At the gates they saw Billet, who had come with the National Guards, ready to follow Gilbert like a dog, to the end of the world.

All was quiet, we repeat, up to three in the morning.

Then arrived a second army from town. The other was composed of women and came for bread; this one came for vengeance and was composed of friends. The leaders were Marat, a hideous, long-legged hunchbacked dwarf named Verrière, who came to the surface from the mud when society was stirred, and the Duke of Aiguillon, disguised as a fishfog.

They came like camp-followers after a battle to fire and pillage.

There had been plenty of killing to do at the Bastile but no plunder, and they reckoned to make up for that at Versailles.

At half-past five in the morning, five or six hundred of this riff-raff forced or scaled the great gate: a sentinel had fired an alarm shot, which slew one of the assailants.

Divided as by a giant swordstroke, the plunderers broke into two gangs, one aiming at the royal plate; the other at the crown jewels. One stormed the Queen's apartments, the other made for the chapel where the King's were.

The sea rose like a high tide.

The guards of the King at that hour were the regular sentry watching at the door, and an officer who rushed out of the ante-chamber with a halberd snatched from the hands of the frightened Swiss porter.

"Who goes there?" challenged the sentinel three times, while leveling his carbine.

226

The officer knew what excitement would result from firearms being shot off there in the private apartments, so he beat up the gun with his halberd and barred the stairs with it clear across as he faced the intruders.

"What do you want?" he challenged them.

"Oh, dear, nothing of course," jeered several voices. "We are old friends of her Majesty, so let us pass."

"You are pretty friends to bring war here!"

There was no reply but an ominous laugh. A man seized the ax-headed spear and tried to wrest it from the officer and as he would not let go, he bit his hand. The officer tore the weapon away, shortened it so as to use it as an ax and split the cannibal's skull with one chop. But the violence of the blow broke the staff in two, made for ornament rather than use as it was.

The officer remained armed with two weapons in one, the ax and the spear. While he used both effectively, the sentinel opened the ante-chamber door and called for help. Half-a-dozen guardsmen ran out.

"To the rescue of Lord Charny, gentlemen," shouted the sentry.

Swords flashed in the light of a lamp in the lobby, and the assailants were given some work to do on either side of Charny. Cries of pain were heard and the blood spirted, while the ruffians rolled down the marble steps which they streaked with gore.

The ante-room door opened and the sentry called out:

"By order of the King, gentlemen, return."

The guards profited by the momentary confusion of these foes to execute the retreat, with Charny the last to enter the haven. The door was hardly closed behind him and the two large bolts shot into the sockets before a hundred blows sounded on it. But they piled up the furniture against it so that it would hold out for ten minutes.

During that time reinforcements might arrive.

Meanwhile the second gang had darted towards the Queen's apartments;

but the stairs were narrow and only two can go up abreast. It was in the corridor that Valence Charny watched.

He fired when his challenge was not replied to.

The door opened and Andrea appeared, having heard the shot.

"Save her Majesty," cried the young man, "they are after her life. I am alone against fifty, but never mind, I shall hold the door as long as I can. Make haste!"

The assailants stole upon him and he banged the door to, shouting:

"Fasten the bolts! I shall live long enough to give the Queen time to flee."

Turning around he ran two wretches through with his bayonet.

The Queen had heard all this, and Andrea found her afoot when she entered her bedroom. Two of her ladies hastily dressed her, and urged her into the private way, while Andrea, always calm and indifferent to danger for herself, bolted each door by which they passed.

At the junction of the communication of the two royal apartments, a man was waiting. It was Charny, covered with blood.

"The King?" cried Marie Antoinette, on seeing this. "You promised to save him."

"He is saved," replied the count.

Looking through the doorways and not seeing among the members of the Royal Family and others, his wife, he was going to ask about her when a glance from the Queen stopped him. He had no need to speak for her gaze plunging into his heart had read his wish.

"Rest easy—she is coming," she said.

She ran to the little prince whom she took in her arms.

Closing the last door, Andrea came into the Bulls-eye Hall like the rest. She and her husband exchanged no word, their smiles were ample. Strange! those long parted hearts began to yearn for one another since danger surrounded them.

"The King is looking for you, madam," replied Charny to the Queen's inquiries: "he was going to your rooms by one corridor while you came to his by another."

They heard the assassins yelling: "Down with the Austrians! Death to Messalina! no more of Lady Veto! let us throttle her—let her hang!"

A couple of pistol-shots were heard at the same time and two holes were bored in the door. One bullet whizzed close to the young prince's head and buried itself in the hangings.

"Oh, heavens, we shall all die," screamed the Queen falling on her knees.

At a sign from Charny, the Lifeguardsmen formed a shelter for her and the royal children.

The King now joined them, pale of face and his eyes full of tears: he was calling for the Queen as she had for him. On seeing her, he ran into her arms.

"Saved," exclaimed she.

"By the count," replied the monarch, indicating Charny: "And has he saved you, too?"

"It was his brother," said she.

"My lord, we owe more to your family than we can ever repay," observed the sovereign.

The Queen blushed as she met Andrea's glance and turned her head aside. The blows on the door resounded.

"Gentlemen, we must hold the post for an hour," said the count. "It will take that time to kill us seven if we hold out stoutly. It is not likely that help will not have come for their Majesties."

With these words he caught hold of an immense sideboard and, his example being followed, a head of shattered furniture formed a wall in which the guards cut loopholes to shoot through. The Queen prayed over her children, stifled their wailing and tears.

The King retired into a closet adjoining, to burn papers which ought not to fall into strange hands. The door was chopped at till pieces fell off every instant, and through the gaps blood pikes were thrust and jagged bayonets which tried to dart death. At the same time, bullets found holes in the breastwork and furrowed the plaster on the gilded ceiling.

At length a bench on top of the sideboard fell down; the buffet lost one panel and bloody arms were plunged in through the orifice to make the crevice larger. The guards had burnt the last cartridge, though not vainly, for through the channel dead bodies were seen strewing the lobby. At the shrieks of the ladies who supposed death was to leap in at the breach, the King returned.

"Sire," said Charny, "shut yourself up with the Queen in the most remote room. Fasten all the doors after you. At each door let two of us stand. I ask to be the last and guard the last. I warrant we shall keep them off for two hours: they take forty minutes full to get through this."

The King hesitated; it seemed so shameful to step from room to room, closing doors on brave men left to die for him. He would not have drawn back but for the Queen. If she had not had her children with her she would have stayed beside him.

But, alas! king or subject, all have a flaw in the iron heart, through which pierces terror when boldness elopes.

The King was about to give the order to retreat when the arms were suddenly retracted, the spears and bayonets disappeared and the shouts and thwarts were silenced. In the instant of stillness all waited with parted lips, listening ears and held breath.

The tramp of regular troops was heard.

"The National Guard!" shouted Charny.

"My Lord Charny!" bellowed a hearty voice on the other side of the door.

"Farmer Billet," cried Charny as a well-known face showed itself. "Is it you, my friend?"

"Yes; my lord. Where is the King, and the Queen?"

"Here, safe and sound."

"God be thanked! This way, Dr. Gilbert!"

Two woman's hearts thrilled variously at this name: Andrea's and the Queen's. Charny, turning instinctively, saw both turn pale; he sighed as he shook his head.

"Open the doors, gentlemen," cried the King. "Here are friends."

The Lifeguardsmen hurried to tear down the remains of the barrier. During their work the voice of Marquis Lafayette was heard:

"Gentlemen of the National Guard, I pledged my word last night to the King that nothing appertaining to his Majesty should incur harm. If you allow his Lifeguards to be hurt, you break my word of honor, and I shall no longer be worthy of being your chief."

When the obstacles were removed, the two first persons seen were General Lafayette and Gilbert: a little to their left was Billet, delighted at having had a part in the King's deliverance. It was he who had gone and roused up the general for this deed.

"Long live the King—long live the Queen!" roared Billet. "Ah, if you had stayed in Paris this would not have happened."

"General, what do you advise?" asked the King of the marquis.

"I think you should show yourself at the window."

Gilbert nodded, and Louis walked straight to the window, opened it and stepped out on the balcony.

"Long live the King!" was the universal shout. "Come to Paris:" added others. While a few, but the most dreadful ones: "Let us have the Queen out here!"

All shivered; the King lost color as did Gilbert and Charny.

She looked at Lafayette, who said:

"Fear nothing!"

"All alone?" she questioned.

With the charming manners he preserved to old age, Marquis Lafayette gently detached the clinging children from their mother and urged them out upon the balcony. He offered his hand to Marie Antoinette, adding:

"If your Majesty will rely on me, all will go well."

He led her out on the balcony above the Marble Courtyard, a sea of enflamed human heads. The yell that burst forth at sight of the Queen was immense but none could say whether it was threat or joy. Lafayette bent and kissed her hand. This time, applause rent the air, for the meanest there did homage to beauty and womanhood.

"Strange people:" muttered the Austrian: "but what about my Lifeguards—can you do nothing for them?"

"Let me have one of them."

Charny drew back, for he had offered himself as the scapecat for the officers' revelry of the First October and he did not want amnesty. Andrea took his hand and also stood back. Again those two had understood each other; and the Queen flashed her eye. With panting bosom she gasped in a broken voice:

"Another."

A guardsman obeyed who had not his captain's reasons. Lafayette led him out on the balcony, put his own tricolored cockade in his hat and shook his hand.

"Bravo, Lafayette! the Lifeguards are not a bad sort."

A few voices remonstrated, but they were drowned by the cheers.

"All is over and the fine weather sets in," said the general. "For the calm not to be broken again, one final sacrifice is necessary. Come to Paris."

"General, you may announce that I shall depart for the capital in an hour, with the Queen and the rest of the Royal Family."

This order seemed to remind Charny of something he had forgotten and he sprang away with alacrity. The Queen followed him, both guided by tracks of blood. The Queen shut her eyes and groping for support met the hand of Charny, which led her on. Suddenly she felt him shudder.

"A dead man," she shrieked, opening her eyes.

"Will your Majesty excuse me taking away my arm? I find what I sought: the remains of my brother Valence."

Here lay the unfortunate young man whom the head of the Charnys had ordered to let himself be slain for the Queen's sake. He had punctiliously obeyed.

CHAPTER XXVI. BILLET'S SORROW.

At the time when the Queen and her consort were leaving Versailles, never more to return under its roof, the following scene was taking place in one of its inner yards, damp with the rain which a bitter fall gale was beginning to dry up.

Over a dead body a man clad in black was bending: a man in the Royal Lifeguards uniform knelt on the other side. Three paces off stood a third person, with fixed eyes and closed hands.

The body was of a young man not more than twenty-three, all of whose blood seemed to have poured out through ghastly wounds in the head and chest. His furrowed and livid white breast appeared yet to heave with the disdainful breath of hopeless defense. The head thrown back and the mouth open in pain and anger, recalled the fine figure of speech of the Ancient Romans:

And with a long-drawn wail the spirit fled to the abode of shades.

The man in black was Gilbert: the Lifeguards officer, Count Charny; the bystander, Billet.

The corpse was Viscount Valence Charny's.

Gilbert regarded it with that fixed gaze which suspends the fleeing soul in the dying and seems in the dead, able to recall the fled one.

"Cold and rigid; he is dead, and really dead," he said at last.

Charny uttered a hoarse groan and pressing the corpse in his arms, emitted so heart-rending a sob that the physician shuddered and Billet went off a little to hide his head in a corner of the quadrangle. Suddenly the mourner raised the body, set it against the wall in a sitting posture and slowly came away, but looking to see if it would not revive and follow him.

Gilbert remained on one knee, resting his chin on his hand thoughtfully, appalled and motionless.

Then Billet quitted the nook and came to him, saying, as he no longer heard the wails of the count which had made his heart ache:

"Alas, Dr. Gilbert, this is really civil war, and what you foretold is coming to pass. Only, the trouble comes sooner than I believed and perhaps sooner then you calculated. I have seen villains slaughter wicked men: I have trembled in all my limbs and felt a horror for such monsters. But yet the men who were killed so far were worthless. Now, as you predicted, they are killing honest folk. They have killed Viscount Charny; I do not shudder but I grieve; I do not feel so much horror for the murderers as fear for myself. The young gentleman has been fouly done to death, for he was only a soldier and fought; he ought not to have been butchered."

He uttered a sigh from his vitals.

"To think that I knew him when a child," he continued: "I can see him now, riding along on his little grey pony, carrying bread round to the poor on behalf of his mother. He was a fine pink and white-faced child, with big blue eyes, who was always laughing.

"Well, it is queer! since I have seen him laying there, bleeding and disfigured, it is no longer as a corpse that I think of him, but as the pretty boy with the basket on his left arm and a purse in his right hand. Really, Dr. Gilbert, I believe that I have had enough of this kind of thing, and I do not care to see any more of it, for as all you foretold is a-coming true, I shall be seeing you die, and then——"

"Be calm, Billet," said the physician, shaking his head gently, "my hour has not struck."

"But mayhap mine has. Down yonder the harvest is rotting; the land is laying unplowed; and my family languishes whom I love, and ten times more fondly since I have seen this corpse for which his family will weep."

"What are you driving at, Billet? Do you suppose that I am going to pity your fate?"

"Oh, no," answered the farmer simply; "but as I must cry out when I am in pain, and as crying out leads to nothing, I want to relieve myself in my own way. In short, I want to go home on my farm, Master Gilbert."

"What, again?"

"Look ye, a voice down there is calling me home."

"That voice is prompting you to desertion, Billet."

"I am no soldier to desert, sir."

"What you want to do is worse than desertion in a soldier."

"I should like that explained, doctor."

"You come to Paris to overthrow an old house and you turn away before the building is down."

"For fear it will tumble on my friends, yes, doctor."

"Rather, to save yourself."

"Why, there is no law against taking care of Number One," said Billet.

"A pretty calculation! as if the stones might not bound in falling and rolling, and kill the runaway at a distance."

"Oh, you know I am not to be scared."

"Then you will remain, for I have need of you here, my dear Billet."

"My folks also have need of me at home."

"Billet, Billet, I thought you had agreed with me that a man has no home when he loves his country."

"I should like to know if you would talk like that if your son Sebastian lay there in that young gentleman's stead?"

He pointed to the corpse.

"Billet, a day will come when my son will see me laid out like that," was

236

the stoical response.

"So much the worse for you, doctor, if he is as cold as you over it."

"I hope he will bear it better than me and be all the firmer from having had my example."

"Then you want to inure the youth to seeing blood flow. At his tender age, to be accustomed to fires, murders, gibbets, riots, night attacks; to see queens insulted and kings badgered; and when he is cool like you and steel like a sword-blade, do you expect he will love and respect you?"

"No; I do not want him to see any such sights, which is why I have sent him down to Villers Cotterets along with Ange Pitou though I almost regret it at present."

"You say you are sorry for it to-day, why to-day?"

"Because he would have seen the fable of the Lion and the Mouse put in action, which would be reality to him henceforth."

"What do you mean, Dr. Gilbert?"

"I say that he would have seen a brave and honest farmer come to town, one who can neither read nor write; who never dreamed that his life could have any influence, good or bad over the highest destinies: he would have seen that this man, who was about to quit Paris, as he wishes once more to do—contribute efficaciously towards saving the King, the Queen and the two royal children."

"How is this, Dr. Gilbert?" asked Billet, staring.

"How sublimely innocent you are! I will tell you. Did you not awake at the first noise in the night, guess that the tumult was a tempest about to break on the royal residence and run to arouse General Lafayette, for the general was sleeping."

"That was natural enough; he had been riding about for twelve hours; he had not been abed for four-and-twenty."

"You led him to the palace," continued Gilbert; "you led him into the thick of the scoundrels, crying: "Back, villains, the revenger is upon ye!" "

"That's right enough; I did that."

"Well, Billet, my friend, you see that you have great compensation; though you could not prevent this young gentleman from being butchered, you did perhaps stay the great crime of the slaughter of the royal family. Ingrate, would you leave your country's service just when such a mighty reward was yours?"

"But who would know anything about it when I never suspected it myself?"

"You and I, Billet; is not that enough?"

The farmer meditated for a while before he said as he held out his hand to the physician:

"I guess you are right, doctor. But, you know, man is a weak, selfish, unsteady creature; you are the only one who is just the other style. What made you so?"

"Misfortune," replied the other, with a smile filled with more grief than a sob.

"Lord, how singular—I thought misfortune soured a man."

"Weak men, yes."

"But if I were to meet misfortune and it was to make me wicked?"

"You may meet misfortune but you will never become wicked. I answer for that."

"Then," sighed Billet, "I shall stay and see the game out. But I shall show the white feather more than once, like this."

"But I shall be at hand to uphold you."

"So be it," said the farmer. Throwing a lazy look on Viscount Charny's body, which servants came to remove, he said: "What a vastly pretty boy he

238

was, with his laughing eye, when he rode along on his little grey with the basket and the purse—poor little master Charny!"

Poor Billet! he had not the mesmerist's prophetic soul, and he could not dream what events we have to trace, now that the King and Queen have started to Paris to follow the road marked by the Revolution's redhot plowshare; now that Charny begins to see what a winsome and noble wife he has; now that our minor characters are standing out; now that poor Ange Pitou, quitting Paris with regret is going to play a grand part in the drama of his own country—our romance is but well on the way. We shall meet our dear old friends and alas! we shall fight our stubborn old enemies in the pages of the continuation to this book, under the title of "The Hero of the People."

THE END.

About Author

His father, General Thomas-Alexandre Dumas Davy de la Pailleterie, was born in the French colony of Saint-Domingue (present-day Haiti) to Alexandre Antoine Davy de la Pailleterie, a French nobleman, and Marie-Cessette Dumas, a black slave. At age 14 Thomas-Alexandre was taken by his father to France, where he was educated in a military academy and entered the military for what became an illustrious career.

Dumas' father's aristocratic rank helped young Alexandre acquire work with Louis-Philippe, Duke of Orléans, then as a writer, finding early success. Decades later, after the election of Louis-Napoléon Bonaparte in 1851, Dumas fell from favour and left France for Belgium, where he stayed for several years, then moved to Russia for a few years before going to Italy. In 1861, he founded and published the newspaper L'Indipendente, which supported Italian unification, before returning to Paris in 1864.

Though married, in the tradition of Frenchmen of higher social class, Dumas had numerous affairs (allegedly as many as forty). In his lifetime, he was known to have at least four illegitimate children; although twentieth-century scholars found that Dumas fathered three other children out of wedlock. He acknowledged and assisted his son, Alexandre Dumas, to become a successful novelist and playwright. They are known as Alexandre Dumas père ('father') and Alexandre Dumas fils ('son'). Among his affairs, in 1866, Dumas had one with Adah Isaacs Menken, an American actress then less than half his age and at the height of her career.

The English playwright Watts Phillips, who knew Dumas in his later life, described him as "the most generous, large-hearted being in the world. He also was the most delightfully amusing and egotistical creature on the face of the earth. His tongue was like a windmill – once set in motion, you never knew when he would stop, especially if the theme was himself."

Early life

Dumas Davy de la Pailleterie (later known as Alexandre Dumas) was born in 1802 in Villers-Cotterêts in the department of Aisne, in Picardy,

France. He had two older sisters, Marie-Alexandrine (born 1794) and Louise-Alexandrine (born 1796, died 1797). Their parents were Marie-Louise Élisabeth Labouret, the daughter of an innkeeper, and Thomas-Alexandre Dumas.

Thomas-Alexandre had been born in the French colony of Saint-Domingue (now Haiti), the mixed-race, natural son of the marquis Alexandre Antoine Davy de la Pailleterie, a French nobleman and général commissaire in the artillery of the colony, and Marie-Cessette Dumas, a slave of Afro-Caribbean ancestry. At the time of Thomas-Alexandre's birth, his father was impoverished. It is not known whether his mother was born in Saint-Domingue or in Africa, nor is it known from which African people her ancestors came.

Brought as a boy to France by his father and legally freed there, Thomas-Alexandre Dumas Davy was educated in a military school and joined the army as a young man. As an adult, Thomas-Alexandre used his mother's name, Dumas, as his surname after a break with his father. Dumas was promoted to general by the age of 31, the first soldier of Afro-Antilles origin to reach that rank in the French army. He served with distinction in the French Revolutionary Wars. He became general-in-chief of the Army of the Pyrenees, the first man of colour to reach that rank. Although a general under Bonaparte in the Italian and Egyptian campaigns, Dumas had fallen out of favour by 1800 and requested leave to return to France. On his return, his ship had to put in at Taranto in the Kingdom of Naples, where he and others were held as prisoners of war.

In 1806, when Alexandre was four years of age, his father, Thomas-Alexandre, died of cancer. His widowed mother, Marie-Louise, could not provide her son with much of an education, but Dumas read everything he could and taught himself Spanish. Although poor, the family had their father's distinguished reputation and aristocratic rank to aid the children's advancement. In 1822, after the restoration of the monarchy, the 20-year-old Alexandre Dumas moved to Paris. He acquired a position at the Palais Royal in the office of Louis-Philippe, Duke of Orléans.

Career

242

While working for Louis-Philippe, Dumas began writing articles for magazines and plays for the theatre. As an adult, he used his slave grandmother's surname of Dumas, as his father had done as an adult. His first play, Henry III and His Courts, produced in 1829 when he was 27 years old, met with acclaim. The next year, his second play, Christine, was equally popular. These successes gave him sufficient income to write full-time.

In 1830, Dumas participated in the Revolution that ousted Charles X and replaced him with Dumas' former employer, the Duke of Orléans, who ruled as Louis-Philippe, the Citizen King. Until the mid-1830s, life in France remained unsettled, with sporadic riots by disgruntled Republicans and impoverished urban workers seeking change. As life slowly returned to normal, the nation began to industrialise. An improving economy combined with the end of press censorship made the times rewarding for Alexandre Dumas' literary skills.

After writing additional successful plays, Dumas switched to writing novels. Although attracted to an extravagant lifestyle and always spending more than he earned, Dumas proved to be an astute marketer. As newspapers were publishing many serial novels, in 1838, Dumas rewrote one of his plays as his first serial novel, Le Capitaine Paul. He founded a production studio, staffed with writers who turned out hundreds of stories, all subject to his personal direction, editing, and additions.

From 1839 to 1841, Dumas, with the assistance of several friends, compiled Celebrated Crimes, an eight-volume collection of essays on famous criminals and crimes from European history. He featured Beatrice Cenci, Martin Guerre, Cesare and Lucrezia Borgia, as well as more recent events and criminals, including the cases of the alleged murderers Karl Ludwig Sand and Antoine François Desrues, who were executed.

Dumas collaborated with Augustin Grisier, his fencing master, in his 1840 novel, The Fencing Master. The story is written as Grisier's account of how he came to witness the events of the Decembrist revolt in Russia. The novel was eventually banned in Russia by Czar Nicholas I, and Dumas was prohibited from visiting the country until after the Czar's death. Dumas refers to Grisier with great respect in The Count of Monte Cristo, The Corsican

Brothers, and in his memoirs.

Dumas depended on numerous assistants and collaborators, of whom Auguste Maquet was the best known. It was not until the late twentieth century that his role was fully understood. Dumas wrote the short novel Georges (1843), which uses ideas and plots later repeated in The Count of Monte Cristo. Maquet took Dumas to court to try to get authorial recognition and a higher rate of payment for his work. He was successful in getting more money, but not a by-line.

Dumas' novels were so popular that they were soon translated into English and other languages. His writing earned him a great deal of money, but he was frequently insolvent, as he spent lavishly on women and sumptuous living. (Scholars have found that he had a total of 40 mistresses.) In 1846, he had built a country house outside Paris at Le Port-Marly, the large Château de Monte-Cristo, with an additional building for his writing studio. It was often filled with strangers and acquaintances who stayed for lengthy visits and took advantage of his generosity. Two years later, faced with financial difficulties, he sold the entire property.

Dumas wrote in a wide variety of genres and published a total of 100,000 pages in his lifetime. He also made use of his experience, writing travel books after taking journeys, including those motivated by reasons other than pleasure. Dumas traveled to Spain, Italy, Germany, England and French Algeria. After King Louis-Philippe was ousted in a revolt, Louis-Napoléon Bonaparte was elected president. As Bonaparte disapproved of the author, Dumas fled in 1851 to Brussels, Belgium, which was also an effort to escape his creditors. About 1859, he moved to Russia, where French was the second language of the elite and his writings were enormously popular. Dumas spent two years in Russia and visited St. Petersburg, Moscow, Kazan, Astrakhan and Tbilisi, before leaving to seek different adventures. He published travel books about Russia.

In March 1861, the kingdom of Italy was proclaimed, with Victor Emmanuel II as its king. Dumas travelled there and for the next three years participated in the movement for Italian unification. He founded and led a newspaper, Indipendente. While there, he befriended Giuseppe Garibaldi, whom he had long admired and with whom he shared a commitment to liberal republican principles as well as membership within Freemasonry. Returning to Paris in 1864, he published travel books about Italy.

Despite Dumas' aristocratic background and personal success, he had to deal with discrimination related to his mixed-race ancestry. In 1843, he wrote a short novel, Georges, that addressed some of the issues of race and the effects of colonialism. His response to a man who insulted him about his African ancestry has become famous. Dumas said:

My father was a mulatto, my grandfather was a Negro, and my great-grandfather a monkey. You see, Sir, my family starts where yours ends.

Personal life

On 1 February 1840, Dumas married actress Ida Ferrier (born Marguerite-Joséphine Ferrand) (1811–1859). He had numerous liaisons with other women and was known to have fathered at least four children by them:

Alexandre Dumas, fils (1824–1895), son of Marie-Laure-Catherine Labay (1794–1868), a dressmaker. He became a successful novelist and playwright.

Marie-Alexandrine Dumas (5 March 1831 – 1878), the daughter of Belle Krelsamer (1803–1875).

Micaëlla-Clélie-Josepha-Élisabeth Cordier (born 1860), the daughter of Emélie Cordier.

Henry Bauer, the son of a woman whose surname was Bauer.

About 1866, Dumas had an affair with Adah Isaacs Menken, a well-known American actress. She had performed her sensational role in Mazeppa in London. In Paris, she had a sold-out run of Les Pirates de la Savanne and was at the peak of her success.

These women were among Dumas' nearly 40 mistresses found by scholar Claude Schopp, in addition to three natural children.

Death and legacy

At his death in December 1870, Dumas was buried at his birthplace of Villers-Cotterêts in the department of Aisne. His death was overshadowed by the Franco-Prussian War. Changing literary fashions decreased his popularity. In the late twentieth century, scholars such as Reginald Hamel and Claude Schopp have caused a critical reappraisal and new appreciation of his art, as well as finding lost works.

In 1970, the Alexandre Dumas Paris Métro station was named in his honour. His country home outside Paris, the Château de Monte-Cristo, has been restored and is open to the public as a museum.

Researchers have continued to find Dumas works in archives, including the five-act play, The Gold Thieves, found in 2002 by the scholar Réginald Hamel [fr] in the Bibliothèque Nationale de France. It was published in France in 2004 by Honoré-Champion.

Frank Wild Reed (1874–1953), the older brother of Dunedin publisher A. H. Reed, was a busy Whangarei pharmacist who never visited France, yet he amassed the greatest collection of books and manuscripts relating to Dumas outside France. It contains about 3350 volumes, including some 2000 sheets in Dumas' handwriting and dozens of French, Belgian and English first editions. This collection was donated to Auckland Libraries after his death. Reed wrote the most comprehensive bibliography of Dumas.

In 2002, for the bicentennial of Dumas' birth, French President Jacques Chirac had a ceremony honouring the author by having his ashes re-interred at the mausoleum of the Panthéon of Paris, where many French luminaries were buried. The proceedings were televised: the new coffin was draped in a blue velvet cloth and carried on a caisson flanked by four mounted Republican Guards costumed as the four Musketeers. It was transported through Paris to the Panthéon. In his speech, President Chirac said:

With you, we were D'Artagnan, Monte Cristo, or Balsamo, riding along the roads of France, touring battlefields, visiting palaces and castles—with you, we dream.

Chirac acknowledged the racism that had existed in France and said that the re-interment in the Pantheon had been a way of correcting that wrong, as Alexandre Dumas was enshrined alongside fellow great authors Victor Hugo and Émile Zola. Chirac noted that although France has produced many great writers, none has been so widely read as Dumas. His novels have been translated into nearly 100 languages. In addition, they have inspired more than 200 motion pictures.

In June 2005, Dumas' last novel, The Knight of Sainte-Hermine, was published in France featuring the Battle of Trafalgar. Dumas described a fictional character killing Lord Nelson (Nelson was shot and killed by an unknown sniper). Writing and publishing the novel serially in 1869, Dumas had nearly finished it before his death. It was the third part of the Sainte-Hermine trilogy.

Claude Schopp, a Dumas scholar, noticed a letter in an archive in 1990 that led him to discover the unfinished work. It took him years to research it, edit the completed portions, and decide how to treat the unfinished part. Schopp finally wrote the final two-and-a-half chapters, based on the author's notes, to complete the story. Published by Éditions Phébus, it sold 60,000 copies, making it a best seller. Translated into English, it was released in 2006 as The Last Cavalier, and has been translated into other languages.

Schopp has since found additional material related to the Saints-Hermine saga. Schopp combined them to publish the sequel Le Salut de l'Empire in 2008.

Dumas is briefly mentioned in the 1994 film The Shawshank Redemption. The inmate Heywood mispronounces Dumas' last name as "dumbass" as he files books in the prison library.

Dumas is briefly mentioned in the 2012 film Django Unchained. The Southern slaveholder Calvin Candie expressed admiration for Dumas, owning his books in his library and even naming one of his slaves D'Artagnan. He is surprised to learn from another white man that Dumas was black. (Source: Wikipedia)